the perfect couple

(a jessie hunt psychological suspense—book 20)

blake pierce

Blake Pierce

Blake Pierce is the USA Today bestselling author of the RILEY PAGE mystery series, which includes seventeen books. Blake Pierce is also the author of the MACKENZIE WHITE mystery series, comprising fourteen books; of the AVERY BLACK mystery series, comprising six books; of the KERI LOCKE mystery series, comprising five books; of the MAKING OF RILEY PAIGE mystery series, comprising six books; of the KATE WISE mystery series, comprising seven books; of the CHLOE FINE psychological suspense mystery, comprising six books; of the JESSE HUNT psychological suspense thriller series, comprising twenty four books; of the AU PAIR psychological suspense thriller series, comprising three books; of the ZOE PRIME mystery series, comprising six books; of the ADELE SHARP mystery series, comprising fifteen books, of the EUROPEAN VOYAGE cozy mystery series, comprising four books; of the new LAURA FROST FBI suspense thriller, comprising nine books (and counting); of the new ELLA DARK FBI suspense thriller, comprising eleven books (and counting); of the A YEAR IN EUROPE cozy mystery series, comprising nine books, of the AVA GOLD mystery series, comprising six books (and counting); of the RACHEL GIFT mystery series, comprising six books (and counting); of the VALERIE LAW mystery series, comprising three books (and counting); and of the PAIGE KING mystery series, comprising three books (and counting).

An avid reader and lifelong fan of the mystery and thriller genres, Blake loves to hear from you, so please feel free to visit www.blakepierceauthor.com to learn more and stay in touch.

Copyright © 2022 by Blake Pierce. All rights reserved. Except as permitted under the U.S. Copyright Act of 1976, no part of this publication may be reproduced, distributed or transmitted in any form or by any means, or stored in a database or retrieval system, without the prior permission of the author. This ebook is licensed for your personal enjoyment only. This ebook may not be re-sold or given away to other people. If you would like to share this book with another person, please purchase an additional copy for each recipient. If you're reading this book and did not purchase it, or it was not purchased for your use only, then please return it and purchase your own copy. Thank you for respecting the hard work of this author. This is a work of fiction. Names, characters, businesses, organizations, places, events, and incidents either are the product of the author's imagination or are used fictionally. Any resemblance to actual persons, living or dead, is entirely coincidental. Jacket image Copyright sergiophoto, used under license from Shutterstock.com.
ISBN: 978-1-0943-7649-3

BOOKS BY BLAKE PIERCE

PAIGE KING MYSTERY SERIES
THE GIRL HE PINED (Book #1)
THE GIRL HE CHOSE (Book #2)
THE GIRL HE TOOK (Book #3)

VALERIE LAW MYSTERY SERIES
NO MERCY (Book #1)
NO PITY (Book #2)
NO FEAR (Book #3

RACHEL GIFT MYSTERY SERIES
HER LAST WISH (Book #1)
HER LAST CHANCE (Book #2)
HER LAST HOPE (Book #3)
HER LAST FEAR (Book #4)
HER LAST CHOICE (Book #5)
HER LAST BREATH (Book #6)

AVA GOLD MYSTERY SERIES
CITY OF PREY (Book #1)
CITY OF FEAR (Book #2)
CITY OF BONES (Book #3)
CITY OF GHOSTS (Book #4)
CITY OF DEATH (Book #5)
CITY OF VICE (Book #6)

A YEAR IN EUROPE
A MURDER IN PARIS (Book #1)
DEATH IN FLORENCE (Book #2)
VENGEANCE IN VIENNA (Book #3)
A FATALITY IN SPAIN (Book #4)

ELLA DARK FBI SUSPENSE THRILLER
GIRL, ALONE (Book #1)
GIRL, TAKEN (Book #2)
GIRL, HUNTED (Book #3)
GIRL, SILENCED (Book #4)

GIRL, VANISHED (Book 5)
GIRL ERASED (Book #6)
GIRL, FORSAKEN (Book #7)
GIRL, TRAPPED (Book #8)
GIRL, EXPENDABLE (Book #9)
GIRL, ESCAPED (Book #10)
GIRL, HIS (Book #11)

LAURA FROST FBI SUSPENSE THRILLER
ALREADY GONE (Book #1)
ALREADY SEEN (Book #2)
ALREADY TRAPPED (Book #3)
ALREADY MISSING (Book #4)
ALREADY DEAD (Book #5)
ALREADY TAKEN (Book #6)
ALREADY CHOSEN (Book #7)
ALREADY LOST (Book #8)
ALREADY HIS (Book #9)

EUROPEAN VOYAGE COZY MYSTERY SERIES
MURDER (AND BAKLAVA) (Book #1)
DEATH (AND APPLE STRUDEL) (Book #2)
CRIME (AND LAGER) (Book #3)
MISFORTUNE (AND GOUDA) (Book #4)
CALAMITY (AND A DANISH) (Book #5)
MAYHEM (AND HERRING) (Book #6)

ADELE SHARP MYSTERY SERIES
LEFT TO DIE (Book #1)
LEFT TO RUN (Book #2)
LEFT TO HIDE (Book #3)
LEFT TO KILL (Book #4)
LEFT TO MURDER (Book #5)
LEFT TO ENVY (Book #6)
LEFT TO LAPSE (Book #7)
LEFT TO VANISH (Book #8)
LEFT TO HUNT (Book #9)
LEFT TO FEAR (Book #10)
LEFT TO PREY (Book #11)
LEFT TO LURE (Book #12)
LEFT TO CRAVE (Book #13)

LEFT TO LOATHE (Book #14)
LEFT TO HARM (Book #15)

THE AU PAIR SERIES
ALMOST GONE (Book#1)
ALMOST LOST (Book #2)
ALMOST DEAD (Book #3)

ZOE PRIME MYSTERY SERIES
FACE OF DEATH (Book#1)
FACE OF MURDER (Book #2)
FACE OF FEAR (Book #3)
FACE OF MADNESS (Book #4)
FACE OF FURY (Book #5)
FACE OF DARKNESS (Book #6)

A JESSIE HUNT PSYCHOLOGICAL SUSPENSE SERIES
THE PERFECT WIFE (Book #1)
THE PERFECT BLOCK (Book #2)
THE PERFECT HOUSE (Book #3)
THE PERFECT SMILE (Book #4)
THE PERFECT LIE (Book #5)
THE PERFECT LOOK (Book #6)
THE PERFECT AFFAIR (Book #7)
THE PERFECT ALIBI (Book #8)
THE PERFECT NEIGHBOR (Book #9)
THE PERFECT DISGUISE (Book #10)
THE PERFECT SECRET (Book #11)
THE PERFECT FAÇADE (Book #12)
THE PERFECT IMPRESSION (Book #13)
THE PERFECT DECEIT (Book #14)
THE PERFECT MISTRESS (Book #15)
THE PERFECT IMAGE (Book #16)
THE PERFECT VEIL (Book #17)
THE PERFECT INDISCRETION (Book #18)
THE PERFECT RUMOR (Book #19)
THE PERFECT COUPLE (Book #20)
THE PERFECT MURDER (Book #21)
THE PERFECT HUSBAND (Book #22)
THE PERFECT SCANDAL (Book #23)
THE PERFECT MASK (Book #24)

CHLOE FINE PSYCHOLOGICAL SUSPENSE SERIES
NEXT DOOR (Book #1)
A NEIGHBOR'S LIE (Book #2)
CUL DE SAC (Book #3)
SILENT NEIGHBOR (Book #4)
HOMECOMING (Book #5)
TINTED WINDOWS (Book #6)

KATE WISE MYSTERY SERIES
IF SHE KNEW (Book #1)
IF SHE SAW (Book #2)
IF SHE RAN (Book #3)
IF SHE HID (Book #4)
IF SHE FLED (Book #5)
IF SHE FEARED (Book #6)
IF SHE HEARD (Book #7)

THE MAKING OF RILEY PAIGE SERIES
WATCHING (Book #1)
WAITING (Book #2)
LURING (Book #3)
TAKING (Book #4)
STALKING (Book #5)
KILLING (Book #6)

RILEY PAIGE MYSTERY SERIES
ONCE GONE (Book #1)
ONCE TAKEN (Book #2)
ONCE CRAVED (Book #3)
ONCE LURED (Book #4)
ONCE HUNTED (Book #5)
ONCE PINED (Book #6)
ONCE FORSAKEN (Book #7)
ONCE COLD (Book #8)
ONCE STALKED (Book #9)
ONCE LOST (Book #10)
ONCE BURIED (Book #11)
ONCE BOUND (Book #12)
ONCE TRAPPED (Book #13)

ONCE DORMANT (Book #14)
ONCE SHUNNED (Book #15)
ONCE MISSED (Book #16)
ONCE CHOSEN (Book #17)

MACKENZIE WHITE MYSTERY SERIES
BEFORE HE KILLS (Book #1)
BEFORE HE SEES (Book #2)
BEFORE HE COVETS (Book #3)
BEFORE HE TAKES (Book #4)
BEFORE HE NEEDS (Book #5)
BEFORE HE FEELS (Book #6)
BEFORE HE SINS (Book #7)
BEFORE HE HUNTS (Book #8)
BEFORE HE PREYS (Book #9)
BEFORE HE LONGS (Book #10)
BEFORE HE LAPSES (Book #11)
BEFORE HE ENVIES (Book #12)
BEFORE HE STALKS (Book #13)
BEFORE HE HARMS (Book #14)

AVERY BLACK MYSTERY SERIES
CAUSE TO KILL (Book #1)
CAUSE TO RUN (Book #2)
CAUSE TO HIDE (Book #3)
CAUSE TO FEAR (Book #4)
CAUSE TO SAVE (Book #5)
CAUSE TO DREAD (Book #6)

KERI LOCKE MYSTERY SERIES
A TRACE OF DEATH (Book #1)
A TRACE OF MURDER (Book #2)
A TRACE OF VICE (Book #3)
A TRACE OF CRIME (Book #4)
A TRACE OF HOPE (Book #5)

PROLOGUE

Even for Suzie, the house was daunting.

As an interior decorator to some of the wealthiest, most powerful people in Los Angeles, it took a lot for Suzie Pearlman to feel intimidated by a home. But this place was something else. After she parked her car across the street and made her way up the long path to the front door, she tried to make sense of how a home like this was in this neighborhood.

Unlike many of the communities she operated in, like Beverly Hills, Brentwood, Santa Monica, and Manhattan Beach, which was just a few miles south of here, El Segundo wasn't necessarily known for its mansions.

Like Santa Monica and Manhattan Beach, it was a coastal community, but its reputation was far less ostentatious. In fact, much of the southern section of town was comprised of an industrial zone, with warehouses, shipping centers, and of course, the massive refinery housing the municipality's largest employer, Metron Oil.

That's why she was here. Just last year, Roger Whitmore, a partner at Daniels, Kramer, Malone & Whitmore and senior outside counsel to one of one of the largest oil and gas companies in the world, had decided to move from his Beverly Hills home and relocate "among the people," living closer to the middle-class folks who worked for his firm's biggest client.

Suzie rang the doorbell and waited, looking around at the nearby homes, many of which might also be classified as mansions, but none of which were as impressive as the half-block long, four story domicile that looked more like a boutique hotel than an actual home. It was situated on a cliff, with a clear view of Dockweiler Beach and the Pacific Ocean, less than a quarter mile west.

After a good minute without an answer, she rang the bell again. It might take a while to get to the door in a house as big as this. She had initially balked at accepting the meeting with Patricia Whitmore. That is, until she discovered who the woman was married to and checked out some photos of their place. Including their two children, only four people lived in the 5200 square foot property with seven bedrooms and nine bathrooms. There was a lot of potential decorating to be done.

Suzie, realizing it had been another full minute without a response, was about to ring the bell a third time when the door opened, revealing a pretty, young blonde woman with ivory skin. Her curly hair, which had obviously been hurriedly brushed, was all over the place and there was sleep in her eyes. She was wearing sweatpants and a t-shirt.

"May I help you?" she asked in an accent that Suzie guessed was Irish.

"Yes. My name is Suzanne Pearlman. I have a 9 a.m. appointment with Mrs. Whitmore to discuss some design ideas for the house."

"Oh, right," the girl replied, her eyes suddenly brightening. "You're the decorator. Trish mentioned you'd be coming by. Come on in."

She opened the door wide and waved toward a large room beyond the foyer.

"I'm Shannon," she said, her burr more pronounced than earlier, "the Whitmores' au pair. I apologize for my appearance. There's no school today and the kids are at a sleepover, so I took advantage of the opportunity to sleep in a bit. I suspect Trish is doing the same. If you want to make yourself comfortable, I'll go get her."

"Sure," Suzie replied. "Do you mind directing me to the kitchen? That was the room that Mrs. Whitmore said she wanted to prioritize first. It would be nice to get a sense of it before she comes along."

"Not a problem," Shannon said, pointing past the living room to a darkened room in the distance. "Can you find your own way from here?"

"Of course," Suzie said, annoyed at the question. She could find her way around any house, no matter how big. That was what she did.

"Right then," Shannon said, seemingly oblivious to her misstep, "settle in. Be back in a bit."

With that, she headed toward the stairs. Suzie wondered how many flights she'd have to take to get the Whitmores' bedroom. When Shannon was gone, she started toward the kitchen. Without the girl around, she noticed just how silent the house was. She walked along the carpeted living room floor, which muffled her footsteps.

As she approached the kitchen, she got an unsettled feeling, as if she was being watched. There was no logical reason for it. The home was open and sunny, but something felt off to her. She was just about to enter the kitchen when she caught sight of herself in a mirror on the wall.

She sighed. At forty-two, she was doing her best to keep up appearances, but the years of scrambling for, and then servicing, difficult clients were starting to weigh her down. She was reaching the point where she might have to consider more drastic measures than weekly facials to keep the lines on her face from becoming more pronounced. Her regularly-dyed, brown hair was looking brittle. Her eyes were slightly red, irritated by her contacts on this gusty, early March day. And her thrice-weekly workouts at the gym with her personal trainer were barely keeping the cellulite at bay. She felt exhausted just thinking about it all.

Suzie forcibly ripped her eyes away from the mirror and returned her attention to the kitchen. As she entered, the feeling that she wasn't alone quickly returned. Somewhere in the house she could hear a clock ticking loudly. In the distance, someone had just started up a lawnmower.

She looked around for the light switch and flicked it on, revealing a massive kitchen with a center island as large as a compact car. There were two double ovens and a giant, Sub-Zero refrigerator. The stove had eight electric burners. All the appliances were modern and the setup was impeccably tasteful. If she was honest, Suzie didn't think the place needed much work at all.

She got out her small notebook to take a few notes when the clammy sensation that there was someone else nearby overcame her again. She was tempted to return to the foyer and wait for Shannon to bring Trish Whitmore downstairs, but she shook off the discomfort and began writing ideas down.

That's when she heard the dripping sound. She checked the sink but nothing was coming from the faucet. She glanced over her shoulder, suddenly fearing that someone was behind her, their sweat trickling onto the floor. But there was no one there.

She put the notebook back in her pocket and carefully moved around the island, her eyes darting everywhere. She had no logical reason to be so jumpy and yet, she couldn't stop herself from eyeing the knife rack on the counter. She briefly considered grabbing one for self-defense.

When she rounded the island to the other side the kitchen, she realized what had been making the dripping sound. For a full second before she reacted, she was able to silently process what she saw.

On the floor in front of her was a woman, though Suzie couldn't determine that from her face, which was mangled beyond identification. Instead it was the long hair and sports bra that gave it away. What was left of the woman's face had been pulverized into a globby mess of blood, bone, and skin. Her skull was cracked open at the forehead. The dripping Suzie had heard was droplets of blood falling regularly from the woman's right earlobe to the kitchen floor. Next to her head, was a long-handled meat tenderizer. Suzie began to scream.

She wasn't sure when Shannon the au pair arrived, but at some point she was conscious of the girl standing beside her. She too was screaming. That was the last thing Suzie remembered before passing out.

CHAPTER ONE

Jessie fought the urge to call again.

She was supposed to be working on her weekly criminal profiling seminar, which was held every Wednesday morning at UCLA. After all, it was already Monday and she still had to nail down the last details of her presentation.

But as she sat at the breakfast table of her mid-Wilshire house, staring blankly at her laptop, her mind kept drifting back to her call with Hannah yesterday. It was actually her seventeen-year-old, younger half-sister who had called her, a rarity these days, and not just because she was currently staying at a residential psychiatric facility.

"Don't freak out," Hannah said to start the conversation, "but someone died here last night and I wanted to make sure you knew about it."

"What?" Jessie asked, trying to keep her voice level. No one had said a word to her.

"I'm sure Dr. Lemmon would have called you," Hannah said, referring to the psychiatrist who they both saw regularly and who had originally convinced her to enter the Seasons Wellness Center in Malibu, "but I heard she was admitted to Cedars-Sinai yesterday with kidney stones. So I thought I should update you before you got a scary call from the administration."

"What happened?" Jessie asked, hoping that her sister's calm tone wasn't merely a cover for possible distress just under the surface.

"A girl named Meredith Bartlett was found in her room last night. It looks like she committed suicide with a shard of glass."

"Oh God," Jessie muttered. Even in a secure psychiatric facility, her little sister wasn't safe from constant death. "Did you know her?"

"Just a little," Hannah said. "She seemed nice."

"I can be there in an hour," Jessie told her. "I was going to come out for our session today anyway."

"They're actually pushing all of today's sessions," Hannah said. "The local sheriff is still wrapping up his investigation and the staff here wants to focus on making sure everyone is engaging in self-care. It's got a lot of people pretty torn up."

"Okay," Jessie said not wanting to push, "should I come out tomorrow instead?"

"Why don't we hold off?" Hannah said. "I'll get in touch with you once the hospital's given the all clear to re-start sessions. Or maybe Dr. Lemmon will feel well enough to reach out to you directly by then. I should go. There's a line of people waiting to use the phone."

"Let me know if there's anything I can do," Jessie said. "I love you."

"Talk soon," Hannah replied before hanging up.

That conversation was yesterday morning, Sunday, when Jessie and Ryan had been relaxing at Peninsula Resort in Palos Verdes after solving a case. And though an administrator with Seasons had called a few hours later to offer a perfunctory, mostly useless explication of the prior night's events and the facility's temporary hold on visitors, Hannah hadn't called again.

Jessie picked up her cell phone and was about to dial the number for Seasons when she heard an imaginary voice. It belonged to LAPD Detective Ryan Hernandez, her fiancé and sometimes work partner, who was currently at the downtown Central Police Station.

She pictured him standing over her disapprovingly and shaking his head as he quietly said, "Don't push her away. Let her come to you."

She put the phone down. Imaginary Ryan was right. Hannah had called her, which was the most voluntary contact she'd had in weeks. It was best not to press for more than that from her now. Jessie reminded herself that she should just be happy that the girl reached out at all. Between that and her seemingly genuine attempts to get better, things were marginally looking up.

Hannah had been at Seasons for over two weeks now, voluntarily (if reluctantly), admitting herself to deal with several issues. Officially, she was there to deal with her difficulty in feeling emotions unless she put herself in heightened, often dangerous situations. That was a legitimate concern.

But what no one at the facility other than Hannah and Dr. Janice Lemmon knew was the other, more pressing reason for her admission. Several months ago, she had shot and killed a serial killer who was hunting her, Jessie, and Ryan in a remote mountain cabin.

While police determined that the killing was in self-defense, the truth was far darker.

The killer, nicknamed the Night Hunter, had already been captured by Jessie and Ryan and was handcuffed and in custody when Hannah shot him. Though she claimed that she worried he would eventually come after them again, Hannah ultimately acknowledged that she'd actually killed him because she wanted to know what it felt like to take a life and assumed no one would miss the guy. Even more troubling, she admitted that the high she got by snuffing him out was massive and that she had a growing desire to recapture the feeling.

That was what Dr. Lemmon was working through with Hannah when they held their private therapy sessions, all in a residential hospital environment where she was removed from the temptations that might make her act on her urges. But with Dr. Lemmon apparently temporarily unavailable, Jessie worried that her sister wasn't addressing the primary reason that she was at Seasons in the first place.

She closed the laptop and stood up. There was no way she was getting any more work done this morning and she needed to do something to get her concerns about Hannah out of her head. She went to the bathroom and threw some cold water on her face.

As she patted herself dry, she looked in the mirror. Just a few months from her thirty-first birthday, Jessie felt pretty good about the woman looking back at her. With Hannah under medical care, she'd gotten more consecutive nights of unbroken sleep in the last two weeks than in the entire prior year. Her skin was vibrant and her green eyes sparkled brightly. Her shoulder-length brown hair looked shampoo-commercial ready. And her daily, five-mile, morning runs had her long-legged, sinewy, five-foot ten frame in the best shape it had been in since she spent ten weeks in the FBI's criminal profiling academy program.

She walked into the backyard and looked at Ryan's set of weights on the patio. She was tempted to do a little lifting to pump out her stress. But with her luck, she feared she might pull something and drop a weight, which her fiancé wouldn't appreciate.

Despite his muscled exterior and stern, square-set jaw, Ryan was a sweet, gentle soul. But he was very particular about his workout equipment, and if she damaged any of it, she'd never hear the end of it. She didn't need the hassle, especially after they'd just worked through a more substantive issue.

As she rolled out a yoga mat to do some stretching instead, she allowed herself a small smile. Just a day and a half ago, their engagement seemed on very shaky ground. Ryan was insisting on a big wedding, stubbornly intent on replacing Jessie's memories of her disastrous first marriage with something bigger and better.

Jessie kept telling him that she wanted something small, the antithesis of the overblown event that wedded her to a sociopath who later tried to kill her. That Ryan didn't seem to get that point gave her increasing pause about whether they should go forward with the thing at all.

Ultimately, after some initial obstinacy, she'd made him understand that she wasn't just playing coy, hoping he'd plow ahead with a huge event over her "feigned" wish for something more restrained. She made it clear that she was the kind of girl who meant what she said and that he ought to know that by now. Luckily, he saw the light.

Now they were in a much better place. In fact, they'd spent part of yesterday looking online at much more modest venue options, places that were suited more to twenty people than two hundred. It was actually borderline fun, although Jessie still would have been just as happy to elope. However, her best friend, private detective Kat Gentry had warned her that she'd kill her if she wasn't invited, so that seemed off the table.

Jessie grinned to herself as she recalled Kat's seemingly complete sincerity when she'd made the threat. Maybe she was just that serious about being in attendance. Of course, it was equally possible that her friend was just surly because she was about to start a new case that would have her sitting in a car for the next few days, eating crappy food while she tailed the trophy wife of a rich guy who suspected she was cheating on him.

Jessie was tempted to call her to see how she was doing when her phone rang. She eased herself out of downward dog and reached for it. The call was from Captain Roy Decker, her supervisor at Central Station. She put him on speaker.

"Hey, Captain," she said, "What's up?"

"Hello, Hunt," he said in his typically gruff tone, "I have Detective Hernandez en route to pick you up right now."

Jessie ignored the fact that the captain wouldn't use Ryan's first name or acknowledge out loud that the guy was her fiancé. That was just Decker's way—all business if he could help it.

"What's going on?" she asked.

"Hernandez can fill you in on all the details," he said. "But the short version is that the wife of a big-time lawyer was found bludgeoned to death in her kitchen in El Segundo less than an hour ago."

"El Segundo?" Jessie repeated. "I thought they have their own police department."

"They do," he confirmed, "but they're handing this one off to LAPD for political reasons that will become painfully clear once you get the particulars."

"You know, Captain," she pointed out, "I'm still only a consulting profiler for the department, at least for a few more weeks. You never even asked if I was available today."

"I know you do those seminars on Wednesdays," he replied tartly. "I assume that as long as the murder takes place any other day of the week, you're in."

"That's quite an assumption."

"Was I wrong?" he asked challengingly. "Are you passing on this?"

"No," she admitted. "I'm in."

CHAPTER TWO

Ryan still had a wry smile on his face when they pulled up near the Whitmores' El Segundo mansion on Hillcrest Street thirty-five minutes later.

"Stop rubbing it in," Jessie ordered.

"I just can't believe he roped you into this thing before you even knew what the case was," he said. "You're such a sucker."

She didn't comment, mostly because it was true. She was an easy mark when it came to this kind of case. And her interest was only piqued more once Ryan had filled her in on the details.

"The victim's name is Patricia Whitmore," he'd explained on the way over. "She had a 9 a.m. appointment with an interior decorator. The au pair let her in and went to find Whitmore while the decorator entered the kitchen. That's where she found the body."

"The au pair didn't stumble across the dead woman in the house prior to that?" Jessie had wondered.

"Apparently she'd been asleep upstairs until the decorator arrived."

"And the woman was beaten to death?" Jessie confirmed.

"Yes," Ryan said, "with a meat tenderizer that the au pair said belonged to the Whitmores."

Jessie shivered at the thought of it. She'd seen lots of horrible things since she started this job, and many more before that, but never ceased to be amazed at the brutality people could inflict on one another.

"Decker said the El Segundo police gave up the case because it was political," she noted. "What's that about?"

Ryan nodded at the assessment.

"Roger Whitmore is a named partner at Daniels, Kramer, Malone & Whitmore. They're outside counsel for Metron, which operates the massive refinery at the southern end of town. I think the local PD considered the possibility that a top lawyer for one of the city's biggest employers would likely be a suspect in this and decided that was too hot for them to handle. So they made some excuse about not having available resources for a case this big and called HSS."

HSS, or Homicide Special Section, was a small, dedicated unit of the LAPD which investigated cases that had high profiles or intense media scrutiny, often involving multiple victims and serial killers. Ryan was the lead detective for the unit. It wasn't unusual for other LAPD stations to ask for help from HSS, but it was far less common for other cities' police departments to defer to the big boys. It almost always meant they didn't want the heat.

That might have explained why several squad cars were already pulling away as Ryan parked his vehicle just outside the police tape line. As he closed the door and walked around to join her, Jessie silently marveled at her fiancé.

Considering that only eight months ago he'd been in a coma after getting stabbed in the chest by her ex-husband, it was amazing that the guy was functioning normally, much less on the job again. But he had moved well beyond that.

He was now almost back to his former chiseled 200 pound, six-foot self. After months of relentless physical therapy, weight training, and cardio, his doctors had declared him 95% recovered. They warned him that he might never get that last 5% back, which he had embraced as a challenge.

Whether he ever achieved the physical excellence he was after, in Jessie's mind, he was close enough. After regaining the weight he'd lost, his gaunt features had been replaced. His cheekbones and eye sockets were no longer pronounced and his lantern jaw and bright, warm, brown eyes had returned. His skin, which had gotten sallow from so much time indoors, had regained its dark tan and even his short, black hair, once limp, seemed to stand at attention. And now that he'd given up his wedding-related stubbornness, he was more attractive to her than he'd ever been.

Jessie saw him notice the same thing she did as they walked over. Several looky-loo neighbors were being held back by a few overwhelmed El Segundo police officers. One of them looked at Ryan and Jessie with trepidation as they approached.

"I'm Detective Hernandez with LAPD HSS," Ryan said, holding up his badge to short-circuit any conflict. "This is our profiler, Jessie Hunt. We're expected inside."

The cop seemed relieved not to have to challenge them and waved them through.

"The crime scene unit is finishing up in the kitchen. That's where you can find everyone," he said.

They passed underneath the police tape and made their way to the front door. As they did, Jessie took in the home. While there were other houses on the block that could reasonably be called impressive, this place was in another category altogether.

Standing on a cliff overlooking the Pacific Ocean, it stood four stories into the air and took up the entire end of the cul-de-sac, curving around the street in a "U" shape. Although it was designed in the Spanish style, it was clearly built very recently with inconspicuous solar panels and what appeared to be an elevator shaft. She also noticed several security cameras placed around the exterior and made a mental note to check on what they might reveal later.

Once they stepped inside, the place continued to impress. Long hallways with stone floors extended out from the foyer in multiple directions like a spider web. The walls were tastefully decorated with paintings interspersed with family photos. The elevator Jessie had seen from the outside stood next to the stairwell, which curled back around above them after reaching the second floor.

They followed the sound of voices until they reached the kitchen. A young, blonde officer standing at the doorway looked at their IDs before allowing entry.

"Who should we be talking to?" Ryan asked.

"The officer in charge is Sergeant Frank. He's over there with the medical examiner," he said, pointing to the far end of the massive kitchen.

They approached the man, who looked to be in his late forties. His belly was fighting his belt and what little hair he had left was more gray than brown. After introducing Jessie and himself, Ryan got straight down to business.

"What have we got?"

"Patricia Whitmore, age 37, went by Trish," Sergeant Frank said in a clipped, staccato tone, nodding at the other side of the giant island where the body, which they couldn't see, was apparently lying. "Found dead by Suzanne Pearlman, prospective interior decorator. She started screaming. The au pair, an Irish kid named Shannon Stanfield who'd been looking for Whitmore upstairs, came back down, saw the same thing, and joined in the screaming. Pearlman passed out. Stanfield called 911 and woke Pearlman up."

"Shall we take a look?" Jessie asked.

The medical examiner, a tall, bony man in glasses with pale skin that matched his straw hair, spoke for the first time.

"Of course," he answered as he led them around the island. "We're basically done here. I understand that LAPD is taking over so we'll send all our preliminary results to your people as soon as we've got them in the system."

They all stopped once Trish Whitmore's body came into view. Jessie allowed herself a second to silently appreciate the gravity of the moment before asking any questions. On the ground before her was a woman lying on her back wearing yoga pants and a sports bra. Other than having short, black hair, there was no way to discern her features above the neck because everything had been bashed in. Had the sergeant not mentioned her age, Jessie would never have been able to guess it. A large pool of blood had settled under the back of her head. A few feet away, in a large evidence bag, was the meat tenderizer. Even from this distance, she could see bits of skin stuck on the spiked face of the long-handled, metal mallet.

"Married nine years, two kids—a girl, age seven and boy, five years old," Sergeant Frank told her, answering the question Jessie had been silently asking. "They were at a sleepover at a family friend's house last night so they didn't see anything. Husband is on the way home now. He was in court downtown this morning. They had to pull him out to tell him."

"Is there any sign of forced entry?" Jessie asked.

"Not that we found," Frank answered. "All the doors were locked and intact. No broken or even open windows."

Jessie glanced over at Ryan and knew he was thinking the same thing: no sign of forced entry greatly increased the likelihood that Trish Whitmore knew her attacker and let them enter the house.

"Okay, do we have sense of time of death?" Ryan asked.

"Body temp suggests between 5 and 8 a.m.," the examiner offered. "Hard to know which blow ultimately did her in, not that it really matters. But we think the first one was to the back of the skull."

"Why is that?" Jessie wondered.

"There's only one back there and there are no defensive wounds on her hands," he replied. "My best guess so far is that the attacker's first blow was when the victim's back was turned. It stunned her, maybe even knocked her out. Once she was down, the attacker went for the face. I count at least seventeen separate impacts but it could more than that."

Jessie didn't say it out loud, but made a mental note: the possibility that Trish had her back to her attacker only reinforced the suspicion that she didn't view her killer as a threat.

"Let's hope she was unconscious after the first one," Sergeant Frank muttered.

From an empathy perspective, Jessie agreed. But for the purposes of investigation, it was a negative. Had Trish Whitmore been alert enough to fight back, she might have gotten some of her killer's skin under her fingernails, or left telltale scratches. Jessie didn't say that. Instead she focused on other methods of identifying the murderer.

"There were several security cameras outside," she noted. "Has anyone had a chance to look at them yet?"

"Not yet," Sergeant Frank answered. "But according to the au pair, they won't be of much use anyway. All the exterior cameras were out of service."

"Seriously?" Ryan demanded.

"According to the girl, the Whitmores decided to switch companies about three months ago. They were able to install the interior cameras themselves. We're getting that footage momentarily. But because the outside cameras required installation by the company, they had to make an appointment. Apparently they'd been dragging their feet on it."

Though she was reluctant to draw conclusions this early on in a case, Jessie couldn't help but be slightly suspicious of the fact that those cameras hadn't been installed. How hard was it to make a call? Was it more than just procrastination?

"Please have the footage sent to Jamil Winslow once you have it," Ryan said, handing the sergeant a card for HSS's brilliant, do-it-all research manager.

Frank took the card and nodded.

"Where is this au pair?" Jessie asked. "I think it's time we had a chat with her."

"She's not here," Frank said sheepishly.

"What?" Jessie and Ryan asked in unison.

The sergeant sighed heavily.

"Before I got on the scene, Mr. Whitmore apparently called her and asked her to go over to take care of the kids. Their sleepover was at a friend's house about a half mile away. I'm afraid my officer didn't feel comfortable insisting that she remain here after Whitmore got him on the phone and started dressing him down. By the time I arrived it was done and I didn't see the point in dragging her back here. If we tried, the kids might want to come too and we don't need to deal with that hot potato. I'll take responsibility for the decision."

As frustrated as Jessie was, she knew that Sergeant Frank was in an impossible position. It was just this sort of thing that likely made the ESPD brass hand the case over in the first place.

"What about Pearlman, the interior decorator?' she asked. "Is she at least still here?"

"Yes ma'am," Frank assured her. "She's out back by the pool. There's an officer with her. She was still a little shaky when I left her."

Ryan glanced over at Jessie.

"Let's see if she's settled down enough to helpful," he said.

Frank guided them through several additional imposing rooms before they arrived at the French doors leading outside. He opened them. Jessie could see Suzanne Pearlman sitting on a patio chair, slumped over with a blanket over her shoulders. A female officer was sitting next to her, holding her hand.

They walked over and gave her a moment to realize they were there. But she was oblivious to their presence, so Sergeant Frank coughed slightly and spoke up.

"Ms. Pearlman," he said quietly. "I have some folks here that need to speak to you. This is LAPD Detective Hernandez and criminal profiler Hunt. They're taking over the investigation."

Pearlman lifted her head and Jessie saw that she'd been crying. Her eyes were red and puffy. Her brown hair was disheveled. Her mouth was pinched with anxiety. Jessie guessed that the woman was in her early forties but right now she looked a decade older than that.

"I know you," she said weakly, fixing her gaze on Jessie. "You're the famous profiler, the one who catches serial killers. Was this a serial killer?"

"We're hoping that you can help us find out," Jessie said quietly, taking the open seat next to Pearlman. "But to do that, Detective Hernandez and I need to ask you some questions. Are you up for it?"

Pearlman nodded, though she still looked unsteady. When she took a sip of water, her hand shook slightly.

"Let's start with how you got in touch with the Whitmores in the first place," Jessie said, easing in.

"I worked on the homes of some of their friends, who recommended me," Pearlman said, seeming to gain strength from focusing on a direct question. "They used to live in Beverly Hills before they moved here."

"Do you know why they moved?" Jessie pressed.

"When we spoke on the phone, Trish Whitmore told me that she and her husband, Roger—he's a big-time lawyer—wanted to get away from the pampered Beverly Hills world. They picked El Segundo because it has a small-town feel with a more economically diverse population, but still has great schools. I don't think it hurt that his firm represents one of the biggest companies in the city. They knew they'd still get a little pampering."

"Did you notice anything unusual when you spoke to Mrs. Whitmore?" Ryan asked.

Pearlman shook her head after thinking about it for a moment.

"No," she said. "We had a pretty standard conversation. We talked last week. She told me how she got my name, explained what she wanted. She was hoping to personalize the home a little more, starting with the kitchen. She told me about the move—all the stuff I was telling you about their reasons. Then we made the appointment for this morning. I texted last night to reconfirm and she said we were still on. That was the last time I heard from her."

"What time was that?" Ryan asked.

"Around six," Pearlman replied. She pulled out her phone and scrolled to the message. It was at 6:04 p.m. and the language was just as she'd described.

"How did Shannon Stanfield seem to you when you arrived?" Jessie wondered.

"Who?" Pearlman asked, perplexed.

"The au pair."

"Oh right," she said, her memory jogged. "I didn't even know they had one. She was nice enough, looked like she'd just woken up and run to open the door. She seemed surprised that Trish wasn't already up and inviting me in."

"And she wasn't with you when you found the body?" Ryan confirmed.

Suzie Pearlman took another sip of water before responding.

"Right. She'd gone upstairs to look for her. I walked into the kitchen and saw her. I kind of lost it and fainted. Next thing I knew I was laying on the floor with a pillow under my head. The au pair was kneeling next to me, offering me some water, this glass actually. She helped me outside. I haven't been back in since." She paused briefly before adding, "Do I have to go back in there?"

"We'll take you back through the house a different way," Jessie assured her. "You won't have to go near the kitchen. So it was Shannon who called 911?"

"Yes," Pearlman said. "She must have done it when I was out of it. She was very clear-headed, much more than me."

Jessie turned to Ryan.

"I feel like it's time we talked to this clear-headed, young woman."

CHAPTER THREE

The drive took less than two minutes.

Jessie and Ryan had left Sergeant Frank in charge of the scene while Trish Whitmore's body was removed and Suzie Pearlman was escorted out. He promised not to let Roger Whitmore enter the house upon his return home until they got back there, no matter how much pressure the man put on him.

Still, they moved quickly, not wanting to leave the police sergeant in the crosshairs for too long. They pulled up at the address they'd been given, a charming two-story Craftsman-style house that would have seemed quite impressive if not for the place they'd just left.

In fact, most of the homes in the community varied from modestly charming to surprisingly outsized. Jessie had always thought of this town as aggressively middle-class. But it was clear that the word was out and this seaside town on the outskirts of a huge city, with a large business district and desirable schools, was pulling in a wealthier crowd than it used to.

When they walked up the porch steps and got to the door, Ryan knocked rather than rang the bell. Jessie knew why. He didn't want to attract the attention of any young, curious children. It didn't take long for it to be opened slightly by a pleasant-looking thirty-something woman with light blonde hair and a scared look on her face.

"Hi," Ryan said soothingly. "Is Shannon Stanfield here?"

"Who may I say is asking?" the woman asked quaveringly.

"We're with the LAPD," he answered. "Did Shannon tell you about the situation from this morning?"

The woman nodded, biting her lip.

"Well, we're investigating what happened," he explained. "And we need to talk to Shannon about what she saw. We understand she came over to keep an eye on the Whitmore children."

"Yes," the woman said, opening the door a little bit more. "I'm Carol Brent by the way. Their children, Tracy and Colin, are friends with my kids. They spent the night because there's no school today."

"Where are they now, Mrs. Brent?" Jessie asked.

"They're all in the family room watching cartoons," she said. "Shannon's with them."

"She hasn't told them anything, has she?" Ryan checked.

"Of course not," Brent said. "She could barely explain it to me. She's just sitting there on the couch, kind of zoned out. I can't say I blame her. I can barely wrap my mind around this. Are you close to solving it?"

"I'm afraid we just got assigned to the case," Jessie informed her. "It could be a while. That's why we're here. Shannon might be able to help us get farther along. Can you please ask her to come out here? Obviously don't make a big deal of it. We don't want the kids to notice anything."

"Sure. If you want to wait in the dining room, I'll get her," Brent said, pointing at the room off to the left. "That's far enough away from the kids that they won't accidentally hear anything."

They took seats at the dining room table. Moments later, Brent returned with an attractive young woman in her early twenties with curly blonde hair and fair skin. She looked shell-shocked.

"Shannon, these are the officers handling Trish's case," Brent said softly. "I'll give you all some privacy."

She hurried off, leaving the young woman standing in front of them awkwardly.

"Please take a seat, Shannon," Jessie said, gesturing to the chair opposite them, where she could best study the girl's reactions. "I'm Jessie Hunt. I consult for the LAPD. And this is Detective Hernandez. We're sorry to meet under these circumstances, but I'm sure you understand that the sooner we talk to you, the better chance we have of finding out what happened."

"Of course," Shannon said quietly as she took a seat, her Irish lilt unmistakable.

"How are Tracy and Colin doing?" Jessie asked.

"They're in the other room watching a show and eating Pop Tarts," Shannon said. "They have no idea their entire world is about to be turned upside down."

"We'll do our best to hold off on that moment as long as possible," Ryan said. "Is that why Mr. Whitmore sent you over here despite the police request that you stay at the house?"

"He just wanted me to check on them, make sure they were okay," she explained. "He didn't know if this was some kind of attack on the family or what."

"I see," Ryan said, apparently deciding to let her having left the scene of a crime go for now. "So let's go back to earlier this morning. Ms. Pearlman, the interior decorator seemed to think you had just woken up when you opened the door for her."

"That's right," Shannon told them. "I was sleeping in because I didn't have to worry about the kids this morning. When I heard the bell ring twice, I knew something was up. Trish never makes anyone wait that long. So I rushed down in my nightclothes."

"When was the last time you saw Trish before you found her body this morning," Jessie asked.

"Last night, before I went to my room," she answered. "It would have been around ten or so."

"Do you know when she usually goes to bed?"

"She and Roger like to turn in early because of the kids and his work schedule," she explained. "It might have been different last night with the kids gone. Roger had a big case he was prepping and Trish is…was an early riser, even on the weekends."

"Did you see or hear anything out of the ordinary last night?" Ryan pressed.

"No, but I wouldn't have. I had my ear buds in, listening to music. I fell asleep with them in."

Jessie paused for a moment, before deciding to go bigger picture.

"Do you like working for the Whitmores?" she asked.

"Oh yes, very much," Shannon replied without hesitation. "They're very generous and the children are quite sweet, especially considering how obnoxious they could be, growing up in the lap of luxury as they do. Au pairs typically stay with a family for a year before returning to their home country. That's Ireland in my case. I've been with the Whitmores for ten months now, and have enjoyed my time with the family so much that I was hoping to extend my stay longer when my J-1 visa expires in May. I have no idea what'll happen with that now."

"How did you like Trish?" Jessie asked, well aware that she was unlikely to hear anything negative but intent on watching Shannon's body language as she answered.

"Very much," the au pair answered, showing no obvious sign of deception. In fact, her eyes got a little misty as she spoke. "She was a very dedicated mother, intent on making sure those young ones don't turn into little monsters. That's why they moved from Beverly Hills. She was very civic-minded, on all kinds of committees and boards. I couldn't keep up with all of them. She could be quite type

A, always on the move. But the great thing was that she didn't expect everyone else to be like that. She knew she was wired differently and had no illusions that others were as gung-ho as she was."

"You told the officers at the house that the cameras weren't working," Ryan noted, intentionally bouncing to a very different topic. Jessie approved. They found that keeping interviewees and possible suspects on their heels made it harder for them to offer pat answers.

"Only the outside ones," Shannon corrected, unfazed by the sudden change in subject. "The ones in the house are fine. I use them sometimes to keep an eye on the kids when I can't be in the same room with them for some reason. I gave the code to the officers so they could check the footage."

"Yes, thanks for that," Jessie said, before again switching topics. "When did Roger leave the house this morning?"

Shannon scrunched up her nose, apparently trying to recall.

"I couldn't say for sure as I was asleep late, as I mentioned. But yesterday evening, he was talking about getting an early start to avoid traffic. He had to be in court today on some big case and I know he didn't want to risk getting stuck on the freeway or anything like that. You'd have to check with him but I'd guess before 6 a.m. for sure."

Jessie looked over at Ryan and could tell that he didn't have any more questions. She wasn't quite done though.

"Just one last thing, Shannon," she began. "Suzie Pearlman said that while she lost it and fainted when she saw Trish's body, you kept your head about you. You called 911, got her a pillow and water, and even with a dead woman nearby, got her outside. How did you manage to stay so calm?"

"Oh, I wasn't calm at all, Ms. Hunt," she insisted. "I heard that woman screaming and my heart was pumping something mad when I rushed downstairs. When I saw Trish, I started screeching myself. Probably would have kept at if the lady didn't pass out on me. I didn't have much choice at that point. To be honest, it was a blessing to have something else to focus on. I kept all my attention on the tasks I could handle. I fixated on one chore, then another, and another, until we were out in that backyard. Once we were there, I got real wobbly, thought I might go faint myself there for a bit. Obviously, I've dealt with little ones who gave themselves a gash with a knife or fell off a play structure and hit their head. You have to stay calm so they will too. But this was something altogether different."

Jessie found her answer compelling and believable. But that didn't absolve her of anything yet. After all, there was no sign of forced entry in the home. And while she claimed to be in her room from 10 p.m. until 9 a.m., a window of time outside the M.E.'s estimated time of death, she had no way to verify that alibi. Until proven otherwise, Shannon Stanfield was still near the top of the suspect list.

Ryan's phone buzzed and he glanced at it.

"It's a text from Sergeant Frank," he said. "Roger Whitmore just got home. We better get back over there."

CHAPTER FOUR

Hannah Dorsey was finding it difficult not to rush the guy.

For fifty-one minutes now, Dr. Ken Tam had been offering her his own special brand of what she liked to call "condescension therapy." He seemed to think that the more he infantilized her, the easier it was to diagnose her, which he had apparently done before their first session even began.

"Would you feel safer if you shared a room with another resident?" he had asked in the wake of Merry's death. "Many people find comfort in the presence of others."

"No," she had told him. "I find comfort in solitude."

"Are there any special meals that might make you happier in this difficult time?"

Really probing stuff.

"No," she assured him, keeping her true thoughts about his therapeutic skills to herself. "I'm good with the kosher meals."

That had been one of Meredith Bartlett's tips in the brief time they'd hung out before she died: always go for the kosher meal. It's less likely to be mass-produced slop. She didn't mention to Dr. Tam that it was Merry's suggestion. That would only lead him to more maudlin questions and she was just trying to get through this.

This was their second chat, but the first since two days ago, when she'd found Merry Bartlett lifeless in her bed with her throat slit and a shard of bloody glass in her hand. Other than being dead, the girl appeared as cheerful as always, wearing a tie-dyed dress, her black hair decked out in pigtails with rainbow scrunchies.

Dr. Tam seemed surprised that, after coming across that scene, Hannah wasn't curled up in the fetal position, mumbling to herself. After all, she was currently a residential patient at the very psychiatric hospital where Merry had died.

She wanted to remind him that she'd seen far worse. In fact, coming across a person *after* they died was infinitely less traumatic than being forced to watch it happen in real time, like when her adoptive parents were slaughtered in front of her by a serial killer who turned out to be her birth father. Then there were the multiple other people she'd seen butchered by another killer, all in a sick attempt to seduce her into joining in the "fun." And of course, there was the murderer she'd shot dead just months ago, simply to watch the light in his eyes flicker out.

If she was still standing after all that, Merry Bartlett's death certainly wasn't going to send her into some kind of spiral, even if they had been on the verge of what normal people might call "friendship." And there was no way that she was going to share any of that with Dr. Tam, who clearly hadn't done his homework.

One thorough review of her file could have told him that she was an expert at navigating the aftermath of death and that treating her like a toddler who lost her dolly was insulting. The guy was an amateur: a squat, dumpy thirty-something with thinning brown hair, a sad mustache, and more arrogance than he was entitled to.

The only thing that was preventing her from taking him down a few pegs was Dr. Lemmon. First of all, she could hear Lemmon's voice in her head, reminding her that baiting someone into a conflict just for the rush of it wasn't helpful to her recovery journey. A big part of the reason that she was in this place at all was because she sought out interpersonal clashes, especially with men who had more power than her, because the high she got from verbally (and occasionally physically) humiliating them was so intense.

The other reason she held back was because she had no idea when Dr. Lemmon would be back. The psychiatrist had been admitted to the hospital with what was rumored to be kidney stones. Supposedly, in most cases, treatment and recovery for that wasn't too involved. But if there were complications, or if the rumors were untrue and she was hospitalized for something more serious, this joke of a therapist might actually have the deciding say, at least temporarily, on her course of treatment, medication, and ability to move about freely. There was no advantage to alienating him right now. So she continued to answer his inane questions.

"If your feelings right now could be described as an animal," he asked sincerely, "what animal would they be?"

She hid the smirk she felt coming on with a heavy sigh.

"Maybe an elephant," she offered, "because it's so hard for me to forget."

He seemed to like that answer, nodding enthusiastically as he scribbled something on the notepad in his lap.

"That's very insightful, Hannah," he said approvingly. "Along those lines, as a way to find an appropriate place to put Merry in your memory, is there anything you'd like to do or say to acknowledge her passing?"

Finally, a halfway decent question, one she had a clear answer to. But there was no way she was going to reveal it to Dr. Tam. She doubted he'd react well if she told him that she was skeptical that Merry had actually killed herself and intended to find out the truth.

He'd have good reason to be dubious of such a claim. After all, Merry had a history of cutting herself and, though she seemed to be a positive, even peppy person, Hannah knew far too well that outward-facing optimism could often mask deep depression.

And admittedly, she had no proof to back up her suspicion. But she did have a wealth of experience with horrific violence. And what she'd seen in that room felt off. The idea that Meredith Bartlett, who found solace in making small incisions in her forearms, suddenly took a chunk of glass and ripped a gaping hole in her own throat, didn't make sense. The wound Hannah discovered when she walked into that room looked messy and rushed and far from self-inflicted. But she couldn't say any of that to this man.

"Let me get back to you on that," she told him meekly, before quickly switching subjects, "or maybe to Dr. Lemmon. Will she be returning soon?"

Dr. Tam looked suddenly uncomfortable and glanced down at his watch.

"I'm sorry, Hannah," he said unapologetically. "But I can't get into the personal circumstances of the staff here at Seasons. In the meantime it appears that our time is up for now. Please do let me know if you have any thoughts about how to honor Merry."

"I'll do that," she replied as she stood up, using every ounce of willpower she had not to make a sarcastic crack about how well the staff at Seasons Wellness Center was doing securing people's personal safety lately.

She left his office, where a chunky, pimply guy about her age was standing anxiously by the waiting room door. He made no effort to move and she had to turn sideways to avoid bumping into him as she slid past. He seemed disappointed that he couldn't manufacture physical contact. Even once she'd gotten by him, she could feel him eyeing her lasciviously.

She half-regretted dressing decently today. Rather than wearing her standard attire for this place—sweatpants and a hoodie—she had decided to "dress up," which in here meant wearing jeans and a presentable top, letting her blonde hair hang loose rather than putting it in a ponytail with a cap, and putting a dash of makeup on her cheeks and around her bright green eyes.

It might have been some unconscious way of being respectful of Merry, who she knew she'd have to discuss with Dr. Tam. But she hadn't considered the unintended consequences. Up until now, she'd hidden herself in bulky clothes and caps, knowing that her tall frame and striking good looks would garner attention that she didn't want. But in an attempt to clean up for the benefit of Merry's memory, she'd sparked the interest of this pudgy mouth-breather with Brillo-pad hair.

It was too much to let go. She turned back around and stared at the teenage harasser-in-training, who looked on the verge of drooling, and waited for his eyes to finish scanning her body and get to her face. When they did, his cheeks turned bright pink, as he realized he was busted. When she spoke, it was with cold precision.

"Maybe if you spent a little less time eating potato chips and playing video games and a little more working out and cleaning up your zit-covered face, girls wouldn't want to vomit when you leered at them. As it is, the sight of you makes me want to take a Silkwood shower."

She turned without another word, just half-glimpsing his jaw drop before she opened the door to leave the waiting room. Behind her, she heard Dr. Tam call out, "I'm ready for you, Niles." Niles was going to have a lot to discuss today.

Hannah felt a half-second flash of guilt. She knew that part of her barbed comment was a result of holding back on them with Dr. Tam for nearly an hour. Beyond that, this was the exact kind of reaction Dr. Lemmon had been working with her to curb. And it had been going so well lately. This was definitely a step back.

Or was it?

How bad was what she said *really*? Yes, she'd been harsh. But she hadn't shamed Niles in front of a large group or accused him of assault or gotten him arrested for a crime he didn't commit, all things she'd done in the past. The only thing she'd done was to remind an aspiring pervert that there were consequences for being unsubtly gross. She was almost doing him a favor.

She was about to leave the administrative office that connected all of the therapists' personal offices when she realized that she was all alone. Elaine, the administrative assistant, was gone. An idea popped into her head.

She waffled briefly, unsure whether she should act on it. But then she asked herself a question she thought she never would: WWJD—what would Jessie do? As much as she currently resented her sister, there was no denying that she was a brilliant profiler and investigator. And the one thing Hannah always observed about Jessie was that she followed her instincts. Sometimes it got her in trouble, but usually it got her an arrest. If Hannah wanted to get to the truth about what happened to Merry, she was going to have to do the same and follow her own instincts.

So, choosing to ignore the caution lights flashing through her brain, she moved quickly to the assistant's desk and tapped the computer keyboard. The screen came to life. The woman either didn't have the desktop password-protected or didn't think she'd be gone long enough to need to lock the screen.

She pulled up Elaine's e-mail and quickly scanned it, looking for anything from the L.A. County Sheriff's Department, which handled law enforcement for the Malibu area. She was hoping that, rather than direct correspondence to any particular doctor, the sheriff's department would send communications to the medical team more generally and let them sort it out.

After a few seconds of scanning, she found that her hope had been borne out. Sitting in the in-box, was an hour-old message titled "Preliminary Sheriff's Department (Malibu/Lost Hills Station) Report/Decedent: Bartlett, Meredith G.," with an attached document. She quickly forwarded the e-mail to an anonymous e-mail account she'd set up last year, and then deleted the forwarded message from the assistant's sent mail. After that, she closed out of the inbox entirely.

She heard the sound of a door creaking open and quickly moved away from the desk, walking purposefully toward the exit. Glancing to her right, she saw Elaine coming out of the women's bathroom down the hall. The woman smiled pleasantly and Hannah gave a little wave before walking out.

As she left, she could feel the old tingle of excitement that she got when she would take chances like this out in the "real world." But she tried her best not to revel in it. She was taking this risk to find out what happened to Merry, not for the cheap high.

She reminded herself of what Dr. Lemmon had told her in one of their sessions last week: "we all feel an adrenaline kick when we're in a tense situation. That's natural. Your goal isn't to avoid those moments entirely. It's to stop actively looking for them." Hannah wondered how Dr. Lemmon would judge her in this moment.

She went straight to the resident communications center and signed the sheet on the clipboard by the door. The facility had strict limits on cell phone use and web services. Residents generally had to use dedicated computers in the communications center to send or receive e-mails. Hannah went to a terminal and pulled up her anonymous account.

Out of the corner of her eye she saw one of the proctors walking casually in her direction, looking over the shoulders of other residents as she passed by. Hannah quickly minimized her e-mail and did a quick web search for California culinary schools. At least that wouldn't look suspicious, as she'd mentioned on several occasions that she was considering trying to become a chef after she graduated from high school in a few months.

She left the search page up until the proctor had passed by and moved into a different row. Then she opened her mail again and went to the sheriff's message. The internet connection was slow and it took forever for the attached police report to load. Once she had it open, she scanned through it quickly.

She had sat at the dinner table with Jessie and Ryan enough times as they reviewed their own reports to know how they were structured. But it turned out that she didn't have to do much of a deep dive to find what she was looking for. Right near top on the first page, she found a line that read: *probable cause of death: suicide.* A few lines below that, the report noted that the only fingerprints found on the piece of glass used to rip open Merry's throat were her own.

Hannah wasn't shocked by the conclusion. If there was an easy explanation for what happened, most people were likely to take it, even cops. She moved to the next page, looking for anything that might cast doubt on that explanation. She found it at the bottom of the page in the preliminary toxicology report. According to the tests they ran, Merry had two medications in her system, neither of which she could easily pronounce. But apparently one was for chronic asthma and another was for depression, both of which doctors said she took on a regular basis.

Hannah finished the report, searching for any other mention of the tox report or the obvious contradiction it revealed, but there was none. She looked at the signature of the sheriff's department investigator, stunned that he had signed off on it without addressing what seemed to be an obvious issue.

Hannah could understand how her new friend might have spiraled downward if she was off her meds, though there was no indication of that in the hours before she died. But if Meredith Bartlett *hadn't* gone off her anti-depression medication, as the toxicology report claimed, why had she killed herself? There didn't seem to be an obvious medical reason. And no personal rationale had been suggested either.

Hannah sat quietly at the computer station, doing her best not to make the same clumsy assumptions that the sheriff's investigator had. And then she realized what she had to do. She needed to do this guy's job for him. She decided that if she was going to prove that Merry didn't kill herself, she needed to come at it backwards and pursue any possible motive she might have had to commit suicide. If she found a credible explanation for that conclusion, then she'd let this go. But if she couldn't, then she'd have a stronger case to take to whoever might actually listen.

It didn't take long for her determine how best to start. She'd talk to the one patient here she'd been scrupulously avoiding, the one she'd almost tossed her hot coffee at just two days earlier. She had to find Silvio Castorini.

CHAPTER FIVE

Jessie felt awful for Sergeant Frank.

Even from halfway down the block, she could see Roger Whitmore in a suit, with his back to them, pointing his finger in the officer's chest. It was clear that he was yelling at him. Though it had only been about four minutes since they got Frank's text saying that Whitmore had arrived home, she suspected that for the sergeant, it had been an eternity. His face was a mask of patient sympathy but she could see little twitches around the mouth that revealed he was churning under the surface.

Ryan pulled up in front of the house and they both hopped out and hurried over just as Whitmore finished a sentence with the phrase "…have no right to prevent me from entering my own home."

"Thanks so much for holding down the fort, Sergeant Frank," Ryan said with confident authority, "but we can take it from here."

"Who the hell are you?" Whitmore demanded, whirling around to face them.

For the first time, Jessie got a good look at him. Roger Whitmore was a big man, easily six-foot-three and two hundred and twenty pounds. He looked to be in pretty good shape, with just the hint of a paunch visible under his suit jacket. Jessie guessed that he was about forty. His brown hair was just starting to recede and he had the first hints of wrinkles at the edges of his eyes, which were red and wet with tears. Other than that and the tight grimace on his face, he was a handsome man.

"I'm Detective Hernandez with the LAPD, Mr. Whitmore," Ryan said evenly, not letting the other man's agitation affect him. "This is Jessie Hunt, a consulting profiler for the department. First of all, we want to offer our deepest condolences on the loss of your wife, sir."

That seemed to set Whitmore back on his heels for a second. Ryan took advantage of the hesitation to continue.

"We work for a unit of the department called Homicide Special Section, which handles…"

"I know who you both are and what your unit does," Whitmore said, cutting him off. "My firm's main office is eight blocks from Central Station. Are you telling me that HSS has been assigned to this case? What about El Segundo's finest?"

He looked over at Sergeant Frank, who clearly wasn't sure if he should respond to the question. Jessie stepped in to save him.

"Mr. Whitmore, your local police department wanted to make sure that all available resources were brought to bear on this case, and since they're a smaller department, they reached out to us for assistance and we agreed. This is what we do."

Whitmore stared at her with watery eyes and she knew that he had seen through her.

"Are you sure, Ms. Hunt," he asked in a tone she imagined he used often in court, "that they didn't hand over the case because when a married person is killed, the spouse is invariably the most likely suspect? And since that potential suspect—me—is also outside counsel for one of the city's most important corporations, it might be awkward for them to investigate me?"

Jessie smiled at him, revealing nothing.

"You'd have to ask them, sir," she said noncommittally. "All I can say is that we're here now, ready to do everything to bring your wife's killer to justice, whoever that night be. Now I think it would be best to continue this conversation inside, don't you?"

He shook his head vigorously.

"I need to see my kids first."

"We've just come from the Brent's house," she told him. "They're fine."

"What were you doing there?" he demanded.

"We needed to speak to your au pair, Shannon," Jessie said. "Right now your children are happily watching cartoons and eating junk food. They know nothing about this. The longer you can let them avoid dealing with this reality, the better. You're going to need the next few hours to process what happened and to make plans as well. You'll want to find a place to stay with them for the next few nights until we clear the house for your return. You're lucky to be able to do that planning without them around. Now I suggest that we go inside. Your neighbors don't need to hear our conversation."

That seemed to click for Whitmore, who nodded and shuffled toward the house. Ryan followed. Jessie gave Sergeant Frank an appreciative nod, indicating that he could go. He didn't need any convincing and headed straight for his car.

"She was killed in the kitchen, right?" Whitmore asked once they got inside.

"Yes," Ryan confirmed.

Whitmore led them to a sitting room in the opposite direction. Jessie couldn't blame him for wanting to talk as far from where it happened as possible. Once there, he sat in an antique chair and they settled in on a couch opposite him. He sighed, rubbed his eyes, and looked up at them.

"Listen," he said heavily, "I'm barely holding it together here. But I know you have a job to do. So before I ask any questions, why don't you get it out of the way?"

"Get what out of the way?" Ryan wanted to know.

"You're going to ask for my alibi at some point," he replied, "so why don't we deal with that now. That way you can have your people start checking it out right away. Then I hope you'll be more forthcoming with me about what happened."

Ryan looked at Jessie, who shrugged. She couldn't think of a reason not to proceed as he suggested.

"That's fine," she said. "Why don't you start by telling us the last time you saw your wife."

He only thought about it for a second.

"Last night around 10:30," he said.

"Not this morning before you left for work?" Ryan asked, surprised.

"This morning," Whitmore repeated, perplexed, "why would you say that?"

"Your au pair said she heard you and your wife talking about you going in early to avoid traffic because you had a big case in court," Ryan said.

"Oh yes, that's true," he answered. "We did talk about me leaving early this morning. But I ultimately decided that it would be better to just spend the night at the firm to avoid the stress of a commute. I have an air mattress in my office for times just like this, so I crashed there and was able to dive into the case right away this morning.

"What time did you leave the house last night?" Ryan asked.

"When I said goodbye to Trish at 10:30," he said. "I got to the office around 11 p.m."

"I assume your building has cameras that can confirm that?" Ryan pressed.

"Yes," Whitmore confirmed, "in the parking lot, the elevators, and the firm reception area. I also had to swipe my access card three times to reach the office. All of that should be logged."

"When was the last time you spoke to your wife?" Jessie wondered.

He thought about it for a second.

"I didn't talk to her last night after I left the house because I knew she'd be asleep by the time I got to work. So I guess it would be when I texted her this morning to check in."

"What time was that?" she asked.

Whitmore pulled out his phone and scrolled through it.

"6:28 a.m.," he said. "She got back to me right away."

He handed over the phone. Jessie and Ryan read the exchange together.

Roger: Morning. Already in the thick of it here. Sleep okay?

Trish: So-so. Forgot the kids weren't here and got up at five like always. Just got out of the shower. You going to be ready when the gavel strikes?

Roger: Fingers crossed.

Trish: Good luck. Keep me posted.

Roger: Will do. Talk later.

Trish: ♥

Jessie handed back the phone as she did some quick math in her head. That last text from Trish came in at 6:29 a.m. Assuming it was legit, that meant Trish Whitmore's time of death could now be shortened to the period from 6:29 until approximately 8:00 a.m. Once they got access to her phone records, they might be able to limit it even more.

Whitmore stared at the phone screen for several seconds, then coughed hard, seemingly trying to cover up a sob.

"What is it?" Ryan asked.

Whitmore shook his head.

"I just realized that the last thing I ever said to Trish was 'talk later.' Not 'I love you' or even 'take care.' Just 'talk later.' It's such a sad, perfunctory final goodbye. It feels wrong."

Jessie wasn't sure what to make of his statement. Was he really in mourning or was this just an act? She couldn't read him well enough yet to make an educated guess. Either way, she wasn't inclined to go down that path with him, at least not until the guy had been cleared of wrongdoing. The best she could do was to allow him a few seconds of respectful silence before pursuing her next question.

"What do you think of Shannon?" she asked bluntly.

He seemed to come out of his reverie and looked up at her.

"She's great," he said distractedly, "loves the kids. They consider her a member of the family, like their cool aunt. In fact, she was trying to extend her stay in the states, which we were fully supportive of. I know you have to look at her as a possible suspect too but it's hard to imagine she could hurt Trish. They got along really well, almost like a big and little sister."

"Is there anyone Trish didn't get along well with?" Ryan wondered. "Anyone she had a conflict with recently?"

"Sure," Whitmore said, "But nothing major. We're talking bureaucratic disputes on a citizens' commission about whether the city should provide complimentary, in-home composting boxes to residents or make them pay for them. Plus, she and another PTA mom disagreed over whether the kids' elementary school library should include books in which animals died. The other mom thought it was too traumatic. Trish felt that excluding them would deprive them of meaningful children's literature options. It was the most polite argument you'll ever see. Those are the kinds of conflicts she had."

"All right," Ryan said. "We'll still need the names of those folks, as well as anyone else she was close to: friends or family she talked with regularly, along with the password to unlock her phone."

"Of course," Whitmore said, "I'll get you all of that. But can you please let me know what happened now? All I was told was that she was killed in our kitchen sometime this morning. I don't know anything beyond that. Every time I asked, I got the runaround."

Jessie looked at Ryan, unsure who should answer and how much they should say. He gave a silent look that indicated he'd take this one. She was glad. He had way more experience in situations like this and if he answered, she could unobtrusively observe Whitmore's reaction.

"You know better than most people that we can't be too forthcoming when it comes to an ongoing investigation," Ryan told the man. "What I can tell you is that your wife was killed this morning. Her body was found by an interior decorator she had an appointment with. I'm sorry to be blunt but you deserve to know—she was beaten to death with a kitchen implement from your own kitchen, a meat tenderizer."

Whitmore made a sound somewhere between a gasp and a gulp. Ryan continued.

"While we can't be certain, the medical examiner thinks the first blow may have knocked her out and that she was unconscious for the remainder of the attack. There was no sign of forced entry. I think that's all I'm comfortable sharing at this point."

Whitmore nodded, not objecting. After several moments of silence, he cleared his throat.

"Can I go see my kids now?" he asked.

"Of course," Ryan told him. "But before you do, I need you to put together the info I asked for on Trish's contacts and phone information. I also assume you won't have any problem with us accessing your phone's GPS, calls, and message data."

"No problem for my personal phone," he said. "If you need to access information from my work phone, that would be a longer process. We'd need to redact some communications with and regarding clients. I'm sure you understand."

"Certainly," Ryan said congenially. "And I'm sure you understand that we'll need for you to remain easily reachable and of course, not leave town."

Whitmore didn't appear offended by the instruction. In fact, under the circumstances, he'd been more than reasonable when it came to all their requests. That, coupled with what sounded like a potentially airtight alibi might have him thinking he was in the clear.

But if he did, he was kidding himself. None of that meant he was off the hook. Roger Whitmore was clearly a smart guy who knew how the system worked and how it could be worked. As far as Jessie was concerned, he was still right at the top of the suspect list. Whether he stayed there or not would depend on the people she intended to talk to next.

CHAPTER SIX

They waited until Whitmore left before talking to the neighbors.

That way, they didn't give him any indication about how they were conducting their investigation. The hope was that someone noticed something or someone unusual this morning that could serve as a fresh lead. Unfortunately, it didn't end up mattering whether Whitmore was there or not.

Because the family's mansion consumed the entirety of the cul-de-sac, neighbors didn't have much reason to wander past it casually. Plus the other homes on the street, which were also big and on large pieces of property, were too far away for anyone not specifically on the lookout for suspicious activity to see or hear much of anything. Every interview they conducted was a bust.

They returned to the Whitmore house. Now that they were alone there, without family, cops, or dead bodies to distract them, Jessie hoped they might pick up on some detail they'd missed earlier. They started in the kitchen.

Jessie walked around the gigantic island slowly while Ryan called Jamil Winslow, HSS's head of research. When he answered, Ryan put him on speaker.

"Did the El Segundo police send you guys the footage from the Whitmore security cameras yet?" he asked.

"Nice to hear from you, Detective Hernandez," Jamil replied sharply.

Jessie couldn't help but chuckle. Since he'd been named Head of Research for HSS, the twenty-four-year old wunderkind had grown in both confidence and willingness to throw good-natured shade at his co-workers.

"Sorry, Jamil," Ryan replied. "How are you and Beth doing on this fine Monday morning?"

Beth Ryerson was the unit's new research hire and Jamil's sole employee. She was also twenty-four, but that's where the similarities between the two researchers ended. Jamil, while brilliant, was almost painfully formal in his personal interactions. He was also short and scrawny, though he was furiously working out as of late to try to fill out a little.

Beth, on the other hand, was casually outgoing, and understatedly attractive with her purple glasses and minimal makeup. A former college beach volleyball player, she towered over her boss at six feet tall. Still in incredible shape, she looked like she could break him in half if she chose to.

"We're good, Detective," Beth piped in. "And we did get the footage. Unfortunately, even though the security system is top-notch, I'm not sure it's going to be all that helpful."

"Why not?" Ryan asked.

"Because there aren't cameras where we need them most," Jamil explained. "There are a ton of them in the main living areas: the family room, the kids' play room, and most hallways. But there aren't any in the kitchen or in the hallway near the primary bedroom."

As Jamil spoke, Jessie opened different doors in the kitchen. One led to the pantry, another to a supply closet. The third, adjacent to the back door leading from the kitchen out to the side of the house, was locked.

"Do we have the key for this?" she asked Ryan.

"No," he said, "but that doesn't mean it can't be opened."

He pulled out a small lock pick and had it unlocked in less than thirty seconds. He opened the door to reveal a narrow staircase that wended up, around, and out of sight. Jessie turned on the light switch by the door and headed up. The stairs spiraled up for what felt like more than one floor. When she finally reached the staircase's end, she found that the door at the top opened directly into the primary bedroom.

"What do you see?" Ryan called out from below.

"The Whitmores' bedroom," she yelled back. "I guess they wanted to be able to get late night snacks without walking down the main hallway and waking anyone up."

She passed through the bedroom and out into the hallway. It was incredibly long, extending a good fifty yards until it curved and opened up near the main set of stairs. Once there, she called Jamil to be conferenced in on the open line that he already had with Ryan.

"Do you guys have a live feed of the house?" she asked, waving her arms over her head. "Can you see me in the hallway?"

"We have a feed," Beth answered. "But we don't have eyes on you."

"Okay," Jessie said, "I'm just going to keep walking. Let me know when I come into view."

She got about halfway down the hall, just past the door for what she assumed was another bedroom, when she heard Jamil's voice.

"We can see you now," he told her.

"What about now?" she asked, taking a step backward so that she was right in front of the bedroom door.

"Not anymore," Beth said. "You're just out of sight."

Jessie opened the door in front of her.

"Whose room is that?"

Jessie almost jumped out of her skin. Ryan had climbed the stairs and was now in the hallway just outside the Whitmores' bedroom.

"You scared the crap out of me," she hissed.

"Sorry," he told her. "I figured why listen to the narration when I could check it out for myself. So whose room is it?"

Jessie looked inside and was confident she knew the answer, even without an Irish flag to tip her off. There were posters of bands she'd never heard of on the wall and many photos of smiling people in pubs, all in their teens and twenties.

"It's Shannon's room," she said.

"You know what that means," Ryan said as he walked over to her.

"I do indeed," she replied.

"I don't," Beth told them. "Care to enlighten me?"

Jamil did the honors.

"It means that even though Shannon Stanfield said she slept in until nine this morning, she could have left her bedroom, gone down the hall, through the Whitmores' room, and taken the stairs into the kitchen, all without being picked up by the cameras or without Trish Whitmore seeing her."

"That's right," Jessie agreed, "and unfortunately for both her and us, it means she can't prove her alibi *and* that we can't disprove it. She could have snuck down and killed Trish. Or she could have been asleep whole time, just as she claims. We're back to square one."

CHAPTER SEVEN

This was it. The big day!

Eden Roth had to use all her self-control not to skip down the street.

After she got out of the cab a block from downtown L.A.'s California Plaza, she walked slowly, trying to time her steps to match her breath in order to control the giddiness that was bubbling up inside her.

It was lunchtime and the plaza was full. The adjoining Cal Marketplace, with over a dozen casual restaurants, was packed as well. Located at the base of the Omni Hotel on Grand Avenue, just down the block from the Museum of Contemporary Art and in sight of the Angel's Flight Railway, this was one of most popular destinations for downtown workers to get a bite. That was especially true today.

It was early March and the mild bite of L.A. winter, which had been slowly relenting over the last few weeks, seemed to have taken the day off completely. It was 71 degrees and sunny, and the plaza was full of people relaxing as they ate.

As she made her way down the funky-looking, wide, stone staircase that led from the street to the food court, she passed several people lying out on nearby, square marble slabs, sunning themselves while reading, eating, or listening to something through their ear buds.

She continued into the interior section of the marketplace, keeping her head down as she walked to the women's restroom. Unlike most folks, she was covered up in a long sleeved top, pants, sunglasses and a cap with the brim pulled down low. It was important that she not be too easily identified later by security cameras.

This was all part of the plan. Back when Eden was a resident at the Female Forensic In-Patient Psychiatric Unit at the Twin Towers Correctional Facility, she'd never have thought she'd be entrusted with a plan by anyone. But that was before she'd met Andrea Robinson.

Andy was the one person who had shown faith in her, who believed that she could be more than what everyone else saw: a mousy nebbish, skinny and short with limp, brown hair, dull, gray eyes, and sickly pale skin.

Maybe it was Eden's degree in biochemistry and placement on the Dean's List, earned before she succumbed to the fantasies that got her locked up, that made Andy believe in her. Maybe it was her fascination with how chemical compounds could affect the human body. Whatever it was that made Andy have confidence in her, that faith had bred devotion in Eden, who committed to the Principles, a series of life instructions that Andy had established for her small coterie of acolytes.

Some were simple and straightforward, like: *Always remember that your mind is your strongest tool. It can take you anywhere if you let it.* Another was: *Don't betray a sister in need; be ready to help a sister complete her deed.*

But the single most important instruction, which Andy referred to as the Primary Principle was as follows: *Protect the Principal, as in never reveal the identity of the group's leader or her teachings, even if it means sacrificing yourself to keep the secret.*

Eden was about to put the Primary Principle to the test. It was possible that this plan she'd concocted could fall apart and that she would fail. Even if she succeeded, she might get caught and be pressed to reveal who had brought her such enlightenment. That was when she would learn what she was really made of. She felt sure she would live up to the moment, but one could never know for certain until the time arrived.

She wished she could have gotten a final message to Andy in her new facility, the Western Regional Women's Psychiatric Detention Center. Eden hadn't seen her in eight months, since she was released from the Twin Towers. And writing, calling, or heaven forbid, trying to visit Andy at the PDC, would have raised too many alarm bells.

So she comforted herself in the knowledge that once she completed her task, Andy would know about it, just as everyone would, and she would be proud of her. After all, she had given Eden complete autonomy as to how to complete her assignment. Eden knew her mentor would be delighted at the deliciousness of it.

Eden had been tossed in the psych ward because she liked to cut her palms, and then go out into public spaces with her red, dripping hands, hugging unsuspecting passers-by and sharing her life-giving blood with them. Now she would take that one giant, beautiful step farther.

The final, majestic twist was that Eden was currently standing just nine blocks from LAPD's Central Station, where Jessie Hunt, the woman who got Andy locked up in the first place, worked. Hunt would inevitably be assigned to this case. She would have to see the carnage. She would have to turn to her old nemesis for help, unaware that she was walking, unprotected, into the lair of the enemy. It was almost too perfect.

Once in the bathroom, Eden found an empty stall, locked it, and hung her small bag on the hook. She giggled silently as she removed the necessary items and put them on the back of the toilet. Out came the latex gloves, followed by the scarf that would hide the protective surgical mask she wore underneath, and finally the special liquid that she had prepared after much time and difficulty.

She removed her sunglasses, put the mask on and wrapped the scarf around her neck and face. After that she snapped on the gloves. When she was sure they were secure, she unlocked the stall door, using her butt to keep it closed. Then she opened the bottle and poured the liquid into her left palm and rubbed it all over the gloves: front and back of the hands, making sure to coat them all the way up to the tips of the fingers.

Once that was done, Eden stepped away from the door, letting it swing open. Peeking under the other stall doors, she saw that she was alone. She tossed the empty bottle in the trash bin and waited by the restroom door. Her heart was pounding so hard in her chest that she could actually hear it. As soon as the door opened and she encountered that first person, there was no going back. Not that she wanted to.

It didn't take long. After ten seconds of anxious waiting, the door opened. Eden stepped forward without even seeing who it was and "inadvertently" bumped into the woman, the back of her left hand making contact with the woman's left forearm. Eden mumbled sorry without ever looking up and stepped out into the crowded food court.

She glanced around, trying to decide the best place to start. The liquid on her gloves only had about two minutes before it began to dry, so she had to move fast. She picked Santa Rosa Farmhouse, the restaurant with the longest line.

She walked over quickly and saw that there was a display case near the front of the line. Pretending to be curious to check out what was behind the glass near the register, she nudged her way past the throng of people, making sure that multiple fingers brushed up against customers with exposed skin. No one seemed to take notice.

After looking at the display for what she silently counted out as seven seconds, she moved on, making contact with a few more people as she left the restaurant. An older man held the door open for her and she gently touched his hand as she said "thanks."

There wasn't much wetness left on the gloves, so she headed back toward the stone staircase she'd used to enter, looking for anyone she could use the last of it on. She saw a janitor and tapped him on the back of neck. When he turned around, she asked "Which street is Grand?"

He pointed in the direction she was already planning to go. She offered a nod of gratitude and moved that way. As she walked, she used the underside of her forearm to adjust her cap upward and tug the scarf down, all in order to make her face a little more visible. In the background, she could hear the beginnings of loud, worried voices from the direction of Santa Rosa Farmhouse, and picked up the pace.

She was just starting up the steps when she saw a couple sitting on one of the large, marble squares. The slightly chunky woman appeared to be crying quietly. The hairy guy in the tank top sitting next to her looked annoyed.

"I'm just saying that if you want to lie out and expose yourself like that for everyone to see, maybe you should lose a few pounds," he said. "Otherwise it's embarrassing for me. Is that such a bad thing to say?"

Eden glanced down and saw that she had one last dollop of liquid left in the palm of her left hand, where she'd originally poured the contents of the bottle. Even though the panicked voices down below had now turned to screams, she couldn't resist one last gift.

She pretended to stumble on one of the stairs and reached out to the hairy guy to get her balance. Rather than try to help, he attempted to ward her off. But he couldn't stop her from clutching his left shoulder with her left hand and smashing her palm hard into his flesh.

"So sorry," she said. "I'm such a klutz."

"No kidding," he shot back, shoving her away hard. He looked like was going to add another comment when his girlfriend interrupted.

"What the hell is going on down there?" she said.

The hairy guy and Eden both looked back down the stairs to where people were streaming out of Santa Rosa Farmhouse. Some were knocked over by the swarm of customers shoving their way out the door. Others were already on the ground, writhing and twitching, with foam coming out of their mouths.

"Dear Lord," the chunky woman whispered as the crowd careened chaotically toward them, "let's get out of here."

But when she and Eden looked over at the spot where her boyfriend had just been, they saw that he'd already abandoned her without a word and was halfway up the stairs. Eden followed right after him, hoping not to get crushed by the advancing horde.

Part of her wanted to stay and watch, but she knew that it would look suspicious to be the one person enjoying the show while everyone else fled. So she darted up the stairs, doing her best to look terrified as people sprinted past her. When she got up the street, she headed left on Grand in the direction of West 4th Street, where she knew she'd have a better chance of catching a cab and clearing the area the cops would soon occupy.

She'd made it about twenty steps when she almost tripped over the hairy main in the tank top. He was lying face down on the sidewalk, his body convulsing up and down, almost like a centipede on amphetamines. His mouth was frothy white. He reminded Eden of a rabid, dying dog.

As she passed by him, she was glad the scarf was still covering her mouth. That way, no one could see her smiling.

CHAPTER EIGHT

It was Beth's idea to go to Roger Whitmore's office.

After they'd come up empty at the Whitmore house, Jessie and Ryan had resigned themselves to going to the El Segundo Police Station to see if the local cops had uncovered anything new.

"What about Whitmore's case?" Beth had volunteered hesitantly. "Is there any chance that his wife was killed to make him drop out of whatever had him in court this morning?"

"That's a great question," Jessie had told her, embarrassed that it hadn't occurred to her to ask it. "Let's find out."

That was why they were currently headed north on the 110 Freeway with the siren on, trying to get to the downtown offices of Daniels, Kramer, Malone & Whitmore as fast as possible. While Jamil and Beth were back at the station reviewing both Whitmore's phone records and financials, Ryan and Jessie used the time stuck in the car to check in with some of the people Roger Whitmore said Trish had been close to.

First they called Trish's Aunt Nancy, whose house Roger Whitmore said he and the kids would be staying at for the next few days. Apparently they were very close and talked almost every day.

"I can't think of anyone she had a serious dispute with," Aunt Nancy said. Even over the phone they could tell she was struggling to keep it together. "Other than occasionally getting annoyed with someone who ran a stop sign or a barista who screwed up her order, she was pretty even-keeled."

"Could anyone connected to Roger's work have been a source of concern?" Jessie asked. "Did Trish ever mention that?"

"We didn't talk that much about his work," Nancy replied. "I know he had a lot of big, corporate clients. I got the sense that it was all pretty dry."

"Did they seem happy?" Ryan asked, switching gears abruptly.

"Yes," she answered without hesitation. "They loved their life, especially after moving from Beverly Hills to El Segundo. Trish grew up here, you know. They were less stressed. The kids seemed happier. They had a solid circle of friends, as well as me as an extra source of support. And based on Trish's cryptic comments, I got the sense that things were still pretty spicy in the bedroom. They absolutely seemed happy."

That was the most salacious thing they got out of her. When they called Michelle McGarry, who Roger said was Trish's best friend, they hoped for something meatier.

"Trish had sharp elbows," she conceded after taking several minutes to recover from the news of her friend's death, "but I never saw anyone get truly angry with her. They just knew that she would stand her ground and not back down when something was important to her. I think any successful woman these days has to have a bit of that in her, don't you?"

Jessie couldn't disagree, though she didn't say so. Instead she asked the same question that Ryan had put to Aunt Nancy.

"How was their marriage?" she asked.

"Good," McGarry said. "They were really into each other, sometimes inappropriately so—lots of PDA. Roger's a bit of a flirt, and he did it right in front of Trish. Half the time it seemed like he did it just to get her riled up. It worked. If he complimented a waitress too much at dinner, it usually meant that he and Trish would be leaving within fifteen minutes. It was like noticing another woman was his surefire way to make sure his wife slept with him that night."

"Did his flirting ever go too far?" Ryan pressed.

"Not that I ever saw," McGarry replied. "It was his way of teasing Trish. She seemed to get off on it. I'm not going to judge. Whatever they were doing, it worked for them."

"And did Trish ever mention any threats that Roger got at work?" he asked.

"Not that I'm aware of," she told him. "I know he made a lot of enemies. But they were the kind who sue, not who murder."

After they hung up, Jessie sat quietly for a minute, the sound of the siren barely registering in her brain as the car neared downtown.

"What is it?" Ryan asked.

She looked over at him.

"I'm not going to dismiss the possibility that this was related to Roger's work," she said, "but I'm more inclined to think this murder was personal."

"Why do you say that?"

"First," she began, "the medical examiner said she was hit at least seventeen times. I suppose it could have been a professional hit and the killer was just going overboard to cover that up, but it sure felt like whoever did this had a beef with Trish Whitmore. Plus, it seems unlikely that she would let someone she didn't know well into her home, her kitchen. That doesn't sound like one of her husband's legal adversaries."

"Well, I guess we're about to find out a bit more about those adversaries," Ryan said. "That's his firm on the next block, in the building so high I can't see the top of it."

*

The law offices of Daniels, Kramer, Malone & Whitmore were located on the 65th floor of the Francisco Building, near the L.A. Live Entertainment Complex. Jessie's last birthday, for which Ryan had thrown her a surprise party, was held at a nearby bowling alley. But she'd never been in this building, which didn't seem like it catered to the bowl and brew set.

They were riding up in a glass, exterior elevator when an alert came over Ryan's radio about a mass casualty event at California Plaza, just over a mile from their current location. He immediately called Captain Decker.

"What is it, Hernandez?" the captain demanded brusquely. "I'm a little busy here."

"We just heard about California Plaza over the radio," Ryan said. "Do you need our help?"

"We've got a Hazmat unit on the scene now," Decker told him. "Chief Laird wants us to take point. I've already assigned Bray, Nettles, and Valentine to the case. You should stick with the Whitmore thing."

"But it sounds like you'll need everyone you can get," Jessie insisted, hoping she didn't sound like she doubted the abilities of the other HSS detectives.

"We're fine, Hunt," Decker said sharply. "We don't even know what we're dealing with yet and the people I assigned are more than capable of determining that. Besides, you two are committed. We already agreed to take over this case from the El Segundo Police. We can't back out now. That's not good form. And if you think Roger Whitmore is just going to sit around quietly while his wife's murder takes a backseat to a sexier case, you are sorely mistaken. Imagine how bad it would look in the media if he did an interview saying HSS doesn't consider her butchering important enough for the likes of Homicide Special Section. No, you stay on that case.

Once you solve it, we'll be happy to have your assistance. Until then, you're spoken for."

She wasn't sure if he hung up or if they lost the cell connection as the fast-moving elevator reached the 65th floor and the doors opened. They stepped out into an expansive, glass encased reception area. People in expensive suits with grim expressions were scurrying about and they had to dodge them to get the reception desk.

"Hi," Ryan said to the receptionist, "Detective Ryan Hernandez and Jessie Hunt from the LAPD. We're here to meet with Charles Daniels. He's expecting us."

The eyes of the young woman at the desk got very wide briefly before she recovered. Jessie suspected that it wasn't everyday that the LAPD showed up to speak to the senior partner of one of the most prominent law firms on the west coast.

"Give me one moment please," she said crisply.

While they waited, Jessie checked her phone.

"Hey, did you see this?" she asked Ryan, showing him the message they'd both received from Jamil.

"No, I missed it."

They read it together. It was brief.

Roger Whitmore's alibi holds up. Phone GPS confirms he was at office all night into morning. So do cameras and security card swipes. Trish Whitmore's phone shows her at home all night and morning as well. No calls or texts in A.M. after final message to husband.

While the information wasn't surprising to Jessie, it was disappointing in that it offered nothing they didn't already know. Trish's phone data kept the window of death sometime between 6:29 a.m. and 8 a.m. And while Roger's data verified his physical location, it didn't absolve him.

Just because he didn't actually beat his wife to death, that didn't mean he couldn't have hired someone to do the dirty work. He would have been able to provide information about the home and access to it. He knew his kids were somewhere else at the time and was able to track Trish's whereabouts. He wasn't out of the woods yet.

Jessie heard a polite cough behind her and turned around to find a small, young woman with short, curly hair and glasses with bold, purple frames standing at attention.

"Hello," she said. "I'm Lynn, Mr. Daniels' executive assistant. If you'll come with me, I'll take you to him."

They followed her down a long hallway that curved back and forth like a snake among the various offices, all of which were glassed in and fully visible to passers-by. One large conference room looked particularly busy, with close to a dozen people bustling about with worried looks on their faces.

"What's going on in there?" Jessie asked.

"Oh, that's the Metron team," Lynn explained. "They're scrambling because Mr. Whitmore had to beg off the case and the judge is only allowing a one-day delay."

"What's the case about?" Ryan asked.

"It's a dispute with an environmental group called Water Warriors over off-shore drilling. They want to shut down one of Metron's proposed operations up along the Central Coast. The wrangling has been going on for years, but since the lease for the drilling expires next month, time is becoming a factor."

They arrived at an office in the far back corner of the floor. Jessie noted that it was one of the few with actual walls instead of glass. The door was closed and Lynn knocked.

"Come in," called out a weathered but molasses-smooth voice from somewhere inside.

Lynn pushed open the door and stepped inside first.

"I have Detective Hernandez and Ms. Hunt for you," she said, welcoming them in.

They stepped inside. It was all Jessie could do to hide her awe. The office was bigger than her backyard, with floor to ceiling windows and a door leading out to a small balcony. The walls were covered in massive, glass-encased canvasses, complete with small informational cards off to the side indicating the provenance of the works. Charles Daniels's desk, was small for the space, but looked to have been carved out of marble. It was immaculate and almost completely devoid of papers.

The man wasn't physically imposing but he had a courtly, commanding bearing. Jessie guessed that he was in his mid-sixties. He was on the smaller side, maybe five foot seven and one-hundred-forty pounds, with neatly parted gray hair and wire-rimmed glasses. His jacket was off but he wore a vest with a bright orange pocket square and a matching tie. The man walked around from behind his desk to greet them and Jessie noted that he moved spryly, like a man twenty years younger.

"Thank you both for coming," he said warmly, his voice enveloping them like a hug as he shook their hands. "We're here to help in any way we can."

"Thank you for responding so quickly," Ryan replied.

"Of course, please sit down," he insisted, leaning against the front of his desk. "I hope you don't mind if Lynn sticks around. That way, she'll be able to expedite any requests that you might have."

"Sure," Ryan said.

"Before you begin," Daniels said, "If you don't mind my asking, do you know where the funeral and memorial service are being held? The firm wants to pay for all of it but we obviously don't want to trouble Roger right now. Everyone is so anxious to lend a hand but we all feel a little helpless at the moment."

"I don't know," Ryan admitted. "But you could reach out to the El Segundo medical examiner. He'll have instructions on where to release the body once the autopsy is done. That's usually to the family's preferred funeral home, but this all so fresh that they might just not know yet."

"Completely understandable," Daniels said. "So how can I help you?"

Ryan turned to Jessie and she launched in.

"Well, as Detective Hernandez mentioned when he called originally, we'd like to look at Roger Whitmore's case files. We don't have a motive yet and it's worth seeing if Trish's death has anything to do with him, if anyone he went up against rings any alarm bells. Plus, it's always a good idea to check if any current or former clients are upset for any reason."

"Certainly," Daniels said, turning to Lynn. "Have we got all that squared away?"

"We do," she said. "All of the files have been set up in the secondary conference room down the hall. They obviously don't include strategy notes or client communications. But there's a full accounting of all his clients and the current status of their cases."

"Wonderful," Jessie said, "we'll head over there momentarily. But as long as we have you, we have a few quick questions."

"Go right ahead," Daniels replied.

"Lynn mentioned that you have a team scrambling to stay on track now that Whitmore is off the Metron case," Jessie noted. "Is it possible that someone involved might have been hoping for just that outcome: for the lead attorney on the case to drop out, putting you at a disadvantage?"

Daniels tried to stifle a chuckle.

"Forgive me," he said quickly. "That was inappropriate. It's just that I find it difficult to believe that our friends at Water Warriors would take such drastic measures. They are unquestionably devoted to their cause, but there's nothing about today's court proceedings so critical that they would engender such an extreme response. Besides, between you and me, they are already virtually certain to win. Almost every court that has ruled on this issue has come down in their favor. As Metron's outside counsel, we are obligated to pursue all legal recourses on their behalf, but at this point we're just playing out the string. The Water Warriors people know that. It wouldn't make sense for them to do something as awful as this when they're so close to winning once and for all."

"May I add something to that?" Lynn asked.

"Please," Jessie said.

"Even if everything Mr. Daniels said wasn't already the case, there's another factor that makes it hard to believe this murder had anything to do with the Metron case. While Roger Whitmore is the lead attorney for the firm, he wasn't scheduled to be the primary litigator on this particular matter in court today."

"Who was?" Ryan asked.

"Joe Lofton," Lynn said. "The only reason he wasn't there was because his wife had their first child yesterday morning. Roger agreed to step in at the last minute because he knows the case backward and forward and was the most prepared to pinch hit. But almost no one else knew that. Not the judge and certainly not the Water Warriors attorneys. They only found out when he walked into the courtroom this morning. I'm not a detective, but if they couldn't have anticipated he'd be there, it seems unlikely that they could have planned something like this."

Jessie had to agree that it was a fair point. What she didn't add out loud was that Trish Whitmore was killed before Roger even entered the courtroom, so the opposing lawyers wouldn't have known about the attorney change until after Trish was already dead. It seemed that researcher Beth Ryerson's theory, while compelling, wasn't panning out.

Impressed with Lynn's thought process, Jessie decided to direct her next question to both Daniels and her. She suspected the executive assistant might be more attuned to answer it than her boss.

"Was Metron happy with your work for them, Roger's in particular?"

"Absolutely," Daniels volunteered. "Not only were they happy, but they were over the moon once they learned his family was relocating to El Segundo. The CEO told me personally that he viewed it as a strong sign of Roger's commitment to them."

"Do you know if he ever faced any threats?" Jessie pressed. "Being the lead attorney for an oil and gas company can't be all rainbows and unicorns when it comes to the public."

Lynn shook her head.

"I wondered that as well and looked through the security files earlier," she said. "Any threat is supposed to be reported to security immediately. I didn't see a single one related to the company. Still, I left the files out on the conference table for you to review."

"Would those files also mention any internal threats?" Jessie wondered. "Rivalries with co-workers that got out of hand? Folks who got passed over for promotions and reacted poorly? That kind of thing."

"Those would be in the security file as well," Lynn said. "I don't recall anything like that in the time that I've been here but you might find something in the files."

"Then I guess we should get started," Ryan said, standing up. "Thanks for your time."

"Glad to be of help," Daniels said. "Lynn will show you to the small conference room. Make yourselves comfortable and let us know if there's anything more we can do."

They nodded and followed Lynn out. Jessie was particularly anxious to get started, and specifically to take a look at those security files. Something the executive assistant had said leapt out at her. While none of the security files related to Metron, there *were* security files. And files meant possible threats, which meant possible leads.

It was all she could do not to skip down the hall.

CHAPTER NINE

Detective Susannah Valentine tried to hide just how overwhelmed she was.

Even on the nine-block drive from Central Station to California Plaza, they were getting a constant, ever-changing flood of information. By the time that she, Detective Karen Bray, and Detective Jim Nettles hopped out of the car on South Olive Street and dashed through the back entrance to the plaza, the number of confirmed dead had risen from three to four and the total count of people either en route to or at local hospitals had climbed from eight to eleven.

When they passed through the food court to the plaza, Susannah had to blink repeatedly to believe what she was seeing. There were at least two dozen uniformed officers on the scene, along with another five in Hazmat suits, though a few of them had removed their helmets.

She saw two human-sized lumps on the ground, covered in sheets, and knew there were at least two more nearby. She could see five other people being treated by paramedics, of which there were at least ten on site. In the distance, on Grand Avenue, she was almost blinded by the flashing lights of an endless stream of ambulances and fire trucks.

"Where should we go first?" Jim Nettles asked, broaching the same question she had.

"Let's check in with one of those Hazmat folks," Karen Bray suggested. "At least they'll know if we should be wearing gas masks or something."

It wasn't so much a suggestion as a politely worded order. Bray had seniority among the three of them and was nominally in charge. Nettles, who had been a street officer for fifteen years before making detective last year at age thirty-seven, was technically next in line, though he didn't seem to care about such distinctions. Burly, grizzled, and taciturn, with flecks of gray in his black hair, he seemed happy to do the job without any drama or power struggles.

Susannah was still considered the rookie in the group. Despite her two years as a detective in Santa Barbara and five more before that as an LAPD patrol officer, she'd only been with HSS for six weeks now and was still trying to earn her stripes. Setting her place in the pecking order aside, Susannah took the lead as they walked toward an authoritative-looking woman in a full Hazmat body suit, wiping sweat from her brow. Susannah refused to let anyone sense the self-doubt that came with being the newbie in the most celebrated unit of the Los Angeles Police Department.

"We're here from Homicide Special Section," she said with a confidence she didn't feel. "I'm Valentine. These are detectives Bray and Nettles. What precautions do we need to take before investigating the scene?"

"Technician Lorna Petty, Hazardous Material Unit," the woman said. "Good to meet you. We've just now established that masks and suits are no longer necessary. Whatever agent was used on these people absorbed into the skin quickly. While I wouldn't touch anyone with your bare hands, it looks like the scene is no longer a threat to anyone who wasn't initially exposed."

"What can you tell us, Lorna?" Karen asked politely.

Susannah had learned quickly not to be deceived by the senior detective's self-effacing manner or petite frame. Karen Bray was a savvy, efficient investigator who didn't take any crap but somehow managed to be diplomatic about it. In her late-thirties, her dirty blonde hair was, as always, tied back in a utilitarian ponytail.

"Not much yet," Petty said. "The folks still being treated here were all injured in the panic right after people started collapsing. Most of them were knocked to the ground. Some were trampled. Everyone impacted by the agent is either dead or at a hospital and none of the latter were in any condition to speak."

"Then how do you know that they absorbed the agent through the skin?" Susannah asked.

"There are telltale marks on the bodies, like acid burns, at least on everyone I've checked out so far."

"Looking at how spread out all the bodies are," Nettles noted, pointing at a third lump in a shaded section thirty yards away, "Is it reasonable to assume that this wasn't some inadvertent chemical explosion or something along those lines?"

"Quite reasonable," Petty agreed. "While initial reports indicate that the bulk of the chaos occurred in the Santa Rosa Farmhouse restaurant over there, we found one body in the women's restroom well off to the right. I leave it to you HSS folks to make the final determination, but based on what we have so far, this feels intentional. These people were killed on purpose."

Susannah felt a chill run up her spine at those words. She pressed ahead with her next question just to avoid the ugly, ensuing silence.

"No idea whether it's a terrorist attack or just some solo psycho?" she asked.

"Not so far," Petty said. "We don't even know what the agent used is yet, which will go a long way to helping make that determination."

"Okay," Karen said. "I think it's time we start doing some of our own investigative work. I was going to check with the security office to see about getting all the camera footage from the area. Maybe that'll offer some clues."

"I can talk to the people being treated over there," Nettles offered. "Maybe a few of them noticed something before everything went to hell."

"And I can check out that body in the restroom to start off," Susannah suggested. "If this was a pre-meditated attack, it makes sense that whoever did it prepped in the restroom and worked their way out from there rather than the other way around. Maybe the dead person in there stumbled on what was happening and ended up being the first victim."

"Sounds good," Karen said. "Let's reconvene here after."

They split up and Susannah headed in the direction where Petty had indicated the restroom was. She showed her badge to the officer at the door, who lifted the police tape for her. As she bent under, she caught a glimpse of him giving her a once-over. She didn't let it bother her, as she'd long ago gotten used to it.

Susannah knew she was attractive. She had hazel eyes, deeply tanned skin and long, black hair. Those features, along with her curvy figure, led to many inappropriately long stares from strangers and fellow cops alike. She didn't resent it. In fact she even cultivated it a little, sometimes wearing clothes that were perhaps half a size too small.

It was all by design. If co-workers, witnesses, and suspects were fixated on her looks, they were more likely to underestimate her and less prepared when she came at them with aggressive questions or, in some situations involving perps, a quick right hook. She knew that some of her female colleagues resented the way she used her sexuality to her advantage. But if they had a problem with it, they could take a look at her record of closed cases and then shut their mouths.

She set all those thoughts aside as she took in the scene in the bathroom. Because there was no concern about dealing with the public or the press in here, the body lying before her hadn't been covered up like those outside. Susannah half-wished it had.

The victim was an African-American woman, probably in her mid-forties. She was dressed in sharp business attire and Susannah guessed that she worked in one of the nearby office towers. She was lying on her back and, other than what looked like a fresh, ugly burn mark on her left forearm; there were no obvious signs of physical trauma. That is, unless one counted the bubbles of spittle drooling down her cheek, the frozen mask of pain on her face, or her, wide, blank eyes.

Susannah sighed quietly, taking a moment to regroup. She looked at herself in the mirror and was pleased to see that none of her uncertainty was visible on the surface. She projected the image of a secure woman at the top of her game. Sometimes it was an accurate image. Other times, like today, she felt like she was acting the part.

As she stared at herself, she wondered how many of the perpetrators of this horror were women? If any were, had they stared at themselves in this very mirror before going out to cause so much carnage? What kind of person would leave this poor woman to die on the floor of a public bathroom? When they looked at their reflections, as she was now, did madness stare back at them? Susannah intended to find out.

CHAPTER TEN

It didn't take long for Jessie's excitement to give way to frustration.

The minute they'd entered the Daniels, Kramer, Malone & Whitmore conference room, she had made a beeline for the firm's security files in the hope of discovering someone who'd threatened Roger Whitmore's family bodily harm. But there was nothing like that.

Most of the incidents referenced were bland threats, spoken aloud in court, by clients on the other side of his cases, and almost always promising to sue him personally or get him fired. In Whitmore's fifteen years at the firm, he'd reported over three dozen such occasions. Some of those people did actually try to sue him. But there wasn't a single threat of violence in the bunch.

After giving up on that dead end, she turned her attention to what Ryan had been working on all along. The detective had spent the last hour quietly poring over case files to see if any of Whitmore's own clients had expressed displeasure at how he'd represented them. Once she dived in, something unexpected became quickly apparent.

"I thought all he had were corporate clients," she said, breaking the silence in the room. "But it looks like that's only a small percentage of his work."

"I know," Ryan agreed. "Apparently the bulk of them are rich and famous types. I've already gone through the files of multiple athletes, celebrities, and power brokers."

"I guess that says something about him as a lawyer," Jessie noted. "At least he had discretion. Even people like Trish's aunt and best friend thought he did boring corporate work exclusively. It sounds like they had no idea that he was rubbing elbows with the rich and famous."

"And getting them off too," Ryan added. "It's amazing how many high profile folks he's managed to get out of court with a slap on the wrist. In many cases, they were acquitted despite solid evidence against them. And I think the reason friends and family don't know about it is because he's rarely the face in court. He leads the team, sets strategy. But he seems to leave the courtroom heroics to others."

Jessie nodded and returned to the files, marveling at how one after another ended in Whitmore's favor. A few clients had to settle cases in civil court proceedings. But those that faced criminal charges seemed to always walk away without doing time. Well, almost always.

She did come across one case that sullied his seemingly perfect record: Palmer George. She knew the name well. An actor who once headlined action films in the nineties and early 2000s, George's star had dimmed even before he got into legal trouble.

Two DUI charges in as many months in 2007 got him dropped from the action ensemble flick, *Grizzled*, about a group of over-the-hill mercenaries coming together for one last job. He never served time, thanks in large part to Whitmore. But the incidents sent him down a bumpy road. The big-money offers stopped coming in, which meant he had to take too many parts in crappy, straight-to-video (and later, streaming) films.

He managed to have a minor career rebirth from 2015-2017 as the male lead in the TV series, "Vice Versa," about a male and female pair of vice detectives in L.A. But the renaissance was brief, as he was busted with cocaine at a club and dumped from the show after its second season. Whitmore managed to get him off with a rehab stint and community service.

But his luck ran out two years ago. While on a hunting trip with his best friend and his wife, Meadow, he shot and killed her. He insisted that it was an accident and that he'd mistaken his spouse for a deer. But after his blood alcohol level was recorded at twice the legal limit and revelations of a tempestuous, sometimes violent marriage emerged, he was charged with manslaughter and criminal negligence.

Reading the file, Jessie considered it an open and shut case, but after a long trial, Roger Whitmore somehow got George acquitted of the first charge. However, even his legal heroics couldn't stop the actor from being convicted on the second charge. He was sentenced to four months in prison and served two, having just been released last week to spend an additional ten days on house arrest. The file indicated that Whitmore had already begun the process of trying to secure a pardon for George from the governor.

"I think we may have a candidate," Jessie said, sliding the file over to Ryan. "Whitmore led the team representing Palmer George in his trial for killing his wife. He just got out after serving his time."

"Has he made any threats?" Ryan asked, looking over the file.

"None that have been logged," Jessie conceded. "But it's not a stretch to think he might hold a grudge against the lawyer that couldn't keep him out of prison. And we both know of his reputation as an unpredictable guy. Plus, look where he lives—Manhattan Beach. That's just one town south of El Segundo, less than a ten minute drive from his place to the Whitmore house. I think it's worth having a chat with him, don't you?"

The fact that Ryan immediately stood up and threw on his sport jacket was all the answer she needed.

"If we move fast and use the siren," he said, "I can get us there in a half hour."

*

Twenty-seven minutes later, they pulled into the driveway behind Palmer George's house. Most of these multi-million dollar, ocean-facing homes had their garages facing alleys behind the houses, so as to get them as close as possible to the beach. George's was no exception.

They had to walk around the block to get to the front door, which wasn't the worst task in the world. The midday sun was out and people were ambling along the Strand, a walking path lining the beachfront homes, only feet from the sand. Folks in bathing suits and wetsuits alike were carrying their surfboards, casually heading toward the sparkling water.

They reached George's address, which, like most of the other homes along the Strand, wasn't gated. They were able to walk right up to his door. As they did, Jessie noted that while the place was impressive at first glance—two stories, with a sundeck on the first level and a large balcony on the second, it had fallen into disrepair.

It desperately needed a paint job. Chunks of the wood trim had broken off, and everything metal looked rusted. She wasn't sure how much of that was due to salty air, his time locked up, or general disinterest, but it gave the place a beach-y, Grey Gardens vibe, which she found disquieting.

Ryan rang the bell but it made no sound. Jessie wasn't stunned. He gave it a few seconds, and then rapped loudly on the door. After waiting a minute and getting no response, he banged on it with his fist, hard and long. She knew what he was thinking. They hadn't come all this way for nothing, and considering that the guy was on house arrest for a few more days, there was no reason he shouldn't be answering.

After another twenty seconds they finally heard a voice from inside.

"Shut up," someone she assumed was George shouted grumpily, "I'm coming."

She saw a shadow pass over the peephole and knew he was checking them out.

"You two look like you're either missionaries or reporters," he grumbled from behind the door. "If you're the first, I'm not interested. And if you're the second, I get paid for interviews these days."

"Two strikes," Ryan said, holding up his badge to the peephole. "LAPD; we need to talk."

For a second Jessie thought he might refuse, but then she heard the lock slide open. He opened the door a crack.

"What the hell?" he demanded. "I haven't left my house in six days. I've called in as required every day. Can't you just let me suffer in peace?"

"We're not here about that, Mr. George," Ryan said patiently. "If you would open the door and let us in, we can explain what this is about."

The man opened the door but stood defiantly in their path.

"We can talk right here," he told them forcefully.

Jessie finally got a good look at him. Palmer George didn't appear much different than he had in the video when he was taken into custody after his wife's death. In his early fifties, his salt and pepper hair was cut short, likely due to prison regulations. He had a few days' worth of stubble and the bleary-eyed appearance of a man who'd already started drinking for the day. He wore sweatpants and a tight, white t-shirt that proved he'd been keeping in shape, even during his incarceration.

"All right," Ryan said amiably, trying to lower the temperature a bit. "Who was your attorney in your recent legal drama?"

"Come on, man," George said irritably. "There's no way you come over here not already knowing that."

"Then I bet you can guess why we're here."

"Not really," he retorted.

"Roger Whitmore's wife, Trish, was brutally murdered this morning," Ryan told him. "You didn't know that?"

George shrugged ambivalently.

"I haven't exactly been keeping up with local news since I got out. And I don't think I'd be the first person Roger would call to share that kind of information with. He was my lawyer but we weren't exactly buds."

"Funny that you should say that," Jessie interjected, speaking for the first time. "Why weren't you buds? Were you pissed that he couldn't get you probation for shooting your wife?"

"Oh, I see what this is," he shot back. "My big-time lawyer's wife dies, and you come hassling me? This conversation is over."

He stepped back and started to slam the door shut. Before he could close it, Ryan stuck his foot out, stopping the move cold.

"Careful, Palmer," he said quietly. "I saw that the rules of your house arrest prohibit the consumption of alcohol and I'm pretty sure that if we conducted a test right now, it wouldn't go so well. So why don't you answer our questions so we can avoid all that ugliness? I'd hate for our little chat to end with you in cuffs on your way downtown."

Palmer George stared at Ryan with fury in his eyes. But her partner and fiancé was unfazed. He'd faced far worse than an aging action star with a record. Jessie decided this might be a good time to step in and short-circuit the testosterone standoff.

"Palmer," she said soothingly, "we're trying to help you here. This looks bad. Your lawyer's wife is killed just days after you get out of prison on a conviction that he couldn't prevent. She lives eight minutes north of where we're standing right now. You have a reputation as a hothead, to put it mildly. If we're asking you questions, don't you think that once Roger Whitmore transitions from the grief phase into anger, he will too? Remember, this is the man who is pursuing a pardon for you with the governor. You think he still does that if he suspects you murdered his wife? Or do you think he joins forces with the prosecution?"

"But I didn't do crap," he blurted out.

"So you say," she continued. "But it sure looks bad. You're just out of prison for your own wife's death. You're trying to rebuild your reputation so you can salvage some semblance of a career. And then you get questioned in the murder of your lawyer's wife? Not to be crass, but I'd say that exhausts all nine of your lives, even in this town. It would be the nail in your coffin. So why don't you tell us where you were this morning between 6 and 8 a.m."

Though he was still trying to look tough, Jessie could see in his eyes that Palmer was making the calculation she'd put in front of him and coming up with the same result she had. His face softened slightly and he stopped trying to force the door closed.

"I was here all morning," he said, "just like I have been for the last week. This thing on my leg should prove that."

He pulled up his sweatpants and pointed at the monitor on his left ankle.

"People with means have been known to use their resources to evade monitor technology," Ryan pointed out.

George shook his head in frustration.

"So you're staying that my big plan was to get out of prison, somehow get this pain-in-the-ass device off my ankle, just so I can go kill, not my lawyer but his wife, even though I didn't even know they lived near me? All that for what—so I can become the number one suspect in her death? How does that help me?"

Ryan looked like he had a comeback but Jessie jumped in before he could reply.

"Palmer," she said firmly. "We're going to check on the records from your ankle monitor. We're going to review footage from nearby security cameras. We're going to look at the GPS data from your phone and cars. And we're going to ask our friends in the Manhattan Beach Police Department to do patrols by here regularly. If we find anything amiss, you better believe we'll be back, and not just to chat. Do you understand?"

"Yes," he said, fairly meekly for him.

"And stop drinking," she ordered. "MBPD will be doing spot checks on that too and if they find even a whiff of alcohol, you can say goodbye to the beach for at least a few more months."

She turned on her heel and headed back down the path to the Strand without waiting for a response. It took Ryan a few seconds to catch up.

"So that's it?" he asked when they were out of earshot, sounding perplexed and annoyed. "You want to just accept that he's on the up and up?"

"Of course not," she said as they returned to the car. "We'll have Jamil and Beth check everything he said, just like I told him we would. And if anything pops, we'll take him down. But I have to say—he made a compelling point. It would be awfully hard for him to do this and in complete opposition to his interests."

"But you're the one who suspected him in the first place."

"I know," she said. "But I've had a change of heart. Look, he's clearly a jerk. And it's possible that shooting his own wife was more than an accident, maybe a moment of anger gone sideways while he had a gun in his hands. I guess we'll never know. But after looking him in the eye, it's clear that he's not a mad man or an idiot. He knows that Whitmore got his sentence reduced about as far as it could go, and that he's been trying to get him a pardon. To come after him in any way, much less through his wife, just doesn't make sense. That's especially true when the guy is on his last legs in this industry. Another hint of controversy would get him blackballed for life. I think this guy's reckless, but I don't think he's that cold-blooded. His problem is that he's too hot-blooded. Besides, can you imagine Trish Whitmore letting that guy into her house, unannounced, first thing in the morning? I may be proven wrong but I don't think he's our guy."

"So what next then?" Ryan asked in a tone that suggested he saw her point, even if he didn't like it.

"I say we go back to Whitmore's office," she replied. "Maybe we missed something in those files. Or maybe we didn't get access to all of them."

"How do you plan to remedy that?" Ryan asked hesitantly, apparently worried about the answer.

"I think it's time we get a little creative."

CHAPTER ELEVEN

They waited until most of the firm's staff was at lunch to put Jessie's plan into action.

After another fruitless search of Whitmore's files at Daniels, Kramer, Malone & Whitmore, she came up with an idea she knew Ryan would hate, which is why she didn't share all of it.

"The less you know, the better," she insisted as a large group of legal secretaries walked down the hall outside their glassed-in conference room. A few moments later, Lynn popped her head in.

"I'm heading out to pick up my lunch order and get some fresh air," she told them. "Can I grab anything for either of you? There's a menu of local restaurants that do take-out in that binder on the table."

"Thanks very much, but we had a snack the way back over," Jessie lied. "I think we're just going to push through here."

"Okay," Lynn said. "If you change your mind, you can have something delivered too. I'll be back in about fifteen minutes."

"Thanks very much," Ryan said. Once the door closed, he turned to Jessie. "Please tell me you not going to do anything illegal."

"I find that 'illegal' is a pretty amorphous term these days, sweetie," she replied, giving him a kiss on the cheek. "I'm going to take a peek at Roger Whitmore's office, something you can't do without a search warrant. That's all I can really share with you at this time, Detective. Now, if you would please change seats and sit at the head of the conference table, you'll find that you can see his office door."

"I'm not liking the sound of this," he muttered.

"Here's all I need you to do. Put in your ear buds. I'll do the same. Call me and keep the line open. If you see anyone passing by Whitmore's office while I'm in there, give me a heads up. If it looks like anyone is about to go in, sound the alarm."

"How am I supposed to do that?" he demanded, exasperated.

"I don't know, fake a heart attack or something."

"I'm begging you, Jessie," he pleaded, actually putting his hands together as if in prayer, "don't do anything that gets me fired or arrested."

"What about me?" she asked, fake petulant, "Aren't you worried about my welfare?"

"You'll get by," he quipped. "But I'm too pretty to serve hard time."

"You are indeed," she said, giving him a kiss on the lips this time before heading out the door. His call came through when she was halfway to Whitmore's office.

"What a delight to hear from you, honey," she said.

"If the door is locked, abort," he replied tersely.

She grabbed the handle and tried to turn it.

"It's locked," she said. "But I learned a few tricks about how to circumvent that problem from a cute guy with a badge. I'm going to use one now. Keep your eyes peeled."

She heard him groan. But he said nothing as she quickly picked the lock, stepped inside, closed the door, and locked it again. The truth was that, despite the show she put on for Ryan, she didn't feel great about doing this. Maybe it wasn't technically a violation of police procedure because of her civilian status. But searching the office of an officer of the court wasn't really defensible in most situations.

To her, this was the exception. The hoops they'd have to jump through to get access to this office legitimately were enormous and she feared it would take forever or never happen at all. Meanwhile a wife and mother who'd been brutally murdered was lying on a metal slab. If doing this got Jessie closer to finding out who put her there, it was worth the risk.

"Here we go," she whispered to both Ryan and herself.

She left the light off as she looked around. In one corner, she saw the air mattress that Whitmore had slept on the night before, complete with a pillow, crumpled sheets, and a blanket. There were sweatpants and a t-shirt on the floor beside the mattress.

She moved quickly to his desk, and sat down. There were multiple photos of his family on the desk, all arranged just so. Jessie peered in, looking at Trish Whitmore, and felt an ache in her chest as she recalled the sight of the same woman from a few hours earlier, so brutally beaten that none of the features in the picture before her were discernible.

She forced the thought from her head. She was here to complete a specific job and she didn't have much time to do it. Sympathy for the victim could come later. For now, she leaned back in the chair, imagining that she was Roger Whitmore, and tried to guess where he might keep his most sensitive material, the stuff he wouldn't dare put in legal or security files.

There was a filing cabinet across the room. She went to it and pulled open each drawer, hoping that one might be locked, indicating that its contents were more valuable than the others. But none were. Every file inside was accessible and seemed relevant to his work.

"Two women are about to pass by," Ryan whispered in her ear.

Jessie stepped behind the filing cabinet and stayed there, unmoving.

"All clear," Ryan said after about ten seconds. "Having any luck?"

"Not so far," Jessie said, looking around and hoping to discover something she'd missed.

"Well, you better find something quick," he told her. "Lynn will be back soon and your absence will be noted."

"Thanks for the reminder," Jessie replied tartly. She was well aware of the time issues.

She looked at the various pictures on the wall. They were all of Whitmore with executives from major corporations. Half of the photos were of him smiling next to Metron execs. Again, she took note of his discretion. There wasn't a single picture of him with an athlete or celebrity, even though he had over three dozen of them as clients.

She returned to his desk and tried to think where a man of such prudence might keep material sensitive enough to put him or his family at risk. His desk had a few files on it related to the Water Warriors litigation but that was about it.

She began opening the drawers of the desk, though she held out little hope that they would reveal something. Like the filing cabinet, none of them were locked. Inside one were more files on the case from this morning. The other drawers were equally innocuous, with office supplies, packs of gum, and a few menus for local restaurants.

"We're closing in on fifteen minutes," Ryan warned her in a hushed voice.

"Understood," she muttered, frustration and anxiousness mixing together in her gut.

Maybe there just isn't anything to hide.

She shook the thought immediately from her head. There was always something to hide. Even the most decent, upstanding of people had secrets they'd prefer never came out. And as a partner at a huge law firm that represented oil companies and entitled celebrities, Jessie didn't buy that Roger Whitmore was as pure as the driven snow.

Based more on instinct than any logical reason, she pushed the chair back and knelt down so that she could see under his desk. It was dark and she had to use her phone as a flashlight. At first she didn't notice anything. But on a second pass, she caught sight of a small shelf on the underside of the desk, just to the right, where it would be accessible to someone who knew it was there.

"Lynn is walking down the hall," Ryan whispered urgently.

"Almost done," Jessie replied, hoping she was.

She hesitantly reached her hand into the dark space of the mini-shelf as if it was a hole in a barren field that might harbor a snake, and carefully felt around. Her fingers immediately landed on something. She knew what it was even before grabbing it and pulling it out—a cell phone. Once she had it in hand, she saw that it wasn't just any phone, but the kind typically used as a burner phone.

Now this is something I can work with.

"She's about to come in the conference room," Ryan hissed. "You're out of time."

"Stall," Jessie muttered back.

She hopped from behind the desk, put the phone in her pocket, and returned Whitmore's chair to its previous spot.

"Hello, Detective," she heard Lynn say. "Everything going okay?"

"Just grinding along," Ryan chuckled.

"Where's Ms. Hunt?"

Ms. Hunt was rushing across the office to the door.

"She'll be right back," Ryan said convincing. "She just ran to the restroom."

"Keep her distracted," Jessie whispered as she grabbed the doorknob, "I'm coming out now."

"That's not a bad idea," Lynn replied. "I think I'll do the same."

"Before you do," Ryan blurted out, "I have a question."

"What's that?"

"Um, where did you get those purple glasses frames?" he asked. "I like the style. They really say 'go for it!'"

Jessie knew that last comment was intended for her and hurriedly stepped out into the hall, closed the door behind her, and made sure it was locked. She glanced toward the conference room, where she saw Lynn with her back to the hallway, taking off her glasses and holding them out to Ryan.

"To be honest," Jessie heard her say. "I just went to a LensCrafters."

"Well, it's working for you," Ryan told her.

Jessie walked briskly down the hall, putting her ear buds away as she went, and opened the conference room door.

"Hi Lynn," she said with all the airiness she could muster. "How was lunch?"

The executive assistant turned around and squinted, apparently struggling to see her without the glasses. Her face was flushed. Apparently a compliment from Ryan Hernandez had that effect on lots of women.

"Haven't had it yet," she said. "I was just showing your partner my glasses."

"Oh yeah," Jessie said, "They're very cool."

"Thanks," Lynn said as Ryan handed them back. "Well, I'll let you two get back to it. Please let me know if you need anything."

Once she was gone, Ryan raised his eyebrows in a silent "Well?"

"Let's check these files one more time," Jessie said. "Assuming we don't find anything, I may have something else that could be of assistance."

"You're not going to tell me what?" he asked incredulously.

"Not until I know if it amounts to anything," she told him. "I don't want you putting yourself at risk professionally unless what I found is really worth the risk."

"You are not filling me with confidence," he grumbled.

Jessie said nothing. Instead she rifled through the last of the remaining files, looking for anything she might have missed before. But it was hard to concentrate, much less ignore the cell phone burning a hole in her pocket.

The sooner they got out of here and she found out what was on it, the better. But doing that meant involving someone else who was even more of a stickler for the rules than Ryan.

CHAPTER TWELVE

Hannah stared at Silvio Castorini, debating how best to approach him.

She'd been anxious to find him but decided to wait until he showed up at the one place she knew he would be. He liked to eat his lunch late, so she waited in the corner of the cafeteria until he eventually appeared. As expected, after getting his tray, he proceeded directly to the small table by the window with the best view of the ocean.

Merry's death didn't seem to have altered how he went about his day. His plate was filled to the brim with pastries, as it was for every meal. She was amazed at how he stayed so skinny on that diet and wondered if it had something to do with his medication or his calorie-burning nervous energy. Even sitting down to eat, he bounced constantly, as if there was an electrical current running through him. His black, buzz cut hair reinforced the perception. Though she knew that he was in his early twenties, he looked much younger.

Hannah walked toward him, trying to look as unthreatening as possible. Their previous interaction on the Saturday that Merry died hadn't gone well. She had unknowingly sat at his preferred table. When he got unusually agitated, she agreed to move, but he insisted that she apologize as well. She had held her tongue, making a concerted effort not to verbally destroy him, even though it would have been both easy and satisfying.

But the situation started to escalate anyway. Only Merry's intervention cooled things down before they got out of hand. An attendant had escorted Silvio out of the cafeteria and he was taken to the Assistance Wing as a precaution. After he was gone, Merry had explained his fixation on that particular table by the window.

"That's where he was last year when he learned his mom had died of cancer," Merry had said. "His dad told him that she'd gone to heaven and every time a wave crashed on the beach, it was her sending a kiss down to him. So he likes to sit there and watch them crash."

Hannah remembered how relieved she'd been that she hadn't gone off on the guy. If she had given him that tongue-lashing, it might have permanently sullied that spot for him. She didn't want that responsibility. Almost as bad, if she had done so, she doubted he would have gotten out of the Assistance Wing after just a day. With her verbal acidity, he might have ended up in restraints, making it impossible for her to talk to him now.

And she really needed to talk to him. It was clear that in his way, Silvio had great affection for Merry. She was the one who'd talked him down the other day. Hannah hoped that whatever connection had made Silvio comfortable with Merry would help her now. Had Merry ever confided in him? Had she shared a story that could help provide a clue of some kind? It was a long shot but right now, it was the only shot Hannah had.

She was just a few steps away when he saw her. His whole body tensed up and his fingers gripped the edges of his tray. His mouth dropped open and bits of the Danish he was eating fell back onto the plate.

"I'm not trying to take your table," she said quickly, realizing that it had been a mistake to walk over so purposefully. He clearly felt threatened.

"This is my table!" he insisted, as more Danish flew out of his full mouth.

"I know," she said, taking half a step back. "Merry explained it to me."

Silvio visibly relaxed at the sound of her name.

"Merry was my friend," he said.

"I understand," Hannah said, staying where she was. "Even though I only knew her for a short time, she was starting to become my friend too. That's what I was hoping to talk to you about. Would that be okay?"

Silvio continued to chew the rest of his pastry as he thought about it. When he was done, he pointed at the closest table, also by the window, with a view almost as good as his.

"You can sit there," he said.

Hannah obliged, moving to the spot he'd assigned her. She sat down and tried not to be thrown by the oddness of trying to have an intimate conversation with a person who was almost ten feet away from her.

"How did you become friends?" she asked, once he seemed confident that she wasn't going to try to move closer.

He was about to take another bite of pastry, when he stopped, the glazed doughnut an inch from his mouth.

"She understood my pain," he said without hesitation.

"What pain?" she asked.

He put the doughnut down and stared at Hannah for several seconds, as if trying to decide if she could be trusted. She waited, sure that he would come to the conclusion that she couldn't. If she was in his place, she wouldn't say a word.

"My mom got cancer a few years ago. It didn't look good but she tried every treatment she could, no matter how painful it was. She knew she wasn't going to make it but she wanted to live long enough to see my twin sister, Sylvie, graduate from college."

Hannah felt a shadow of foreboding envelop her as he spoke, but she tried to hide it, saying nothing, not even changing her expression.

"But Sylvie couldn't handle knowing that Mom wouldn't survive," he continued, his voice flat and emotionless. "So on the night before she was supposed to graduate last May, she took a bunch of pills. I lived at home and she was staying there that night in her old room. I went in to wake her up the next morning and found her lying there. Her eyes were closed so I shook her, thinking she was just sleeping in. But she was really cold. My mom was at the doctor and my dad was at work. I was the only one home. I had to call 911. I saw the ambulance come. I saw them take her out in a black bag. As they drove her off, I realized that I had lost my sister and I was going to lose my mom soon too. Something inside me just cracked open. That's the last thing I really remember from that day. I guess I collapsed and the paramedics who were still there took me to the hospital. I got transferred here a little while later."

"I'm so sorry, Silvio," Hannah said.

"Yeah," he replied, finally taking a bite of the doughnut. "Anyway, I met Merry after that. I'd been here a few months when she showed up. She was in my therapy group so she knew what my issues were. We'd talk outside of group sometimes. I think those talks helped me more than the official sessions did. She really seemed to get it. That's why it hurts so much."

"Why?" Hannah asked, though she thought she knew the answer.

"Because she did the same thing as my sister," he said darkly. His eyes were wet. "I know it's not true, but part of me thinks it's my fault because I couldn't stop her, just like I couldn't stop Sylvie. I failed them both."

Hannah wasn't sure she had the wherewithal to process that comment, much less the expertise to help him. On top of everything else he was dealing with, this kid was walking around feeling responsible the deaths of two people. At this rate, she doubted that he'd ever get out of here.

She felt the strong inclination to just push past what he'd said and get to what had brought her to see him in the first place. But some part of knew that he needed something to cling to.

"Silvio," she said, uncertain if she was about to make things better or worse, "not too long ago, my adoptive parents were murdered by a serial killer, right in front of me. I'm not great with emotions, but I'll tell you this: there's not a day that goes by that I don't wonder if there was something I could have done to save them. It's a constant battle against the guilt. But the truth is, I couldn't save them. It was out of my hands. Just like what Sylvie did was out of yours. You need to let yourself off the hook."

He looked back at her with a mix of gratitude and pain, tears streaming down his face. Somewhere deep inside her, Hannah had the odd stirrings of something she hadn't thought she was capable of: empathy.

"Thanks," he whispered.

She nodded silently, not sure what to say next.

"You said that you and Merry talked outside of group therapy," she finally reminded him, moving on quickly as she shoved the unfamiliar feeling down where it couldn't mess with her. "Did she ever mention wanting to kill herself?"

She watched him process the question. When he did, his expression turned dark again.

"No," he said so emphatically that his voice echoed throughout the cavernous cafeteria. He seemed to sense that he was risking a return to the Assistance Wing and spoke more quietly when he continued. "She told me that she would cut her forearms because, for a little while, the physical pain made her forget the emotional pain she felt all the time. Plus, she said the pain made her feel more alive. She *wanted* to be alive. At least that's what I thought."

Hannah wasn't sure how to broach her next question, and she certainly didn't want to ask it from ten feet away. Finally, she decided to just be straight with the guy.

"Silvio," she said as quietly as she could, considering the distance between them. "I have an important question for you, but it's very sensitive. May I please join you at your table for a minute?"

His whole face clenched up as if he'd just sucked on a lemon. She watched as he tried to control himself. After a good five seconds, he nodded reluctantly. She came over, grabbed the chair opposite him, moved it slightly back from the table so she wouldn't be right on top of him, and sat down.

"I know this is a weird question," she whispered, "but do you think there's any chance that someone else might have killed Merry?"

His face immediately clenched up again, only this time it turned red as well. It looked like he was on the verge of a full-fledged meltdown.

"Are you accusing me?" he demanded, again entering near-shouting territory.

"No, of course not," she said quickly in a hushed voice. "I would never."

That wasn't entirely true. Silvio, with his quick-trigger temper and personal connection to Merry, would normally be a prime suspect. But because she knew definitively that he was being held in the secure Assistance Wing at the time Merry died, he was in the clear.

Hannah looked around to see several residents and attendants staring at them. One of the attendants, a tall, skinny guy with glasses whose name she couldn't remember, started to head in their direction.

"Silvio," she said under her breath, "you need to chill. If you keep blurting stuff out, you're going to end up right back in the Assistance Wing. I know you don't want that. So when this attendant comes over, you have to convince him that you're okay. Can you do that?"

There wasn't time for him to respond because the attendant was almost there.

"Is there a problem?" the tall guy, whose nametag read "Brian", asked.

Hannah looked over at Silvio, who appeared frozen with fear. She decided to step in.

"We're good, Brian," she said, offering him her most effective "sweet girl" smile. "I was just playing around, asking Silvio if he stole one of my pastries. But he's not the best at picking up on sarcasm. So we had a moment. But we're cool, right buddy?"

Brian looked over at Silvio for confirmation. Hannah thought he might start blubbering right in front of them. But instead, he inhaled deeply, exhaled dramatically, and answered.

"She wanted to know if I snagged her bear claw," he explained. "But this place doesn't even have bear claws. It took me a second to get the joke. But now I do. Pretty funny, right?"

Brian the attendant didn't seem amused or totally convinced, but since both of them were sticking to the story and no one was yelling anymore, he was stuck.

"Let's just keep our voices at a normal conversational level, okay?" he requested.

"Not a problem," Hannah promised.

"Okay," Silvio agreed.

Once Brian was out of earshot, Hannah picked up where she'd left off.

"So, do you think it's possible that someone here—a resident, a staff member, even a visitor—might have had something to do with her death?"

"Why are you asking that?" he wanted to know.

"It's like you said, Silvio," she reminded him. "She didn't give you any indication that she was even considering taking her own life. I didn't get that feeling either. That's not proof of anything, but I'm sorry to say that I've seen a few dead people in my time and this just doesn't feel like a suicide to me. Did she ever say if she had any conflicts with anyone?"

"Not that I remember," he said. "She was nice and everyone here mostly is too."

Hannah wasn't sure how true that was but let it lie for now. Before she could think of anything else to ask, Silvio added something.

"What if no one did anything?" he wondered. "What if something just went wrong?"

Hannah looked at him sharply.

"What do you mean?"

Even though there was no one anywhere near them, Silvio looked around suspiciously. When he felt safe enough to continue, his voice was barely audible.

"These are just rumors," he whispered. "But I've overhead some residents talking about how doctors might be secretly testing out new medications, especially on Assistance Wing patients."

"What kind of medications?"

"Anti-depressants," Silvio murmured. "I heard they might be using unapproved drugs and checking the effects on people without reporting their findings. What if it's true and someone gave Merry one of these medications? What if she took it and had a bad reaction? What if instead of helping her, it made her worse and she killed herself? Some of these drugs can affect people really fast. She might be fine in the afternoon and then be in bad shape just a few hours later."

Hannah considered the theory. It wasn't crazy. The toxicology report hadn't mentioned the anti-depressant in her system being experimental, but the results were only preliminary. Maybe the medical examiner didn't know enough to make that claim, or maybe a potentially experimental medication looked the same as another one on initial inspection.

"Anyway," Silvio added, pulling her back into the moment. "It's just a rumor."

He was right. There might be nothing to it. Merry could simply have been struggling more than anyone knew. But if there was any truth to this unapproved medication story, that was something else. If that's what happened, it might still technically be a suicide, but one facilitated by medical malpractice. If so, someone needed to be held responsible.

Hannah was more than willing be the person to make sure that happened. She just needed to figure out how.

CHAPTER THIRTEEN

LAPD's Central Police Station was hopping.

The California Plaza attack had everyone bustling about, shouting out updates to each other. Jessie had to dodge a few folks who rushed past her with their heads down, staring at documents. She looked over at Ryan, who was staring at a woman in a Hazmat suit, sipping coffee in the corner.

"I didn't realize the magnitude of this thing," he said.

"Are you sure we shouldn't shelve this Whitmore case for now?" she pressed.

"No way," Ryan replied definitively. "Decker's right. This Plaza thing may be more of a headline-grabber right now, but a mother of two, who was married to one of the most influential men in the city, was bludgeoned in her own home this morning to the point of being unrecognizable. On a normal day, *that* would be the headline-grabber. And if we don't handle it properly, the headlines will be bad for HSS. We can't just bail to go after the newer, shinier object."

"That was harsh," Jessie said.

"I'm sorry," he told her. "I don't mean to be. But it's true. And if you bring it up again with Captain Decker, I promise he'll be a lot blunter than I am. Let's focus on getting justice for this woman. If Decker needs us, he'll let us know."

"Fair enough," Jessie said, feeling a little guilt seeping in. Trish Whitmore did deserve their time just as much as anyone else. Besides, if they could solve this thing soon, maybe they could assist on the Plaza case. That meant finding out what was on Roger Whitmore's burner phone. "I need to go talk to someone. You should do…something else."

"That was cryptic," Ryan replied, with a crooked smile. "I guess I'll see if Decker has two spare minutes for me to brief him on where we're at. Let me know when it's safe to be around you again."

"Will do," Jessie said and headed for research. As she passed by HSS's section of the bullpen, she saw Jim Nettles on the phone at his desk, but Karen Bray and Susannah Valentine were nowhere to be found. Nettles hung up as she passed by and she took advantage of his brief pause to butt in.

"Sounds like you've got a live one," she said.

"You wouldn't believe," he told her after taking a glug of water and picking up the phone again. "We're up to five dead and ten more at the hospital."

"Is that where Bray and Valentine are now?"

"Yep," he said, dialing a number. "They're hoping someone regains consciousness long enough to say what happened. Meanwhile, Jamil is going over every camera angle from the Plaza, hoping to find anything worthwhile. I'm sorry Jessie, but I've got to get back into it."

"No problem," she said and continued on her way. But as she continued down the hall to the research department, she could feel frustration set in. Jamil was her best bet to crack this burner phone. If he wasn't available, she wasn't sure what to do.

She got to the door and poked her head in. Sure enough, Jamil was working three monitors, all with different camera angles. He was concentrating hard, his eyes darting from screen to screen.

"The final security camera angle just came through," Beth said from across the room. "I'm sending it to you now."

A second later, an image popped up on Jamil's previously blank fourth monitor.

"Thanks," he muttered distractedly.

"Now that that's done, I'm running to the restroom," Beth said. "Be back soon."

Jamil was so focused that he didn't respond. Jessie wasn't sure he'd even heard his fellow researcher. As she walked to the door, Jessie decided to take a flyer. She had no idea what the new girl's technical skill set was, but she was smart, and just as important, temporarily available. The big question was now: was she willing to bend the rules after being on the job only three weeks?

"Mind if I walk with you?" she asked as Beth joined her in the hallway.

"Sure," the young woman said with a curious look on her face, one of the few female ones that Jessie actually had to look up at. "But why do I feel like this isn't going to be a 'get to know you' moment?"

"Because you're no dummy, Beth. I have a favor I need to ask but it's a little complicated."

"How so?" the researcher asked with a look that was more intrigued than apprehensive.

"A few reasons," Jessie replied. She waited for the uniformed officer hurrying down the hall to pass by before offering them. "First of all, I don't even know if you have the technical know-how to complete this task."

"So you're going to start off by insulting me?" Beth asked, though she was smiling.

"Apparently so," Jessie replied before continuing. "Secondly, I can't really tell you what this is about. You'd be doing this blind, based only on my say-so. That's for your own protection, but I could see how it might not seem that way."

"Okay," Beth said, still smiling. "Is there a third reason?"

"There is," Jessie told her. "You've been in this job less than a month and I'm—.'

"A famous, celebrated criminal profiler who has caught multiple serial killers and attracts camera crews like moths to a flame," Beth interrupted. "You're worried that I'll feel pressured because of the huge power imbalance."

"Something like that," Jessie conceded.

"Got it," Beth said. "I'm in."

Jessie was unable to hide her surprise. Her mouth dropped open. When she managed to reply, she made sure to be clear.

"Are you certain?" she asked. "I'm just a consultant, not an LAPD employee. You don't answer to me and aren't obligated to accept any request that makes you feel uncomfortable."

Beth forced her mouth to stop smiling and did her best to put on a serious expression.

"I hear what you're saying," she said slowly, "and I understand. Now what do you need me to do?"

*

Jessie was impressed.

Beth managed to unlock the phone in ten minutes. She might not have been as fast as Jamil, but no one was as fast as Jamil, so she had nothing to be ashamed of.

"Here you go," she said, handing it over while making an elaborate show of not looking at anything on the screen.

"You almost done over there?' Jamil asked from across the research office.

Beth had told him she needed fifteen minutes to handle a tech issue for Jessie. He'd been so immersed in his own work that he hadn't asked any questions.

"Just finished," Beth announced. "What do you need?"

Jessie mouthed a silent "thank you" and headed out unobtrusively. Beth beamed back at her, seemingly over the moon to finally be the point person on something, even something apparently so simple and straightforward. Then she turned her attention to Jamil, who was talking to her with such jargon-heavy terminology that it almost sounded like a foreign language to Jessie.

She hurried to the women's restroom and locked herself in a stall, where she knew no one could catch a peek at what she was looking at. Once there, she began to scroll through the phone. What she found made her jaw drop.

Roger Whitmore wasn't communicating with clients surreptitiously. He was communicating with women. That wasn't even the real shocker. Jessie had anticipated the possibility. What had her agape was the sheer number of them.

As she went through his texts and photos, of which there were hundreds, she counted at least eleven different women going back eighteen months, and that was just on this phone. Who knows how many there were on previous burner phones that he might have dumped?

The texts were direct and graphic: usually describing where an encounter would take place and what he hoped would be involved. The photos were equally explicit, always from the women, never from him. That and his use of initials for himself were the only tactics he employed to protect himself if the phone was discovered.

As she pored over the messages, it became clear that Whitmore wasn't just a serial philanderer with a multitude of mistresses, but that he reveled in the activity. There was no hint of shame or guilt at what he was doing. He was more brazen than just about any adulterer she'd encountered in her career.

There were no references to meeting at his office and taking advantage of his air mattress. Apparently that was a bridge too far. But that seemed to be his only concession to propriety. In additional to hotel meetings, there were multiple references to these women coming to his home. Jessie wondered how he coordinated their comings and goings without getting caught. Maybe that was what the secret staircase from the primary bedroom down to the kitchen was for—to let his mistresses sneak out the back way without Trish discovering them.

The women were apparently equally untroubled. They were happy to hook up wherever he preferred, regularly or just on occasion, depending on his preferences. Actually, that wasn't quite true. As Jessie finished skimming the texts, concluding with the most recent one, she saw that there was one woman who didn't seem as copacetic with the arrangement.

Her exchanges with Whitmore started out much like the others. But in the last few weeks, they'd gotten more intense, with demands to meet at times and places of her choosing. Just three days ago, he'd sent her a text saying: *I think that we've come to a natural end point in our relationship. It would be best to stop seeing each other.*

She didn't react well. Her first text expressed shock: *This is coming out of leftfield. Why?* When she got no response, she moved onto to disappointment: *I thought we had a good thing going. Will you please tell me what I did wrong? This isn't what I want.* That too went unanswered, leading to: *This is unacceptable. I deserve an explanation. In fact, I demand one.*

That got a terse reply from Whitmore that said simply: *It's over. Don't contact me again.* That didn't go over well. Her most recent response, yesterday afternoon, was: *Unacceptable. You will give me what I want or I will make things very difficult for you.* There was no subsequent communication from Whitmore.

Jessie put the phone back in her purse and hurried out of the restroom. She had two stops to make. The first was to get the address of the woman in the texts, whose name was Kimberly Kelly. The second was to find Ryan and tell him, without explaining how she got it, that they had a new lead and had somewhere to be.

CHAPTER FOURTEEN

One of the victims had woken up.

Detective Karen Bray waited impatiently for the doctor to give her the go-ahead to talk to the woman but so far hadn't gotten approval.

She and Detective Susannah Valentine had spent most of the afternoon at Dignity Health California Hospital Center, where the victims of the California Plaza attack had been sent for treatment. But with all of them unconscious, they could only use their bodies as leads. So they did the best that they could, studying the wounds on their skin, all of which looked like small but ugly burns.

The crime scene techs had taken samples and hurried them off to the lab, though they warned that results were unlikely to come today. Better news came from the HSS head of research, Jamil Winslow.

"I've isolated the source of the attack," he'd told them when he called. "It looks like there's only one culprit. Every one of the victims had physical interaction with this person before they collapsed."

"What can you tell us about them?" Susannah Valentine had demanded before he even had a chance to continue.

"It's very likely a female," he had said with what Karen could tell was slight irritation. "Her face is almost completely covered by her cap and she's wearing a scarf and oversized coat that makes it hard to know for sure. But at one point, more of her face, near the eyes and bridge of the nose, became visible and it's a 92% match to a woman. Plus, based on comparative analysis of the people near her, she looks to be about five-foot-two. Also, it's not exactly scientific, but Beth says she walks like a girl."

Despite the situation, Karen half-chuckled at that last bit of analysis. While it wasn't definitive, this was more than what they'd had before. Now they knew they were hunting one person, almost certainly female.

"Unfortunately," Jamil had added, "in in the crush of people escaping the Plaza, I lost track of her on nearby available cameras."

"You did the best you could," Karen told him. "Now just keep in close contact with CSU. If they get any hits on the substance she used, I want you to help narrow down where it might have come from."

"Will do," he had promised just before the forty-something, gray-haired nurse, Dolores, told them that a woman named Holly Valdez was starting to wake up.

But she wouldn't let them in to see her until the doctor had done an initial evaluation. After five minutes, Karen had lost patience. She was just thinking about how best to convey that to the medical personnel when Susannah sighed heavily.

"I've had enough of this," she huffed and started for the patient's door.

"You can't—," Nurse Dolores began to say, but it was too late. Susannah was already in the room. Karen and Nurse Dolores followed quickly behind. By the time they entered, things had already gotten heated.

"You need to wait outside," a young male doctor with bleary eyes and disheveled hair ordered.

"We've waited long enough," Susannah shot back. "We've got five dead people and the imminent threat of many more. Your patient may have information that can help us, so whether she's feeling super duper or not, we're going to chat."

Karen studied the woman in the hospital bed. She looked like she'd been in a fight. Her face was ashen in the spots where it wasn't blotchy red. She had black circles under her unfocused eyes. Her brown hair was bedraggled. It appeared that her mid-section was wrapped. There was a bandage on her left hand. She seemed confused about what was going on and why people were yelling all around her.

"I need to evaluate her further," the doctor insisted. "We need to make sure she's stable enough to talk. She might not be in any condition for this yet."

"Doctor...Mahajan," Karen said soothingly, looking at his name tag as she stepped forward, "we understand that you're in a difficult position and we appreciate that you have a duty to your patient's well-being. We respect that. And I'm sure you respect our need to keep this city safe from potential future attacks. So maybe we can work together. You continue your evaluation while we ask some questions. If at any point, you feel that she's in distress, let us know and we'll back off. How does that sound?"

From his expression, she could tell that Dr. Mahajan was relieved to at least be dealing with someone who wasn't yelling at him. Susannah Valentine was a tough, dogged detective, but sometimes her "bull in a china shop" determination could be counter-productive when it came to getting the help they needed.

"I suppose we could try that," Dr. Mahajan said begrudgingly, giving Susannah a sideways glare.

"All right," Karen said, walking around the hospital bed so that she was on one side while the doctor did his thing on the other. The woman, whose eyes were a little clearer now, opened her mouth.

"What's happening?" she croaked.

"Can you please get her some water?" Dr. Mahajan asked Nurse Dolores before turning his attention back to the patient. "Holly, you're in the hospital. You've been unconscious for the last four hours. How are you feeling right now?"

Before she replied, Nurse Dolores held out a cup with a straw. Holly took several long sucks before speaking.

"Wiped out," she told them in a gravelly voice, "It's like my insides were scooped out and then dropped back in. Everything is raw. And I'm so confused."

"What do you remember before coming here, Holly?" Karen asked, trying to keep the questions vague at first so as to not draw the ire of Dr. Mahajan.

"Um, okay," she said, her forehead wrinkling as she recalled what happened. "I was hanging out in the Plaza with my boyfriend, Alonzo. We were getting some sun. Then all of a sudden, there was this commotion coming from the restaurant area. People started screaming and running away from that whole section. I got up to do the same thing. Lonzo was already headed up the steps. I chased after him—."

She started to cough as she inhaled a big breath, then winced in pain.

"Take your time," Dr. Mahajan said, looking concerned. "You have several broken ribs so you're going to need to go slow for a while. Have some more water."

Holly took another few sips and several deep breaths. Karen saw Susannah fidgeting nervously next to the doctor, clearly frustrated at the pause in the flow of information. Luckily, she managed to avoid verbalizing her annoyance.

"Why are her ribs broken, Doctor?" Karen asked, giving Holly time to gather herself.

"At first I thought someone had stepped on her," he replied, "but the bruising isn't consistent with that. Oddly, it's as if she was asphyxiating and the associated body spasms were so severe that the contractions cracked her ribs."

"What would cause that?" she pressed.

"I'm not sure," he answered. "That isn't even common among people having epileptic seizures."

"You were saying you chased after Lonzo," Susannah said brusquely, refocusing attention on Holly. "What happened next?"

"By the time I got to the top of the stairs, it was a madhouse," Holly continued. "I couldn't find Lonzo. People were slamming into each other. I almost got knocked down twice as I ran away. Then I saw him, almost tripped over him. He was on the ground, on his stomach. He was…twitching and stuff."

She made a sound somewhere between a hiccup and a sob. Nurse Dolores gave her more water and she used that as an excuse to regroup. After several seconds she resumed, unprompted.

"I knelt down and rolled him over onto his back," she said quietly. "I noticed that the spot on his shoulder where I turned him over was like, sizzling or something. I tried to talk to him but he couldn't speak. His eyes rolled up in his head. And he kind of went limp, like he'd passed out. I started screaming for help, asking if anyone knew CPR, but no one stopped. In fact, one woman slammed into me and sent me sprawling off the sidewalk into the street. I was just getting back up when I started feeling really bad, like my insides were burning. I remember my legs wouldn't do what I wanted and I collapsed back down on the street. I was flat on my back with people running by me, not even looking down. I started shaking and twitching like Lonzo did. I couldn't breathe, couldn't make my body respond to my commands. That's the last thing I remember before waking up here."

Everyone in the room was quiet. Karen wondered if the others were, like her, wondering how awful those last moments must have been for the victims who didn't survive. Holly seemed to read her mind.

"Is Lonzo here too?" she asked, looking directly at her. "Is he awake yet?"

Karen glanced over at Dr. Mahajan, who shook his head faintly. Holly saw it too and pressed.

"Where is he?" she demanded.

"Your boyfriend's name is Alonzo Huertas?" he asked.

She nodded apprehensively.

"I'm afraid he didn't make it," Dr. Mahajan said gently. "He passed away a few hours ago."

Instead of wailing as Karen expected her to, Holly just lowered her head and sniffled quietly. When she looked up, her eyes were wet but focused.

"He was an asshole, but I loved him," she said quietly, and then with more intensity. "Who did this?"

Susannah, who had shown considerable restraint for her up to this point in the interview, saw her moment and leapt at it.

"Holly," she said, stepping forward, "we think this was a planned attack by one individual, a woman. She very likely bumped into Lonzo at some point and wiped some kind of poisonous substance on him, probably in the shoulder area you said was sizzling. That's almost certainly how you got sick too. You must have touched that area when you turned him over. The poison was no longer concentrated enough to kill you but it still landed you in here. In addition to Lonzo, four other people died and nine others are here in the hospital with you. That woman is still out there, maybe planning another attack right now. That's why we're here. I know you're not feeling well, but we need your help to stop her."

"How?" Holly asked without hesitation.

Susannah looked over at Karen, who knew what that meant. She pulled out her phone.

"We think this is the person who poisoned Lonzo," she said, displaying the clearest image that Jamil had managed to get as a screenshot on her screen. "Does she look familiar?"

Holly squinted at the photo briefly before looking up.

"I recognize her. She stumbled into Lonzo while she was walking up the steps, just before all hell broke loose down below. It seemed like an accident at the time but I remember she put her hand on his shoulder to steady herself."

"What do you recall about her?" Susannah pressed. "Are you sure it was a woman?"

"Yes," Holly said. "She was wearing that big coat, which I thought was weird considering the weather. She was tiny. And when she apologized for bumping into him, her voice was definitely female. It was really timid-sounding. Also, I couldn't see much of her face, but she had gray eyes and her skin was real pale. That's all I noticed before things started going crazy. Does that help?"

"It does," Karen assured her, and that wasn't a lie.

They could now officially confirm Jamil's suspicion that their suspect was a woman. And they had the beginnings of a physical sketch: she was small, with gray eyes, pale skin, and maybe a meek voice, though that could have been for show.

The truth was that unless they had the woman in right front of them, it wasn't of much use. There were tens of thousands of women in Los Angeles who met that description. No—in order to move forward they were going to need a break on the poison: what it was, where it came from, or who had access to it.

Without those kinds of details, they were still flying blind, while a woman who killed five people in less than a minute with just her hands was moving about freely, ready to strike again at any minute.

CHAPTER FIFTEEN

Jessie and Ryan pulled up in front of Beverly Yoga, on Brighton Way, not far from Rodeo Drive, and waited for Kimberly Kelly's class to end. Jessie could feel her fiancé's eyes boring a hole into the side of her head and she turned to him.

"What?" she asked.

"So we're sure this is where we're going to find her?" Ryan asked.

"According to Beth, yes," she told him. "She checked her social media and there was a post right outside this place an hour ago, saying she was, and I quote, 'about to get her butt toning on.' She's tall and blonde, and she's wearing hot pink yoga pants and a black sports bra with a purple, Lakers zip-up sweatshirt. I think we should be able to find her."

"And you still don't want to tell me anything about how you got access to her text exchanges with Whitmore?" he asked for the third time since they'd left the station. "What if she asks how we know about her?"

"We just stick with the old 'we're not at liberty to say' line," Jessie recommended. "She's in no position to object. We don't need to make specific references to the texts, just to the tenor of their interactions. I'm happy to take point on this if you're uncomfortable with it."

"I'm uncomfortable because I don't know everything you know and I don't like to go into an interview unprepared," he told her. "It's obvious that you somehow accessed the guy's phone and it's clear that Beth was your point person on that. Is she going to get in trouble for this?"

"I've kept her in the dark even more than you," Jessie replied. "If anyone takes a hit on this, it will be me. Having said that, you'll probably want to put in a search warrant request for Roger Whitmore's office. That way, this will all be retroactively legit."

"You realize that it doesn't work that way, Jessie," he chided her. "I sure hope you know what you're doing."

"I guess we're about to find out," she said, pointing at a woman just leaving the yoga studio. "That's her."

They got out of the car and walked casually toward Kimberly Kelly, as if they were tourists on a romantic stroll. The act was easy to sell, and not just because late afternoon was bleeding into early evening as the sun started to set while palm trees swayed lazily in the gentle breeze. It was also because they were adjacent to a street with some of the most expensive real estate in the world, with five-star restaurants, haute couture shops, and famous jewelry stores. This felt like a good couples stroll spot.

Kimberly Kelly walked to her car with her head down, looking at her phone, oblivious to everyone around her. That allowed Jessie to get a better sense of her. She guessed that the woman was in her early thirties. Her blonde hair appeared be natural and she had yet to take advantage of the plentiful plastic surgery options available to her in this town. Close to six feet tall, she was beautiful in a confident, statuesque "I used to be a model" kind of way. The giant ring on her finger suggested that she'd married well enough not to have to work for a living anymore.

She seemed to be enjoying the perks. Jessie surmised that her outfit—the pink yoga pants, black sports bra, and sneakers—cost over $500. Her small handbag looked like it went for over $1500 all on its own. The silver Tesla she'd stopped at cost a pretty penny too.

She reached into her handbag for her keys. But to Jessie's surprise, she spun around, pulling out a can of pepper spray instead.

"Take one more step and you'll regret it," she shouted, pointing the can at them with a shaky hand.

"Hold on, Kimberly," Jessie said, holding her palms up in front of her. "Spraying the LAPD with that is assault. Even for a woman of means like you, that has consequences."

Kimberly paused for a moment, unsure how to proceed, before recovering.

"How do I know that you're really who you say you are?" she demanded.

"We're going to pull out our IDs," Ryan said slowly. "Just take it easy."

They both took out their identification and held them out to her. Ryan showed her his badge as well. Only after looking at each closely did she lower the pepper spray.

"Thank you," he said. "Now I need you to either hand that over or put it on the roof of your car while we continue this conversation."

"What conversation?" she asked, putting her phone in her purse. "Is this about those parking tickets? That hardly seems worthy of involving a detective, especially since I'm disputing some of them."

"How many are you disputing?" Jessie asked, incredulous.

"Eight," Kimberly said matter-of-factly as she handed the spray can to Ryan.

"And how many do you have total?" Jessie continued.

"Unpaid? In the last year? That I'm not disputing?"

"Sure," Jessie said.

"Maybe five or six."

Jessie wanted to ask how it was even possible to get that many parking tickets in such a short period, but managed to stay on task.

"This isn't about parking tickets, Kimberly," she told her.

"What then?"

"Do you know Roger Whitmore?"

"Why?" Kimberly asked, her eyes narrowing.

"Just answer the question please," Ryan requested firmly.

"Obviously you must know that I do or you wouldn't be talking to me," she said, finding some of her haughtiness again. "What's this about?"

Jessie looked over at Ryan, whose expression indicated that this was her rodeo and she should proceed, so she did.

"His wife, Trish, was murdered this morning in her home."

She watched Kimberly's face closely for any sign that this wasn't news to her. The woman inhaled suddenly, seemingly stunned by what she'd heard. But it quickly turned into a cough. She put her hand to her mouth and bent over, making it impossible for Jessie to get a clear look at her. When she "recovered," she looked up again with watery eyes that Jessie suspected were due to the cough more than to grief.

"I'm sorry to hear that," she finally said.

"Did you know her well?" Jessie asked.

"I was familiar with her."

"What does that mean?" Ryan wanted to know.

Kimberly shrugged ambiguously.

"We definitely interacted on a few occasions," she said carefully before deciding that she should be offended. "Are you suggesting that I was involved in this somehow?"

"You threatened Roger very recently," Jessie reminded her.

Kimberly waved her hand dismissively.

"Are you talking about the text stuff?" she said. "That was just me expressing my frustration. I don't kill people I'm upset with. I sue them."

"Where were you this morning?" Jessie asked with more aggression than she'd used up until now.

Kimberly seemed briefly taken aback.

"So I'm really a suspect here?" she wondered. "Should I be calling my lawyer?"

"That depends on where you were this morning between 6:30 and 8 a.m. and if you can prove it," Jessie told her.

The frown on the woman's face softened at that. She started to reach into her purse but stopped when Ryan stiffened.

"I'm just reaching for my phone, Detective," she said, almost smiling. "Please don't shoot me. I only want to show you my alibi."

Ryan nodded and she pulled out the phone. After a few taps she showed them the screen. It was a photo of her at some kind of banquet event, seated at a table with several other women.

"What's this?" he asked.

"It's me at the Beverly Hills Scholarship Breakfast," she explained. "I joined the executive committee a few years ago because my soon-to-be-ex thought it would make us seem more philanthropic. The marriage didn't last—we're separated—but I found that I actually liked the adoring looks those kids gave me when I announced their scholarships. You may not believe this, but I don't typically get thanked for my good works, mostly because I don't do many good works."

"Shocking," Ryan muttered under his breath.

"Anyway," Kimberly continued, oblivious to his comment, "this is where I was this morning, at the Peninsula Hotel. I met the caterers there at 7 a.m. to make sure everything looked good. The breakfast started at eight. I'm not allowed to post the event photos until tomorrow—some embargo until the local paper runs the story online later tonight, or else you'd have already seen where I was on my Insta. This photo is from 8:06 a.m. You said Trish was killed at her house. Since you asked me where I was from 6:30 to 8, I assume she died in that timeframe."

"Correct," Ryan told her.

"I've been to their house. If you think I could get from residential El Segundo to Beverly Hills in thirty minutes during morning rush hour, you haven't been in L.A. very long."

"Did you go to their house a lot?" Jessie wanted to know.

"A few times," she admitted.

"How did Roger coordinate that without his wife finding out?" Jessie asked, pursuing the question that had been eating at her ever since she found out how many affairs he had.

"Oh wow," Kimberly said, shaking her head in amazement. "You have no idea, do you? If you think this was done by someone he'd been with, you two really have your work cut out for you."

"What does that mean?" Ryan asked.

The woman seemed to realize she'd gotten too comfortable and tried to walk it back.

"Nothing," she replied quickly, "just that he had a lot of affairs."

"We already know that," Jessie said sternly. "But you're the only one of them we can find who threatened him. Clearly you meant something by that crack, so what was it?"

Kimberly looked up and down the street apprehensively even though there was no one else nearby.

"Listen," she whispered loudly. "Roger knew I was just blowing off steam with that text. He didn't really think I was seriously threatening him. I tend to get a little dramatic from time to time. But if I talk to you guys, *really* talk to you, he'll come after me. And in case you haven't figured it out, he's a very powerful man. Crossing him could have unpleasant consequences that I don't think I'm ready to deal with."

Jessie and Ryan exchanged a look and she immediately knew that even though he'd told her that she should take the lead on this interview, he wanted to handle this one point.

"Are you under the impression that *we're* not powerful, Ms. Kelly?" he wondered, using her last name for the first time to let her know the dynamic had shifted to something more formal. "We represent the Los Angeles Police Department in a murder investigation. If you don't answer our questions, we may have to consider that obstruction and haul you in. It's after 5 p.m., so court business has closed down for the day. That means that you and your hot pink yoga pants will have to spend the night in a holding cell at our downtown Central Police Station until you can get a bail hearing in the morning, assuming you get it at all. Someone was killed, after all."

"You wouldn't—," she started to say.

"Oh yes he would," Jessie interrupted. "Have you ever shared one toilet, sitting out in the open, with ten to fifteen other women—women who are mostly dealers, junkies, hookers, and probably some junkie hookers? It's an adjustment. And here's the worst part. When Roger learns of your arrest, he's going to assume you'll talk, just to avoid another night in there. So clamming up will have been for naught. But there's another option."

"What?" Kimberly asked, her face chalky white.

"You tell us why you said we have our work cut out for us. If we find your information useful, you go home instead of to jail. If we can find a way to follow up without mentioning your name, Roger might never know where we got the lead. Hell, we might even talk to our friends in the Beverly Hills Police Department about giving you a pass on those parking tickets. Now which of those options sounds better to you, Kimberly?"

It only took the woman a fraction of a second to make her choice.

"The reason Roger didn't have any trouble hiding his affairs from his wife was that he wasn't hiding them. In fact, they weren't affairs at all."

"What?" Jessie asked, not sure she was totally getting it.

"Trish knew all about them, every single one," Kimberly said. "In fact, she liked to watch. She'd give him suggestions for which girls to hook up with. I don't know if she was swiping through Tinder with him or what, but she definitely had strong opinions."

Jessie's brain was swimming at this gusher of information but Ryan managed to speak.

"Did she—?" he started to ask.

"Participate?" Kimberly anticipated. "Never. But that didn't mean she wasn't involved. She'd sit just off to the side, giving tips, advice on what she wanted to see. And she could be *very* critical if she wasn't happy. I remember one time when Roger and I had a threesome with this other, much younger girl. Trish was calling her out, pointing out places where she had cellulite, criticizing the shape of her breasts. The poor kid had tears in her eyes."

"Did she ever do that to you?" Jessie asked.

"Criticize my body—no way," Kimberly said, insulted. "I mean, look at me. She wouldn't dare. But if I wasn't performing a particular act just so, she'd let me know very directly."

"That didn't bother you?" Ryan asked.

"I didn't care," she said. "It was nothing worse than my ex said. But he was gross about it. Roger and Trish somehow made it hot. I got off on it. But I doubt every other woman did. Everyone thought they were the perfect couple, pillars of the community, but it was

91

more complicated than that. That's what I meant by having your work cut out for you. I was thinking of all the girls they were with. If Trish was as brutal with them as she was with the girl in our threesome, I could easily see one of them wanting to take her out."

"Do you remember the girl?" Jessie asked.

"Not really. It was over a year ago. She was a brunette, I think. We only did that once. It wasn't the sexiest vibe with four of us in the room."

"Was it always at the house?" Ryan wanted to know.

"Not always. We'd meet in hotels too. I know they preferred the house because they could usher me out through the kitchen without risking the kids seeing me. But El Segundo's a trek for me so we'd mix it up. In fact, we got together a few times at the very hotel where I had the scholarship breakfast this morning—kind of kinky."

"That's lovely," Jessie said, trying not to sound too puritanical. "But I'm wondering, if you were so casual about this arrangement, why the threatening text?"

Kimberly looked a little sheepish when she answered.

"It started off casual." She said without any of her usual arrogance, "but after a while, I began to develop feelings for Roger. I started to imagine what it might be like if it was just the two of us, if he left Trish. I know that sounds like I'm providing you with a motive, but it wasn't that. I think I just got tired of the whole thing and figured maybe if I gave him an ultimatum, he'd choose me. But he didn't. I wasn't really shocked."

"Why not?" Ryan asked.

"Because he *liked* all her instructions," Kimberly explained. "He followed them enthusiastically. They were a good match. I know that sometimes they would keep the party going after I left. I could hear them going at it as I walked down the stairs. In their unconventional way, I think they really loved each other."

Jessie allowed everything she'd heard to wash over her. It all made sense. His brazenness with these women was because his wife already knew everything. He likely used a burner phone to keep things from work, not Trish. The secret stairwell leading to the kitchen and back door exit was no longer a mystery.

But it opened up a new one. It now appeared far less likely that the murder was a way to get back at Roger or make him drop out of a case. Trish wasn't just a proxy victim. She was the target all along. And that opened up a whole new pool of suspects.

CHAPTER SIXTEEN

It was well into the evening and Jessie was getting frustrated.

Things had started off well enough. Ryan got the search warrant for Roger Whitmore's office. When they went to execute it, Jessie searched under his desk and "found" the burner phone. The look on Ryan's face when she made her discovery wasn't hard to read. He was disappointed at what she'd done and didn't like being used to cover for her questionable activity, even if it had sent them down this new investigative path.

Jessie felt the same pang of guilt that she'd had when she first snuck into Whitmore's office. But again, she reminded herself that it had been for the greater good. Without that phone, they wouldn't know anything about his extracurricular activities.

She had some concern that the folks at the firm would let Whitmore know about the warrant, despite him being in mourning with his kids. But even if they did, she doubted there was much he could do. He had to have anticipated that his office would be searched. And what was he going to do—ask Lynn the executive assistant if she happened to notice them collecting a burner phone he'd hidden under his desk? That would cause him more problems than the question was worth. No, for the time being at least, he'd keep a low profile and hope for the best.

Ryan was quieter than usual on the ride to the police station, but seemed to warm up once they settled in and started going over the names in the phone in more detail with Beth and Jamil, who was at an impasse on the Plaza killings and had some free time.

They went through the names in the phone in greater depth than Jessie had been able to earlier, hoping to identify each woman and build a profile of her. It was more difficult than one might expect, as Kimberly Kelly seemed to be the rare exception that didn't care if she was found out. With everyone else, Roger Whitmore only used initials and little personal information was ever shared in the texts. Discussion focused almost exclusively on what was going to happen and where. Some of his paramours used burner phones as well, which added to the challenge.

"You should plug the photos that Whitmore received into the facial recognition database," Ryan suggested to Jamil, who blushed deeply at the thought of studying a series of images with naked women in quite literally compromising positions.

"I can do that," Beth offered, sensing his discomfort with the idea.

While the system searched, they did the laborious work of going through each text, looking for context clues that might more quickly identify who the Whitmores were involved with. While that was proving largely fruitless, one thing had become clear to Jessie.

"All of these women seem perfectly happy to participate in this," she noted. "I haven't read one comment that suggests coercion, or any threats of retaliation like the one from Kimberly Kelly. No one seems upset at all, much less angry enough to want to kill Trish Whitmore."

"You're right," Ryan agreed. "If something happened to set one of these women off, it doesn't look there's a digital footprint of it."

And yet, Jessie couldn't shake the feeling that Trish's murder was somehow connected to the Whitmores' nocturnal adventures. It was hard to buy that they could have so many potentially fraught interactions without there being any blowback. Not everyone was as emotionally calloused as Kimberly. Someone had to take issue with Trish's brutal assessment of her body or skill set during her most vulnerable moments.

Jessie closed her eyes for a second to regroup. When she opened them again, they felt heavy. She realized that she didn't know how long she'd drifted off for. No one seemed to have noticed so it couldn't have been long, but it was definitely a sign that her exhaustion was starting to compromise her investigative sharpness.

She looked at the clock. It was approaching 8 p.m. Under most circumstances she would have just pushed through. But there wasn't much more they could do tonight. Starting fresh tomorrow was the smart move. It was time to go home.

"I think I'm tapped for the day," she said to Ryan. "What do you say we go home and pick this up in the morning?"

Her fiancé, who looked equally beat, nodded in worn out agreement. There was just one issue. She wanted to leave the phone and its contents in Jamil's capable hands. But after the rough day he'd had working the Plaza killings, she was worried he might be too burned out to focus.

"Go ahead, leave the phone here," Beth said, seeming to read her mind. "Don't worry. He's not going to sleep much tonight anyway. You may as well put him to good use."

Jessie looked at Jamil, who nodded. "I'm too wired to sleep, whether I'm twiddling my thumbs or working. So I may as well be working."

Jessie didn't need to be told twice. She and Ryan said their goodbyes, and then headed out, making it to the car in record time.

*

It was almost 10 p.m. and Jessie couldn't sleep.

She'd drifted off briefly on the ride home but since then, the unsettled feeling in her gut had made it impossible to get comfortable. She lay in bed beside Ryan, who had conked out within seconds of his head hitting the pillow.

She listened to his quiet, rhythmic breathing as she scrolled through her phone, looking for something to take her mind off the case. At one point she texted Janice Lemmon to see how she was feeling after her hospitalization. The therapist answered but the brevity of her response suggested that she was as exhausted as Jessie was.

Her eyelids were just starting to droop when the phone buzzed silently. It was Hannah. Jessie hopped quickly out of bed, closed the bedroom door, and moved to the kitchen, where she answered.

"You okay?" she asked.

"Yeah, I'm fine," her sister assured her. "I just need your help with something."

"Okay," Jessie said, sitting down at the breakfast table. She couldn't remember the last time Hannah had said anything remotely like that. "What can I do?"

"First of all, this isn't specifically about me," Hannah said, "So don't worry. And I can't get into specifics, so please don't ask. I just need some advice on some big picture stuff. Can I ask you that without being interrogated?"

"Yes," Jessie said, though she wasn't actually sure that was possible. But apart from the obligatory call yesterday to let her know that a girl at Seasons had committed suicide, this was the first time in weeks that Hannah had initiated any kind of dialogue with her, so she wasn't going to hedge.

"So what do you do in your cases when you know something isn't adding up but you don't have anything tangible to back up your suspicions? What steps do you take?"

Jessie immediately guessed what was troubling her. She was trying to reconcile how she could have missed the signs that the girl at Seasons was going to kill herself. She wanted to tell her little sister that it wasn't her fault, that sometimes there are no obvious signs, and that even if you know a person well, you might miss the subtle ones. But answering a question that Hannah hadn't asked would only alienate her. So she stuck to the one on the table.

"Well," she said. "I try to figure out what's eating at me, what's making me think things aren't quite right. I might not be able to pinpoint the reason that something feels off, but I can narrow down the universe of what's giving me pause."

"What do you mean?" Hannah asked.

"For example," Jessie said, "I'm working a case right now involving a wife and mother who was viciously beaten to death in her kitchen. I initially thought it might have to do with her husband, who is very powerful. Maybe someone was trying to get back at him. But her face was unrecognizable, as if the perpetrator wanted not just to kill her, but to punish her, to humiliate her. And then we learned that the couple was involved in a variety of—," she trailed off, not sure how to broach the topic with her seventeen-year-old sister.

"I know this is all off the record, Jessie," Hannah said, irritated. "I'm not going to tell anyone."

"It's not that. There are just some elements of the case that are unsavory."

"Are you kidding?" Hannah asked, half-chuckling. "I've gotten into a knock-down, drag-out fight with a pedophile. I acted as bait to bust a sexual slavery ring. I think I can handle it. Don't get chaste on me now."

"Okay," Jessie said, unable to argue the point. "This couple liked to engage in sex games with other women. The wife was often verbally vicious with them. Now I feel certain that her death is somehow related to the way she treated these girls. But nothing we've found in the evidence so far supports that."

"Then why keep pushing that angle?" Hannah asked.

"Because not yet having the smoking gun doesn't mean I'm wrong. It might mean we haven't found the crucial clue yet, or maybe I'm circling around the truth but missing the bullseye.

Whatever the truth is, I believe it has something to with the way the wife treated these women. It's like a jigsaw puzzle where you're missing a piece. You know the shape of it and where it's supposed to go. But there are so many options to choose from. You just have keep plugging them in until one fits. Sometimes it's frustrating and laborious, but eventually that piece is going to click into place and you'll be able to see the whole picture."

Hannah was quiet for a moment and Jessie knew that what she'd said had connected. Then she asked another question.

"What if finding that piece reveals something that no one really wants to look at? What if the final picture is too ugly and seeing it could hurt lots of people?"

Jessie's internal alarm bells were ringing loudly. What exactly had her sister gotten herself into? As she'd just admitted, she had a history of putting herself in harm's way. Oftentimes it was to right a perceived wrong, but that didn't make it any less worrying.

But the very fact that Hannah was coming to her was a heartening sign. She wasn't just diving into the situation, whatever it was, headfirst. She was trying to game it out. Jessie considered that a sign of growth and, uncomfortable as it was for her, she decided that the best response was to give her sister her honest opinion and trust her instincts.

"Sometimes the truth is ugly," she said. "But if you truly believe that revealing it is for the greater good and not just an act of spite or vengeance, then I won't tell you to stop. You just have to constantly ask yourself what your own motives are and make sure you're coming from a genuine place. Use your best judgment."

Again Hannah was quiet for longer than Jessie expected. When she spoke again, her tone had changed, as had the subject.

"How is Dr. Lemmon?" she asked. "They won't tell us anything here."

Jessie fought down her desire to ask more questions and reminded herself that Hannah asking about another person's well-being was also a sign of growth that she should nurture.

"She's going to be okay," she said. "Everyone thought that she went into the hospital for kidney stones. But I just checked with her and it turned out that she slipped a disk in her lower back while boxing, if you can believe it. The woman's pushing seventy and she still gets in the ring to spar. She had been dealing with it for a week before finally consenting to get it checked out."

"Is she out of the hospital?"

"They gave her a steroid injection. They're keeping her a little longer for observation, but she texted me that she's already itching to get back to work. I wouldn't be surprised if you see her in person later this week."

"I'd like that," Hannah said, again stunning Jessie. This was the first time she'd ever heard her sister mention looking forward to meeting with a therapist. "Anyway, I have to go."

"Wait," Jessie said, despite herself, "can't you talk a little longer?"

"They just made the announcement that lights out is in five minutes," Hannah said. "If I'm not in bed by then, I lose media privileges for the next day. And you know I can't live without my super-slow internet connection."

"Okay. Well, take care."

"You too, talk later," Hannah said quickly before abruptly hanging up.

There were no goodbyes and certainly no "I love you," but Jessie was happy to take what she could get. When she went back to bed, she fell asleep right away.

CHAPTER SEVENTEEN

Andy Robinson lay in her bed at the Western Regional Women's Psychiatric Detention Center. It was after lights out but she couldn't sleep. Something wasn't right.

She'd watched the news religiously today, so she knew that Eden had finally struck. Based on the footage Andy had seen, it looked like the attack had been incredibly successful. The latest tally was five dead and ten hospitalized, with a few of those in critical condition.

There had been no way to safely communicate in the days prior to the attack without risking revealing their shared connection, so the method of Eden's assault came as a pleasant surprise. Though Andy was still putting the pieces together based on incomplete information, she could draw some conclusions.

It appeared that Eden had gone to a busy, shared public space to take out her victims. No one interviewed afterward mentioned gunshots or anything out of the ordinary prior to people around them dropping like flies. That suggested a stealth measure was used, either a toxin in the air or a poisonous substance passed via touch.

The first seemed unlikely. Eden would have needed to wear a gas mask to disperse an airborne toxin without putting herself in danger, which would have attracted notice. Since no one mentioned seeing anything like that, physically touching the victims made more sense. She could have simply walked into the crowded area, "inadvertently" bumping into multiple people without drawing attention to herself.

Andy couldn't help but admire the synergy of the act. Eden had cleverly managed to use a variation on the very behavior that had gotten her confined to a psychiatric prison in the first place. Back then, she liked to cut her palms, go into public areas, and hug strangers, covering them in blood. This simply took that proclivity to the next level.

But it served an additional purpose. By using a method similar to what originally got her incarcerated, Eden was leaving investigators a trail of bread crumbs to her identity. And since the crime took place only blocks from where Jessie Hunt worked and it was exactly the kind of crime that HSS took on, she was sure to be assigned to it.

That meant that, because Jessie was superb at her job, she would inevitably make the connection between Eden's prior crimes and this one, especially after she was eventually identified on one or more of the dozens of cameras at California Plaza. HSS would do facial recognition, get her name and learn where she'd done her time—the Female Forensic In-Patient Psychiatric Unit at Twin Towers—the same facility as Andy.

Once all those pieces came into place, Jessie would have no choice but to come to her and ask her for any insights she might have into Eden Roth, just as she'd done with Livia Bucco, another former inmate who recently committed a brutal crime.

That was their deal after all. Andy offered any intel she had on crimes committed by patients she had awareness of at any facility where she'd stayed. In exchange, Jessie got her into a nicer prison hospital, and additional perks while there. Since there were five dead people and potentially more in the near future, Jessie would have no choice but to ask Andy for help.

Of course, Jessie didn't know that there was an ulterior motive to this help. Andy hoped to make herself invaluable, eventually win back her former friend's trust, and maybe get released one day. It was admittedly a long game. One couldn't murder the wife of the man one was sleeping with, and then, after befriending the profiler on the case, try to kill her once she solved the murder. Well, one could, but not without there being blowback to the friendship. Still, Andy was committed to finding a way back into Jessie's life, no matter what it took.

But there was a problem, which was why Andy lay in bed, staring a hole into the ceiling above her. The attack was almost twelve hours ago. Jessie should have come to her for help by now.

At this point, HSS should have identified Eden, discovered the connection between this attack and her previous M.O., found out where she'd been previously locked up, and seen that she was there at the same time as Andy.

The fact that she hadn't received any visitors yet suggested one of two possibilities, either of which would complicate matters. First, Eden screwed up. Maybe she'd been too careful in her preparation and failed to leave traces to her identity. Had she covered up her face? Forgotten to leave fingerprints? Avoided interacting with anyone who could later describe her?

Andy had specifically instructed her to commit an effective crime but not a perfect one. Had Eden forgotten that? It wasn't inconceivable. The little hobbit was brilliant when it came to biochemistry but an idiot when it came to functioning normally in the world, not to mention being a literal mental patient.

The thought of that fragile, little troll ruining her plan was infuriating. She hadn't let Eden lie next to her in bed, listening to the sycophantic nut job wax rhapsodic at her "golden" blonde hair, her "piercing" blue eyes, and her "resplendent, feminine figure" just for the ego-stroking. She already knew those things about herself. She'd suffered through that intimacy, among others, because it served her purposes. And now those purposes might be thwarted.

The other possibility for why Jessie hadn't come to see her was equally troubling: what if the profiler was onto her? What if she'd identified Eden, but instead of coming to Andy for help because she might know the girl, she'd gotten suspicious of her for that very reason?

Two women committing violent murders within weeks of each other, both of whom served time with Andrea Robinson, might not seem to be a coincidence. Yes, Eden had been released a full eight months ago and had not caused a peep of trouble since. But Jessie was a cynical person who might assume that Andy, rather than seeking redemption and rehabilitation, had a long-term plan that involved activating Eden long after she'd re-entered society. It was a dark way to look at the world, even if she would be right.

Though Andy feared the second possibility more, she thought the first was far more likely. After all, even if Jessie suspected a connection between Andy and Eden, she'd almost surely still have come to talk to her. Five people had been killed and the murderer was still at large.

Jessie was prideful, but there was no way she would refuse to come here and bend the knee out of spite or arrogance if lives were at stake. And it would be investigative malpractice not to at least speak with a person she thought could help catch the culprit, even if she suspected they were in cahoots. Besides, for a case this huge, the powers that be would demand it of her.

"Put aside your history with this woman," they would order, "and get this case solved."

No—if Jessie had made a connection between her and Eden, she'd be here by now, which meant that Eden had messed up somehow. Andy would have to remedy the situation.

She considered calling Jessie directly to mention that she'd noticed a connection between these killings and Eden's prior behavior. It was a little on the nose, and might raise the very suspicions that Andy wanted to avoid, but at least it would get the ball rolling in the right direction.

And if that didn't work, there was always the backup plan. It wasn't ideal, as it had more variables than she usually preferred. But this was a fluid situation that might require improvisation. If she had to pull the trigger on plan B, there would be one bonus: the side effects would be delicious to watch unfold.

Suddenly, Andy felt sleepy. Now that she had a plan of action, her stress faded away and she began to drift off. One way or another, tomorrow morning would be interesting.

CHAPTER EIGHTEEN

When Jessie and Ryan arrived at Central Station, it wasn't even 7 a.m.

She had woken up early that morning, then tried to roll over and go back to sleep, but it didn't work. She was too restless to stay still and eventually popped out of bed. Ryan had apparently been feigning sleep because he got up a second after she did.

They weren't the only ones. Jamil had clearly been awake most of the night. By the time they stepped into the research department, he'd already definitively identified all the women from Roger Whitmore's burner phone. There were actually fourteen of them in the last eighteen months, rather than the eleven Jessie had originally counted. He'd also compiled a database with crosstabs showing their shared connections. One link among the women became immediately obvious.

"You see it?" Jamil asked after giving them a few moments to review the database.

"Yes," Jessie said. "Eight of the fourteen women work as au pairs."

"Exactly," Jamil replied excitedly. "And there's more, of those eight, three are from Beverly Hills, where the Whitmores used to live. But the five he texted with in recent months are all from the El Segundo area. And not just that, they're all listed on a website that works with au pairs and local families. I think he was using the site to troll for potential hookups."

"This makes for a perfect pool of potential partners," Jessie said, talking out her theory as it came to her. "The very fact that these women are open to uprooting their lives and moving to a foreign country for a year or more to live with total strangers shows that they have adventurous spirits, though this arrangement took that concept to another level."

"Plus, they all live in the neighborhood," Ryan added. "They'd be available to meet up regularly after their families' children went to bed."

"Right," Jessie agreed. "And it's not a stretch to think that the Whitmores were willing to pay them for their participation."

"Which would substantially supplement their income," Jamil noted, "during my research I learned that in most cases, other than room and board, these girls just get pocket money."

Jessie looked over at Ryan and could tell he was thinking the same thing she was.

"And assuming she was interested, there was one au pair Whitmore didn't even have to text with to set up get-togethers," she said, "the one who lived under their own roof: Shannon Stanfield."

"The very person who was there every day," Ryan expounded, "living under the same roof as them, sharing meals and who knows what else."

"Yes," Jessie said. "Remember she talked about how happy she was to be there. And Roger vouched for her, spoke of her glowingly. Now we know why. There's no way the Whitmores could have kept their proclivities from Shannon all this time. She had to know and she almost certainly had to be a participant. Maybe the relationship turned sour or Trish offered one criticism too many."

"Plus she was there when Trish's body was found," Ryan reminded her. "I think we may have found our killer. She was right under our noses the whole time."

"I think it's time to go to El Segundo," Jessie said.

*

They turned off the siren a few blocks before they got to Aunt Nancy's house.

Nancy Bell, the older sister of Trish's dad, only lived a quarter mile away from the Whitmore house. Her home was much more modest than most in the neighborhood, more of a large cottage than a traditional house. Jessie imagined it was a tight fit for her, Roger, the two kids, and Shannon. But as a temporary reprieve from the horrors of the Whitmore place, they would make do.

They knocked on the door and didn't have to wait long until a sixty-something woman with short gray hair and a warm smile opened the door.

"Are you Aunt Nancy?" Ryan asked.

"I am," she replied. "What can I do for you?"

"I'm Detective Hernandez with the LAPD and this is Jessie Hunt," he explained. "You might remember that we spoke on the phone yesterday."

Nancy's smile faded and her eyes grew wet.

"Yes, of course," she said. "Roger mentioned that you might stop by at some point. Do you need to speak to him now? I can get him but he's sleeping. He had to take something so he might be a little fuzzy."

"Not right now," Jessie said. "Actually, we were hoping to talk to the au pair, Shannon."

"Oh, she's not here right now."

"Did she take the kids somewhere?" Jessie asked.

"No, they're still sleeping too, thank goodness. You can imagine how hard yesterday was for them."

"Of course," Ryan said. "Where is Shannon then?"

"She said she was going back to the house to get some essentials that she didn't have time to grab yesterday."

Jessie didn't mention that going to the house without permission was a criminal offense. No one other than law enforcement was supposed to enter a crime scene until authorized. It might have been an innocent oversight by a young foreigner unfamiliar with the law, or it might be something more nefarious.

"How long ago did she leave?" she asked casually.

"Not more than twenty minutes ago," Aunt Nancy said. "She took my car. You could probably wait here if you like. She said she'd be right back. I could make you some coffee. You'd just need to keep your voices down."

"Thanks very much," Ryan said. "But it's so close. We'll just catch her over there to save time. Thanks so much for yours."

Jessie was impressed that he managed to keep his tone relaxed, considering that he was probably thinking the same thing that had her anxious: it was entirely possible that Shannon Stanfield had no intention of coming back at all. She might be making a run for it.

"Of course," Aunt Nancy said as they started back down the path to the car. "Should I have Roger call you when he wakes up?"

"That's okay," Jessie said. "Let him sleep. It sounds like he could use the rest. We'll check in with him later."

She didn't add that as long as Whitmore was asleep, he wasn't looking into the details of the search warrant executed on his office, whether they'd found the burner phone, and if they'd learned its contents.

Once they heard the front door close, both broke into a sprint to get to the car. If Shannon did intend to run for it, she had a big head start, and every second counted. Ryan drove away as quickly as he could without peeling out.

"Do we want to call for backup?" Jessie asked as he sped down the road to the Whitmore house.

"Not at this point," he said. "She's a quality suspect but I don't think we have enough yet to justify support. She could theoretically be doing what she told Aunt Nancy: gathering essentials for an extended stay at another house."

"Do you really believe that?" Jessie asked they whizzed by neighborhood homes.

"No," he admitted. "But if you and I can't handle a 115 pound au pair on our own, we're in the wrong jobs."

They arrived on Hillcrest Street and parked a half block down from the cul-de-sac the house dominated. They jogged the rest of the way. Jessie noticed a Subaru Outback in the driveway and kicked herself for not asking Aunt Nancy what kind of car she drove. When they got to the front door, they found it locked.

"What about the side entrance by the kitchen?" Jessie suggested.

Ryan nodded and they walked around the house to the side gate. It was closed but unlocked. They opened it and proceeded along the side of the house to the kitchen door; Ryan turned the knob. The door opened. He unholstered his gun and Jessie did the same.

They stepped inside and listened for any noise. There was none. They split up and searched the first floor of the house, meeting up again by the stairs after finding nothing. They were just starting up the stairs when there was a loud thud from one of the upper floors.

They both darted up as fast as they could without making noise. Jessie led the way and passed the second floor entirely, confident that she knew where Shannon was. When they got to the third floor, she peeked around the banister and down the hallway toward the bedrooms. The au pair was almost certainly in one of two places: her bedroom or the Whitmores'.

She glanced back at Ryan, who indicated that he was on the same page. She started forward but he grabbed her forearm.

"Not all of us run five miles a day," he whispered, his breath laboring slightly. "Besides, in general, the cop should enter the dangerous situation first."

"Are you sure that you're saying that out of policy and not chivalry?" Jessie whispered back, though she wasn't going to fight him on this. If Shannon did have a gun, Ryan was a better, more experienced shot. Jessie wouldn't let her pride get in the way of good judgment and stepped aside, letting him pass.

He led the way, hugging the wall with his back and she stayed close behind. As they moved forward along the hallway, she noticed one of the security cameras mounted on the wall just above her, pointed down the hall at an angle. She remembered seeing it on Jamil's monitor yesterday and that its view extended halfway down the hall, across from Shannon's room.

They moved methodically until they were just inches from her eggshell-colored door. Ryan was about to kick it open when Jessie stopped him and pointed at a wall-mounted mirror across the hall.

"Just open the door gently," she whispered. "We can use the mirror to see where she is in the room."

Ryan nodded and used one finger to push it open. As it swung inward, they saw Shannon with her back to the door, shoving items into a large backpack. As far as they could tell, she was unarmed. They stepped into the room behind her.

"What fell?" Jessie asked.

Shannon screamed as she jumped two feet in the air. When she turned around, her eyes almost popped out of her head at the sight of two people with guns pointed at her.

"Oh my Lord, you scared the piss out of me," she said. "What are you doing here? And why do you have guns?"

"We could ask you the same thing," Ryan said before pointing to a laptop on the ground as he holstered his gun. "I think that's what fell. You must be in a real rush to knock over something as sensitive as a computer and just leave it lying on the ground."

Shannon's pale skin turned bright pink.

"I'm not in a rush," she insisted. "I'm just freaking out being in the house where my boss was killed."

"That makes sense," Jessie acknowledged, holstering her own weapon as she and Ryan entered the room. "Although you know you're not supposed to be here while the investigation is ongoing. Please put your arms above your head while I search you."

"I'm sorry," Shannon said, flinching as Jessie ran her arms up and down the girl's body. "But I needed some things. I had to leave so fast yesterday that I didn't think to grab the essentials."

"She's clean," Jessie told Ryan before nodding at the backpack straining at the seams and noting, "Are you sure you're not planning an extended trip?"

"What do you mean?" Shannon asked, eyeing Ryan as he walked into her bathroom.

"You didn't just grab a few toiletries," he called out. "This counter is bare."

Jessie moved past Shannon and opened her closet.

"Same thing in here," she noted, looking at the unused hangers. "You cleared everything out."

She was about to put the pressure on and see if Shannon, who seemed very on edge, might crack. But before she could say anything else her phone rang. The caller ID simply said PDC. Those were the initials for the Western Regional Women's Psychiatric Detention Center. There was only one reason she ever got calls from that place. And the reason was always named Andy Robinson.

But this wasn't the time. She sent the call to voicemail and looked up, prepared to resume putting the screws to Shannon. But while the girl's backpack was still lying on the bed, she was gone.

"Where did she go?" Ryan asked, stepping out of the bathroom. They both heard feet running down the hallway in the direction of the Whitmores' bedroom.

"She might be making a break for it," Jessie said, both surprised and mildly impressed.

"You think?" Ryan said, hurrying past her and out into the hall. Jessie joined him just in time to see Shannon close the Whitmores' bedroom door. She heard it click as the girl locked it.

"You follow her," she said. "She's going to take that hidden staircase down to the kitchen. I'll take the main stairs and try to cut her off."

Ryan was running down the hall before she even finished talking. As she reached the main stairwell, she could hear him kicking at the Whitmores' door. After two kicks, it cracked. After three, she heard it slam open.

She took the stairs three at a time. When she got to the bottom, she didn't even try to go to the kitchen. That wouldn't be Shannon's final destination. Instead, Jessie ran down the main hallway to the front door, unlocked it and threw it open. From there she dashed through the front yard and past the driveway. She made it to the side gate they'd used to access the kitchen just as the girl yanked it open and stopped, frozen in shock.

"Don't make me tackle you, Shannon," Jessie said wearily. "You'll never make it to Aunt Nancy's car, and if you try, you'll end up getting charged with assault in addition to the other trouble you're in."

"What other trouble?" Shannon asked, though it was clear she knew the answer.

"Let's start with murder," Ryan said, appearing from behind the gate.

As he slapped the cuffs on her wrists, Shannon Stanfield started to cry.

CHAPTER NINETEEN

They let Shannon stew in the interrogation room for a good half hour before going in. It wasn't just to unsettle her. They needed that extra time.

Jessie's eyes started to get blurry as she tried to reconstruct the girl's last twenty-four hours. With Jamil busy helping the team investigating the California Plaza killings, she and Ryan worked with Beth to pore over Shannon's GPS data, call and text log histories, and social media posts. The more they knew when they questioned her, the more effective it would be.

When they finally entered the room, Jessie saw that Shannon was in bad shape. Her eyes were puffy and her skin was blotchy. A snot bubble sat unresolved in her nostril. Jessie wondered if the girl's upset was a result of guilt over what she'd done, fear of what was coming her way, or something else entirely. She handed her a tissue and sat down across from her. Ryan took the other chair.

"You remember the rights I read you on the way over?" he asked.

Shannon nodded silently.

"They still apply," he reminded her. "Did you make your phone call?"

"Yes," she replied. "I called Roger but it went straight to voicemail."

That reminded Jessie that she had a voicemail of her own she should check after they finished this interrogation.

"You can wait for him to wake up, eventually notice the call, and drive all the way downtown," she said faux sympathetically. "Of course, we'll have to put you in a cell while you wait. Or if you think it will help, you can tell us your version of events right now. It's up to you."

"I'm willing to talk," Shannon said without hesitation, "because I didn't do anything."

"That's kind of hard to buy, Shannon," Jessie countered. "You were packing everything you owned in a backpack. It sure looked like you were fleeing to me."

"It's like I said before," the girl said unconvincingly, "I was just getting my stuff to have it at Nancy's."

"That's odd," Ryan noted, "because we just discovered that you bought a ticket back to Ireland this morning. The flight's supposed to the leave in four hours. I'm not sure that Aunt Nancy was expecting to find her car at the airport."

Jessie watched Shannon's jaw drop and decided this was the time to push harder, and to take a risk.

"This doesn't look good, Shannon," she said forebodingly. "You were in the house during the murder. In fact, you were the only other person we know that was definitively there. There's no sign of a break-in. And amazingly, you somehow didn't hear a woman being beaten to death with a meat tenderizer. And all of that is before we add the small detail that you were sleeping with the victim's husband. A jury's not going to need much time with this one."

If possible, Shannon's jaw seemed to sink even lower. In that moment Jessie knew in her bones that her accusation—that Shannon was involved with Whitmore—which was only a suspicion until now, was spot on. Her bluff had worked.

There was a long pause. The she started crying again. Neither Jessie nor Ryan tried to console her. Instead, they waited until she had regained control. She wiped her nose on her sleeve, inhaled deeply, and spoke.

"All of that is true," she admitted quietly, "except I didn't kill her."

"Then why did you run?" Jessie wanted to know.

"Because I knew it was only a matter of time before you learned about the unusual relationship I had with the Whitmores. I realize it looks bad, that you'd probably think I wanted to take Trish's place in the family and jump to me as a suspect. I don't know exactly how the legal system works here. But I had nightmares last night that I was about to become the Irish Amanda Knox. So I panicked."

"If you were innocent, you should have just come forward yesterday and told us the truth," Ryan told her.

"Really?" Shannon shot back incredulously. "I had just come across the body of a woman I'd spent endless hours with over the last year. I couldn't even recognize her. I was being asked to collect two little ones and care for them until their father figured out a way to tell them that their mother was dead. And you're saying that was the ideal time for me to acknowledge that I had a sexual relationship with them?"

"It would have put you in a better position than you are in now," Jessie informed her.

"Maybe, but I wasn't thinking about it in that moment. I didn't consider it to be anything worthy of suspicion."

"A threesome involving the employers you lived with and whose children you cared for didn't seem relevant to our investigation?"

"First of all," Shannon said. "It wasn't a threesome. Trish never participated. She only…instructed. And I know it sounds weird but our arrangement worked. I liked being with them. It was exciting. I felt edgy for the first time in life."

"You weren't jealous of the other women they were with?" Jessie asked.

"No. They told me up front when they made the proposal that regardless of what I chose, I should expect to see strange women in the house on occasion. It was less uncomfortable than I expected because they made it so matter-of-fact. They said if I felt awkward, they'd find me a new family."

"So you stayed?" Ryan asked.

"Yes," she answered. "I was intrigued. Plus, they were extremely generous financially. I know the weekly stipend they gave me was more than quadruple what most other au pairs in the neighborhood received. And on top of all that, I loved the family. I especially adore Tracy and Colin. I know it sounds horribly inappropriate, but it worked for us."

Jessie was debating whether to ask anything else when Shannon volunteered one more thing.

"I looked up to Trish," she said pleadingly. "I thought she was so cool. She had it all together: good family, good life. And she was so self-assured in her sexuality. It was actually inspiring to me. You have to believe me; I would never kill her."

Jessie glanced over at Ryan to see if he had anything further. He shook his head.

"Sit tight," Jessie said as they both stood up and left the room. "We have to figure out what to do with you."

They went to the observation room and studied Shannon through the one-way mirror. The girl sat with her elbows on the table and her head in her hands.

"What do you think?" Ryan asked.

"I think she's very compelling," Jessie said. "But then again, so are many of the killers we've questioned."

"I wish those video cameras from the house had a clear view of her room," Ryan muttered. "That way we'd know for sure if she left it that morning. I don't want our whole case to be dependent on whether we believe the claims of a sex-game loving au pair."

Jessie sighed, sharing Ryan's frustration. As of now, they had enough to hold Shannon, maybe even to charge her. But whether it would stick in court was another matter. And somewhere deep in her gut, Jessie felt that familiar stirring that usually meant she was overlooking something important.

She thought of what she'd told Hannah last night. "I try to figure out what's eating at me," she had said, "what's making me think things aren't quite right."

She had the feeling that something here wasn't quite right. It had started when Ryan mentioned wanting something more definitive than Shannon's word to go by. What about that had her insides churning?

She set the thought aside for a moment, hoping that taking a brief mental break might make it emerge on its own. Instead, another thought shot to the center of her mind. She had a voicemail to check.

She pulled out her phone and played it apprehensively, fearing it would be another mind game from Andy Robinson, which she didn't need right now. Sure enough, she heard Andy's voice, oddly warm and chipper considering her current living conditions.

"Hi Jessie," she said, "sorry to bother you but I was watching the news yesterday and something jumped out at me. I think I might have some useful information regarding the case you're currently working. Please reach out when you get a chance."

That was the whole message. No clever quips, no pleas to visit her in person. No requests for additional perks if her information bore fruit. The lack of any telltale "Andy" maneuvering was actually more disconcerting than when the woman tried to manipulate her outright.

Still, she wasn't inclined to drop everything and call her. It was unlikely that Andy Robinson, who had been in psychiatric facilities for the last year, would know much about the current state of the El Segundo au pair world. And Jessie didn't even recall the story making the news yesterday. They'd done a pretty good job of keeping things buttoned up on this one. It was possible that Andy was just lonely and looking to re-engage with her old sparring partner. Jessie decided that she might reach out if they hit a wall, but not before.

"I know you're a criminal profiler," Ryan said, interrupting her thoughts. "But I need a break from delving into the mind of a potential murderer. Let's check back in with Beth to see if she found anything interesting in Shannon's personal history. Maybe she has a history of torturing small animals back in Ireland. Or maybe her stepmom was bludgeoned to death with a leprechaun."

"Okay," Jessie said, putting Andy out of her head and starting down the hall to the research department. "I'm sure your leprechaun theory is going to break this case wide open."

CHAPTER TWENTY

Hannah tried not to look too squirrelly.

It was hard to appear casual while staring at the staff directory in the therapy wing of a psychiatric facility, but she did her best. She looked at each name, matching them to the biographies of the doctors that she'd just read online, using one of the painfully slow computers in the resident communications center.

She reminded herself of the purpose of this endeavor: to determine if there was any legitimacy to the rumors that Silvio had mentioned involving the use of unapproved medications on patients. The only way to do that was to check the medical files, and that meant accessing the restricted area of the building.

She could immediately dismiss some of the people on the directory. There were six full-time therapists at Seasons Wellness Center, to go along with over a dozen nurses and almost twenty attendants. But only doctors could prescribe medication and there were only five full-fledged psychiatrists on staff. One of them, Dr. Lemmon, who held an emeritus position, could safely be crossed off the list. If she was involved in anything like this, it was more than Hannah was prepared to process, so she chose not to.

Of the remaining four, one was still in training and didn't yet handle cases as acute as Merry Bartlett. That left three doctors. Dr. Cyrus White specialized in eating disorders, and at least according to Silvio, had never worked with Merry. Still, she couldn't dismiss him.

Dr. Rose Perry was the senior psychiatrist on permanent staff. That was who Dr. Lemmon preferred Hannah see when she wasn't available. Their occasional sessions together had been as useful as was realistically possible, considering that Dr. Lemmon had instructed her not to mention to anyone here that she'd enjoyed killing a man and longed to recapture the feeling.

While Dr. Perry seemed on the up and up, this was an investigation, and assumptions like that could lead to mistakes and false conclusions. She had to do her due diligence to make sure the woman was clean.

That left Dr. Tam. Hannah didn't have much respect for his psychiatry skills but incompetence didn't mean he was involved in anything sketchy. Still, as the junior doctor on staff, he might be the most likely to cut corners to get recognition or get paid. As such, he was her prime suspect and she'd be checking to see if he was prominent in Merry's file.

The big problem was how to access Merry's medical files without getting caught. Even when the doctors weren't around, there were nurses and, of course, the administrative assistant, Elaine. Hannah didn't want to resort to any drastic methods that could get her in real trouble but those were all that came to mind right now.

She stepped outside of the therapy wing and considered her options. She could call in a bomb threat from an interior phone line. She could start a fire in a trash can, setting off the alarm and causing an evacuation. But both of those were actual crimes that wouldn't just get her kicked out of Seasons, but arrested as well.

And then it hit her. She was over-thinking things. She didn't need to start a fire. She could go with one of the oldest tricks in the book and just pull the fire alarm. It was equally effective, less dangerous, and far less criminal.

She took a casual stroll around the area. It didn't take long to find an alarm in an ideal location. The therapy wing was just across the courtyard from the secure Assistance Wing of the facility. That made sense, as it allowed staff to take more challenging patients directly to their sessions without having to interact with the rest of facility population.

It also served Hannah's purposes. If she pulled an alarm in the Assistance Wing, it would be less suspicious. Staffers would invariably assume it was done by one of the patients there. Hannah wanted to feel bad about possibly subjecting those residents to undeserved questioning, but determining if Merry's death was really a suicide took precedence over their emotional well-being.

She stepped into the closest women's restroom and put on the nondescript, gray hoodie she'd brought on the chance that she'd need it for some semi-nefarious purpose. She was well aware that the Seasons surveillance camera system only operated in certain areas, due to privacy restrictions. One of those areas was the Assistance Wing.

She left the bathroom and stood outside the entry vestibule of the wing, waiting until the interior reception area was empty. It took a few minutes. Knowing she might not get another chance anytime soon, she took a deep breath and moved.

She tugged the sleeve of her hoodie over her hand so that she wouldn't leave any fingerprints, and opened the door. Once inside the vestibule, she pulled the fire alarm. Just as quickly, she was out the door and walking back to the restroom. Once inside, she tore off the hoodie, shoved it to the bottom of the trash can, and walked outside.

She did her best to look concerned as she passed people hurrying down the outside corridors. She stopped and waited behind a pillar near the therapy wing entrance. When there was no one else in sight and she was confident that everyone had exited the building, she darted inside.

She ignored the P.A. announcement instructing everyone to go to the parking lot in a calm orderly fashion and walked briskly to the medical records room. Of course it was locked.

She rushed back to Elaine's desk and scanned it for the key. There was nothing on top, so she began yanking open drawers. To her amazement, there it was, on a key ring in the top drawer, in little basket with a Post-It taped to the front marked "medical records room."

She grabbed it and hurried over to the door. There were three keys on the ring. One was marked "door." The second read "gray cabinets" and the final one was labeled "black cabinets." She unlocked the door and stepped inside.

It wasn't hard to know where to go. The eight gray cabinets were along the longer wall, which had a printed sheet of paper taped to it that read "former patients." The sign on the shorter wall, which had three black cabinets, read "current patients." They couldn't have made it much easier for her.

Don't get cocky!

She shook her head, frustrated with her lack of self-discipline, and focused on the task. The "current patient" file drawers were all alphabetized and she went straight to the one labeled "AU-BO." Flipping through, she got to the appropriate spot and found that there was no file for Meredith Bartlett. She stared at the drawer in disbelief.

If it wasn't there, that meant it was likely in the care of one of the doctors. That meant it could be in an office or a briefcase, or in a worst case scenario, intentionally "misplaced" to hide something untoward. If that was the situation, then she was screwed. A missing file was suspicious but it was also a dead end. She slammed the drawer shut, turned around and leaned against it.

Unless...

She stared at the gray cabinets and wondered if it was possible. Might the staff here have been so cold as to simply have moved Merry's file from "current" to "former?" She had to hope they were.

Dashing over, she found the right cabinet, unlocked it, and opened the drawer where the file should be. To her shock, it was there. She set aside her disgust as she grabbed it and opened it.

The file wasn't as thick as she'd expected. She flipped through the pages, ignoring much of the jargon as she looked for two things: language suggesting Merry had suicidal ideation or a change in her prescription medication in the last few weeks by any of the staff doctors. When she got to the last page, she didn't know whether to be relieved or troubled. There was no reference to either.

Her mind raced. Was it possible that one of the psychiatrists had just changed her meds without noting it in the file? While they might not want the use of an experimental drug to be put down in writing, the doctors didn't administer the meds, nurses did. There would need to be some written order for the change, if only to formally protect those nurses from blame.

Would one of the docs avoid that by administering the medication during a session, when no one else could see? That seemed unlikely. For one thing, patients saw different psychiatrists all the time. There was no way a doctor could guarantee that he or she would see Merry regularly, which would defeat the purpose of using the drug in the first place.

For that matter, if one of the physicians was hoping to get plaudits or money for proving the efficacy of a medication, they'd need a paper trail to show its usefulness. Secretly using an unapproved drug and then touting its value after the fact seemed more like a path to getting a medical license revoked than getting a grant. The more she thought about it, the less this whole "drug experimentation" theory made sense. It sounded more like the paranoid raving of a mental patient than a legitimate lead. Of course, that might be exactly what it was.

The fire alarm was still ringing but Hannah wasn't sure for how much longer. Frustrated, she put the file back, locked the cabinet, and left the room. The therapy wing was still empty.

She dashed over to Elaine's desk, returned the key, and was about to leave the building and try to inconspicuously join everyone in the parking lot, when she noticed that Dr. Tam's office door was open. Against her better instincts, she headed that way.

Once inside, she started rifling through his drawers, not even sure what she was looking for. They were filled with nothing more than extra pens, snacks, and tissues. That is, until she got to the bottom one on the left, which was locked. She was about to begin searching for the key when the alarm turned off.

"There is no fire," came the announcement over the P.A. system. "This was a false alarm. It is safe to return to the facility. Please re-enter at the direction of nearby staff."

Hannah knew she didn't have long. She took a step back to get a full view of the desk. Maybe she was missing something. Did he have a tchotchke on his desk that seemed out of place and might hide a key to the drawer? Might it be somewhere else in the room? But nothing jumped out at her.

That's when she heard stirring in the outer office. Tiptoeing over to the door, she saw the one person she hoped to avoid. Dr. Tam had just walked through the main entrance door and was headed directly for her. There was no way to get out of his office without him seeing her.

She turned around to see if she could escape through his window, but the blinds were down. By the time she pulled them up, unlocked the window, and left, he'd be sitting in his desk chair. She heard his footsteps getting closer, mere feet from his door. Trapped, she did the only thing she could thing of: fake a breakdown.

She leapt onto the loveseat against the wall, curled up in ball, and started whimpering. She closed her eyes and hid her head just as the door opened so he couldn't gauge her expression.

"What the hell?" he demanded once he saw her.

Hannah looked up suddenly, as if startled by his arrival. He appeared unsure whether to be angry or sympathetic. She immediately sent him down the latter path.

"Oh, thank God you're here, Dr. Tam," she exclaimed, jumping up and squeezing him tight. "I thought it would never end."

"What are you doing in here, Hannah?" he asked as he disentangled himself from her.

"I was in the bathroom nearby when the alarm went off," she explained through sniffles. "It was so terrifying."

"Why? It's just a fire alarm."

"You don't understand," she insisted tearfully. "When I was kidnapped and groomed by the serial killer, Bolton Crutchfield, he used to intentionally turn on the fire alarm at all hours to freak me out. He'd do it at one in the afternoon or four in the morning, just keep me off balance and deprive me of sleep. So now anytime I hear an alarm like that, I go into panic mode."

Absolutely none of what she'd just said, other than being kidnapped and groomed, was true. But she said it with conviction, as if remembering a vivid nightmare.

"I'm sorry," he said, sounding genuinely concerned.

"By the time I got out of the restroom, everyone was gone. Then I saw the therapy wing and came in, hoping someone was here to offer support. I came into your office because you're such a caring doctor and I hoped you'd be here. But you were gone too. That when it all became too overwhelming and I just curled up on the couch until it was over."

"Okay," he said soothingly, "well it's over now. Why don't we get outside into the fresh air, maybe over to the cafeteria for a bite to eat? You'll feel better once you're up and moving."

She nodded without speaking, offering him a timid but hopeful smile. As he guided her out of the office, it took all her willpower not to look back at his desk and that locked drawer. She was now fairly certain that neither Dr. Tam nor any of the other doctors were prescribing experimental meds to patients that might lead Merry to suddenly kill herself, but that didn't mean he was off the hook.

There was something in that locked drawer that he didn't want anyone to see. Maybe it was just a laptop or a wad of cash that he didn't want to leave out in the open. But something told her he was hiding more than that. And she intended to find out what.

CHAPTER TWENTY ONE

Jessie was having doubts.

Beth's search of Shannon Stanfield's personal history hadn't turned up anything suspicious.

"She was a good, if not great student," the researcher explained. "She had a seemingly stable home life."

"So there was no record of harming animals or leprechaun bludgeoning?" Jessie asked, casting a sideways glance at Ryan who pretended not to notice. Beth looked confused.

"What?" she asked.

"Never mind," Jessie said. "So the girl seemed to have led a normal, if unremarkable life, which reinforces her claim that she was drawn to the Whitmores because their unusual offer provided her with a chance to explore a side of herself that she'd never been able to back home."

"Maybe," Ryan conceded, "but none of that mitigates the circumstantial evidence against her. In fact, when I was giving Captain Decker a progress report on the case while you two were researching her background, he was inclined to charge her right now and have us start helping out on the Plaza killings."

Jessie shook her head.

"As much as I'd like to sink my teeth into that case, I don't think we're done here. Something just doesn't feel right."

Before she could pursue that thought any further, they heard a ruckus in the hallway as an officer loudly told someone they didn't have permission to be back here. A second later, Roger Whitmore appeared in the doorway, followed by a young, flummoxed-looking uniformed cop.

"I'm sorry," Officer Garrett Dooley said. "He just barged right through."

Jessie felt bad for the straw-haired, gangly kid. He was normally a fount of enthusiasm but right now he looked completely thrown.

"That's okay, we'll take it from here, Dooley," Ryan said calmly before turning his attention to Whitmore. "Get some decent sleep?"

Whitmore looked like he hadn't. He was dressed in jeans and a t-shirt, His hair was only half-brushed and he hadn't shaved. His eyes were red and tired-looking.

"I woke up to a message from Shannon saying she'd been arrested for Trish's death," he said tightly. "Care to explain that?"

"She hasn't been formally charged yet," Ryan told him, "But she's definitely a person of interest. No alibi, potential motive, plane ticket back to Ireland, leaving today—we didn't have much choice."

Whitmore appeared briefly thrown by that last fact but quickly recovered.

"There's no way she could have done this," he insisted. "Shannon is a good kid who doesn't deserve to have her life ruined. She's part of the family."

"Yes," Jessie noted drily. "We understand that you and your wife were very close with her."

That briefly silenced the man.

"You should have told us about your arrangement," she told him.

"Why?" he demanded, getting his voice back. "What does it have to do with anything?"

"You and Trish were involved in a complicated sexual relationship with a young woman who lived under your roof. Then your wife was killed. You didn't think that relationship was worth mentioning to investigators?"

"It was none of your business," he shot back. "Besides, I didn't want Trish's memory sullied by being turned into a tabloid thing."

"It might be an important lead," Ryan said, "one you kept from us."

"I genuinely didn't think it was relevant," he told them. "Where is Shannon now? I'm acting as her attorney and I don't want her to say another word to you."

"You're going to serve as the lawyer for the woman who's under suspicion in the murder of your wife?" Ryan asked. "You can see how that might strike us as odd, Mr. Whitmore, can't you?"

"Frankly, I don't care how it strikes you," he retorted. "To be honest, it strikes me that you're attempting to railroad an innocent woman. Now please take me to my client."

Ryan looked over at Jessie. She could tell he had the same concern that she did.

"We can take you to her," she informed Whitmore. "But you won't be allowed to speak to her privately at this time."

"Why the hell not?"

"Because frankly, sir," she said, standing to her full height and fixing him with a hard glare, "you choosing to represent Shannon is pretty suspicious. We're investigating her for murdering your wife *and* you had a sexual relationship with her. Your motives are in question and we can't allow you to potentially coordinate with her."

"Are you accusing me of something?" Whitmore demanded.

"Not yet," she replied, unfazed. "But any future prosecutor would have our heads if they found out that we'd given you time to privately discuss the crime with a potential co-conspirator. So here are your three options: talk to her with law enforcement present, get her another lawyer, or don't talk to her at all. Which do you prefer?"

Whitmore looked at her incredulously for several seconds before responding.

"My understanding is that you are a consulting profiler for LAPD," he said. "As such, you don't have the authority to make determinations like that."

"You're right, Mr. Whitmore," Ryan said sharply. "But *I* do. And my determination is that you have three options: talk to her with law enforcement present, get her another lawyer, or don't talk to her at all. Now which do you prefer?"

After taking a beat to process the futility of his situation, Whitmore answered.

"I'd like to speak to her now," he said, defeated.

"Of course, Mr. Whitmore," Ryan said. "We'll find someone to stay with you while you chat with her. We'll also need to make sure the recording equipment is on. Please come with me."

He led Whitmore out of the room, leaving only Jessie and Beth. Jamil was off in the bullpen, giving some kind of report to the Plaza case detectives.

"What now?" Beth asked.

"What now," Jessie replied slowly, "is that something Ryan said a while back has been eating at me and I want to get a handle on it."

"What was that?"

"That he didn't want our whole case to be dependent on whether we believed the claims of a sex-game loving au pair," Jessie replied quoting him verbatim. "He wanted something more definitive."

"We all would," Beth agreed.

"Right," Jessie said, feeling the thought that had been nibbling at the corners of her brain start to take center stage. "But he specifically mentioned wishing the surveillance video camera footage from the Whitmore house had been more definitive, that it had a clearer view of Shannon's room so that we could tell if she ever left it the morning Trish died."

"I remember," Beth said. "But the way the camera angled down that bedroom hallway, it stopped just short of her room."

"That's true," Jessie acknowledged. "But when I was there earlier, I noticed something I missed before. Are you able to pull up the footage from that camera angle starting at around 8:58 a.m.?"

"Sure," Beth said, moving over to Jamil's monitor and hitting a few keystrokes. "What am I looking for?"

"I'm not a hundred percent sure yet," Jessie admitted.

Beth pulled up the footage and let it play. The door to Shannon's room was just out of sight but Jessie already knew that. Instead, she focused in on the wall opposite the door, specifically the mirror nearby. At 9:02 a.m., she saw something. A moment later, Shannon appeared, rushing down the hall.

"What was that about?" Beth asked.

"That was after the interior decorator rang the bell multiple times," Jessie explained. "Shannon was hurrying downstairs to answer the door. But can you rewind the footage back ten seconds?"

Beth did as she was asked, and then leaned in close to try to catch what she'd missed the first time around. This time she saw it too.

"There was a change in the light in the mirror," she said excitedly, "like a shadow passed by before Shannon comes into view. What is that?"

"That is evidence," Jessie said confidently. "The camera isn't at the right angle to see the mirror reflecting directly across to Shannon's room. But it did pick up something: the change in color as Shannon opened up her eggshell-colored door, revealing the dim interior of her room. In the darkened hallway, on a distant security camera, what looks like a shadow passing by is simply the change in color from light to dark as she opened the door."

"Okay," Beth said, getting it, "so how does that help us?"

"In a big way," Ryan said from behind them, startling them both as he re-entered the room, "because we now know what it looks like in that mirror when Shannon opens her door. If we review the window of death from 6:30 a.m. until 8 a.m. and don't find a similar shadow, it means that Shannon didn't leave her room during that time."

Jessie smiled at her fiancé.

"When did you come back in?" she asked.

"Just in time to watch you figure that out," he replied. "I guess all you needed was a break from my presence to have your 'a-ha' moment."

"We haven't proven anything yet," Jessie reminded him.

"Hopefully we're about to," Beth said, typing away. "I'm going to set the system to play back that stretch of time and look for any variations in light or shadow. It should only take a minute now that we know what we're looking for."

Jessie turned back to Ryan.

"How did it go with Whitmore?" she asked.

"Unpleasantly," he replied. "He's in there now, along with Officer Dooley. I told him that if he mentions anything specific about the case, he'll end up being held in a cell too."

"Okay," Beth said, 'the program is running. We should have an answer in about…now."

"What does it show?" Ryan asked excitedly.

"There's no gradation in the colors that appear in the mirror—no shadowing at all—during the time in question," Beth explained. "The door never opened, so unless she climbed out the window, I don't see how she could have gotten out of that room."

Everyone was quiet for a moment.

"Should we let her go?" Jessie finally asked.

"Not yet," Ryan replied. "While this looks good for Shannon, it isn't definitive. She lived in that house for a year. We can't assume she didn't figure another way out of that room, even if it seems unlikely at this point. But there are other reasons to hold her for now."

"Like what?" Jessie wanted to know.

"For one thing, it keeps her and Whitmore out of our hair," he said. "If they're here instead of out in the world, it makes everything less complicated, at least in the short term. More importantly, if Shannon's innocent, that means the killer is still out there, probably keeping tabs on our comings and goings. If we hold Shannon for a bit, maybe whoever did this lets their guard down, makes a mistake. But if they see that she's been released, who knows what they'll do? If they feel like the hunt is still ongoing, maybe they pack up and leave. They could be settling into a non-extradition country before we find out it was them."

Jessie didn't love the idea of keeping Shannon Stanfield locked up and terrified if she was in the clear, but Ryan's logic made sense.

"Then we better move fast," she said. "I say we go back to that au pair list that Jamil put together."

"Why?" Beth asked.

"Because once we fixed in on Shannon, we kind of dropped it," she explained. "But if we thought she might kill Trish to take her place in the Whitmore household, it's not unreasonable to assume another au pair he was sleeping with felt the same way. Plus, let's not forget what Kimberly Kelly said. Trish could be brutal in her assessments of these girls. Maybe one of them reacted especially badly."

"I think I may have found something," Beth said excitedly.

"What?" Jessie and Ryan asked in unison as they looked over her shoulder at the monitor.

"Before Jamil had to focus exclusively on the Plaza killings," she explained. "He set up an extra search field. We didn't have the data at the time but it's come in now."

"For what?" Ryan asked.

"He got access to the bank accounts of every au pair mentioned on the texts in Roger Whitmore's burner phone," Beth said. "In recent months, he communicated with five women in El Segundo. All of them received large deposits in their accounts. But here's the odd thing. Four of them got multiple payments. One got two. Two girls were paid three times. Another one was paid four times. But one of them was only paid once, last Friday. And it looks like she wrote a check for the exact same amount, $5000, the very next day."

"To whom?" Jessie asked.

"To a women's shelter," Beth answered.

"That sounds like someone who felt dirty keeping the money," Ryan suggested. "Maybe it didn't sit right to keep it after what Trish said to her."

"And a woman who felt strongly enough to give away the money might also be upset enough to take more personal action," Jessie noted. "What's her name, Beth?"

"Regan Navarro. The family she works with lives six blocks from the Whitmores."

"Can you text us the address?" Jessie asked before turning to Ryan. "We should go now."

They were just leaving the research office when Officer Dooley poked his head in.

"We've got a problem, Detective," he said.

"What's wrong?" Ryan asked.

"Whitmore just left the interrogation room and went to confront Captain Decker," he said. "I could hear him screaming about everything from shoddy investigating to destroying a family in mourning to making an enemy of a huge law firm and a major local corporation. He also mentioned that you were potentially starting an international incident with a foreign country."

"So what?" Ryan said. "People bluster all the time. Decker's not one to back down."

"I'm not so sure," Officer Dooley said. "He sent me to get you. He demanded to see both of you in his office right now."

"Thanks, Dooley," Ryan said coolly. "Tell him I'll be right here."

The officer nodded and headed down the hall. When he was gone, Ryan turned to Jessie.

"I don't know if Decker's just placating Whitmore or if he's really feeling the pressure," he said. "Either way, once we're in his office, it's going to be extremely difficult to extricate ourselves easily. That's why I'm going solo."

"What do you mean?" Jessie protested. "I can't let you take all the heat by yourself."

"It's not that," Ryan insisted. "We have the name of a possible suspect. It's a credible lead and I don't want to let her slip through our fingers while we're wasting time here. You go. I'll say you were already gone when Dooley came by. The kid won't contradict me. Talk to Regan Navarro; see if there's anything there. I'll stall here, and then try to catch up once I smooth things over."

"How long do you think you'll be?" Jessie pressed.

"I don't know, but you better get out of here fast," Ryan warned. "If Decker sees you, he'll pull you in too and this lead might dry up."

Jessie didn't need to be told twice. She peeked out into the hallway. Once she was sure the coast was clear, she dashed over to the stairwell, glancing back briefly at Ryan, who blew her a kiss. She returned the gesture, and then hurried down the stairs, hoping to get out of the police station garage before Decker knew she was gone.

CHAPTER TWENTY TWO

Jessie parked her car and sat quietly for a minute, allowing her body and brain to reach some kind of equilibrium.

Everything had been so "go go!" since leaving Central Station that she hadn't had time to put the pieces together. Now that she was parked on a quiet, tree-lined street in El Segundo, she allowed herself that time.

She rolled down the windows and let the early March ocean breeze blow through the car. The house where Regan Navarro was staying was just up the block and she'd parked far enough away that anyone looking out their window suspiciously wouldn't notice her.

All the houses on West Acacia Avenue were nice, many two stories high with expansive front yards and even a few tree houses, but none approached the grandeur of the Whitmore place. There was a buzz and Jessie looked down to see another text from Beth.

The researcher had been sending her updates on the drive down. First was the address for the Cranes, the family the au pair was staying with, along with a description of the family: *Husband, Alton, is an engineer at Metron. Wife, Dorian, is a home-based accountant. Three children, ages nine, six, and four.*

Next she had shared that Ryan was still in Captain Decker's office, though Roger Whitmore had returned to talk to Shannon, still under police supervision. Now she got a brief bio on Regan Navarro.

Twenty-three years old. From Guadalajara, Mexico. Father died when she was five. History of abuse at the hands of her stepfather, who was imprisoned when she was fourteen. Moved in with grandmother the next year. College softball player. Planning to attend veterinary school at the end of her time in the U.S., which concludes in June.

It sounded to Jessie like Regan had overcome some serious obstacles to get where she was now. To risk all that for a moment of vengeance suggested that Trish must have been especially cruel to her. Had she donated her money to the women's shelter, hoping it would put the matter behind her, only to find that the fury she felt at being judged so harshly still burned inside her?

Jessie decided it was time to find out. She left the car and walked up to the Crane house. School was back in session today so at least she wouldn't have to worry about navigating curious children. She rang the bell and stepped back, waiting to see if anyone peeked through the curtains in one of the windows on either side of the front door. There was no movement but she did see the light in the peephole disappear as someone checked her out. A moment later, the door opened.

"May I help you?" asked a put-together woman in her late thirties with brown hair, a sensible haircut, and glasses. Even though she worked from home, the family matriarch still wore slacks and a professional-looking top.

"May I help you?" she asked again, hesitantly.

"Dorian Crane?" Jessie confirmed.

"Yes."

"My name is Jessie Hunt," she replied, holding up her ID. "I work with the Los Angeles Police Department. I was hoping to talk to Regan Navarro."

"Why?" Dorian asked cautiously. "Is she in some kind of trouble?"

"No, of course not," Jessie lied. "We're investigating an issue with another au pair who lives in the area and we think talking to others in the neighborhood might be helpful."

"Can't you tell me what it's about?"

"I'm afraid not," Jessie apologized. "We're sticklers about protecting people's privacy."

Dorian still looked hesitant to answer.

"To be honest," Jessie said, leaning in conspiratorially, "it's likely nothing. My captain sends me on a lot of wild goose chases. But this is the chase I've been assigned so I have to do the job, you know? I doubt I'll need more than five minutes of her time. Is she here?"

Dorian finally seemed to relent at Jessie's manufactured chummy-ness.

"She's actually at a doctor's appointment right now," Dorian whispered, even though there was apparently no one around.

"Oh my goodness, is she okay?"

"She's fine," Dorian assured her, before reluctantly conceding, "It's just that she hasn't been to a gynecologist since she moved here. In fact, she told me that she's never been to a proper one ever, just to a nurse at her university back in Mexico. I insisted that she see mine, got her an appointment right away. She took a rideshare over about forty-five minutes ago."

"That's very considerate of you, Mrs. Crane," Jessie said. "Can I get the name of the doctor please?"

"Of course, but I'm sure she'll be back soon. Wouldn't you just rather wait here than go looking for her in a busy office building?"

"Normally, yes," Jessie told her. "But this is a little time sensitive, as in my boss is on my butt. So I'd just as soon go to her."

"Okay," Dorian Crane said as she pulled out her phone and sent the info to Jessie.

"By the way," Jessie asked, as if the thought had just occurred to her. "Do you have a photo of Regan that you could send me too? I'd hate to walk around an OB/GYN office tapping every girl asking if her name was Regan. It might weird them out."

"Good thinking," Dorian said, scrolling through her pictures and sending a nice full-body shot of Regan at Disneyland with the three kids.

"She's beautiful," Jessie said and she meant it. Regan had long, black hair down to her mid-back. Her dark eyes sparkled in the sun. The photo had been taken in the summer and she was wearing a floral skirt with a tank top that revealed a curvy body and arms that still looked muscled enough to throw a softball or swing a meat tenderizer. It was clear why the Whitmores would have been drawn to her.

"Please go gentle when you talk to her," Dorian asked. "She's had a rough few days."

"Why is that?" Jessie wondered, pretending to be only casually interested in the answer.

"She said that she's been feeling homesick lately, even mentioned going back early. We hope it's just a passing thing."

Jessie seriously doubted that homesickness was the issue plaguing Regan Navarro but she kept that to herself.

"I'll be as sensitive as I can," she said, before saying thank you and goodbye, and heading out.

She waited until she heard the door behind her close before breaking into a jog, hoping to get to the doctor's office before Regan left for who knows where.

CHAPTER TWENTY THREE

The doctor's office, like everything in this community, was only a few minutes' drive away.

That was just long enough for Jessie to call Beth and update her so that she could do the same for Ryan when he finally got free of Captain Decker.

Dr. Lydia Lyman's office was on the seventeenth floor of a huge office tower on the corner of Sepulveda and El Segundo Boulevards. Jessie took the elevator up and walked briskly to the door. Before opening it, she instructed herself not to give off too strong a law enforcement vibe when she walked in. She didn't want Regan to pick her out in the waiting room and do something rash.

She opened the door and the five women in the waiting room looked up at the same time. Jessie quickly scanned them. None was Regan Navarro. She walked over to the reception window slowly, trying to get a sense of the place.

Dr. Lyman clearly catered to a well-off clientele. Her practice was in a desirable community, in a giant, pristine tower. The furniture in the office wasn't cheap and the place exuded a relaxed, unhurried energy. The music was smooth jazz and the art on the walls was modern but not too avant-garde. The receptionist, a friendly-looking woman in her late twenties with blue-dyed hair and several tattoos, smiled at her.

"Checking in?" she asked.

"Actually, no," Jessie said in a hushed tone. "I'm looking for a patient named Regan Navarro."

The woman looked startled at the request.

"I'm sorry?"

Jessie pulled out her ID.

"I need to speak to Regan Navarro," she repeated. "Is she still here?"

"I'm afraid that I can't talk about potential patients, ma'am," she said emphatically after looking at the ID.

"I'm not asking about her medical records," Jessie replied. "I just need to talk to her."

"I can't reveal anything about a patient, and certainly not just because someone walks in flashing some identification. I have no idea if you are—"

"Is there a problem, Justine?" someone asked from behind her.

Jessie looked up to see a plump woman in her early forties wearing a lab coat, with grayish-blonde hair and light blue eyes.

"Are you Dr. Lyman?" Jessie asked.

"I am," the doctor answered warily.

"My name is Jessie Hunt. I work with the LAPD. We need to talk about one of your patients."

Lyman eyed her calmly before glancing back at the receptionist.

"Let her in, Justine," she said.

Justine buzzed the door and Jessie entered, following the doctor back to her office. Lyman waited until she was inside, and then closed the door. She didn't offer her a seat.

"What is this about, Ms. Hunt?" she asked.

"I'm investigating a murder, Dr. Lyman," Jessie explained. "I believe that Regan Navarro may have valuable information about the case. I just came from Dorian Crane, who told me that she'd made an appointment for Regan with you this morning. Is she here?"

"She was," Lyman said without putting up an argument. "But she left a little while ago."

"How long ago?"

"I don't know. Maybe ten minutes? I wasn't paying close attention."

Jessie sighed. She could try to access the building's camera footage but wasn't sure how much good it would do. It would take time and even if she saw the girl, that wouldn't reveal where she'd gone from here.

"Dr. Lyman," she said, knowing her next request might not be received well, "I need to know why Regan came to see you. Dorian said it was just because she'd never been to a proper gynecologist but I suspect there's more to it than that. Was she concerned about a possible pregnancy?"

"You know I can't tell you that," Lyman scolded.

"Not even if it involves life and death?"

"Ms. Hunt," the doctor said, her blue eyes steely. "If you get a court order, maybe we can revisit this conversation. But you know as well as I do that it's a HIPAA violation for me to tell you anything about a patient's medical information."

"Listen, Dr. Lyman," Jessie said coolly, knowing that raising her voice to this woman wouldn't do any good, "I understand the rules and I wouldn't ask if this wasn't such a serious situation."

Lyman didn't answer but she didn't kick her out either, so Jessie continued.

"I'm about to share confidential details with you that I'm not supposed to reveal to anyone," she said quietly. "A woman was murdered yesterday in her own home, less than three miles from here. Her face was hammered to a pulp with a meat tenderizer. She leaves behind a husband and two young children. I have reason to believe that Regan knows something about it and I'm pretty sure her visit here today is connected to what happened. She slept with the husband last week. Now I don't know why she came here—whether she's worried about getting pregnant or contracting an STD. But I know it's not a coincidence that she came to see you. I'm asking for your help. I will keep whatever you tell me off the record. It won't go in any report until I can corroborate it through other means. But we're talking about a vicious crime here. I need your help to solve it."

Dr. Lyman looked torn. Jessie could tell that she wanted to reveal what she knew but couldn't get past the ethical complications. Finally she sighed and Jessie knew, even before the doctor spoke, that she hadn't convinced her.

"I'm sorry, Ms. Hunt," she said. "I just can't. Get that court order and I'll open up my records, but not until then."

It was Jessie's turn to sigh heavily.

"Thank you, Doctor," she said, opening the door. There was nothing more to say.

She trudged out of the office, feeling like there was an anvil tied to her back. There were still ways to find Regan, but if she was responsible for what happened to Trish, every second that she was on the street meant someone else might be in danger. If she lost it again, or just felt desperate enough, there was no telling how she'd react.

Jessie left the waiting room and made her way back down the long hallway to the elevator. She pushed the button and pulled out her phone. There was a text from Beth that read: *Detective Hernandez finally left Decker's office. I filled him in. He's en route.*

A second text from Ryan had arrived a few minutes later. It read: *Beth updated me. On my way. Meet you at the Cranes' house.* The elevator arrived and she stepped inside. The doors were just starting to close when she heard a voice call out.

"Ms. Hunt!"

She looked up. It was Dr. Lyman, hurrying down the hallway toward her. Jessie put her hand between the doors just before they met and they retracted. She stepped out of the elevator and waited. It took a few seconds for the doctor to catch her breath. When she did, she spoke quickly and quietly.

"Do I have your word that you will not reference how you got access to anything I tell you?" she asked. "That you'll find another way to get the information for any report or potential trial and that if you can't, you will promise not to use the information at all?"

"I promise," Jessie assured her.

"It will be as if this conversation never happened, right?"

"Right," Jessie repeated, hoping she could live up to the agreement.

"I'm trusting you with my career, Ms. Hunt," Dr. Lyman said. "The only reason I'm even considering this is because I'm well aware of you and your reputation. I believe you to be a force for good in this city, someone who advocates for victims, both alive and dead. Please don't make me regret that trust."

"I won't."

"In that case," she said, appearing pained at the words she was speaking, "Regan Navarro didn't come to see me out of fear of getting pregnant or an STD, although those are real concerns for her. She came to see me because she was raped."

"What?" Jessie said, her mind suddenly swimming.

"She didn't admit that," Lyman quickly added, "but she had all the telltale signs. There was vaginal bruising and swelling. When I started asking questions, she conceded that things had gotten physical, though she didn't get more specific than that. When I started to do a rape kit, she got spooked, asked who it would go to. After I told her the police would get it, that I was required by law to turn it over, her demeanor changed. She looked terrified and insisted that there was no need for a kit, that everything was consensual, that it was just rough sex. I pressed her on the matter but she got upset and said she'd leave if I tried to submit the kit. So I backed off. She was in bad shape and I didn't want her to just run out before I could do anything for her. But I've been doing this for fourteen years and what I saw was definitely rape."

Jessie's stomach turned as she nodded silently, trying not to visibly reveal her horror in front of the doctor. This woman was taking a huge professional risk confiding in her and she needed to know she was dealing with a professional.

It all made sense now. Regan wasn't just upset because Trish had said cruel things to her while she was with her husband. Roger Whitmore had raped her while Trish sat in the room, doing nothing to stop it. No wonder she was filled with such rage.

"How long ago do you estimate the rape occurred?" Jessie asked, keeping her own fury out of her voice as best she could.

"Three or four days, tops," Dr. Lyman said, "So probably Friday or Saturday."

According to Regan's bank account information, that fit the window when she would have met with, and later been paid by the couple.

"Did Regan say how she planned to proceed?" Jessie wanted to know.

"At her request, I gave her medications to address both a potential pregnancy and most STDs. But she didn't say much after that. I'm sorry."

"That's okay," Jessie said. "You've been very helpful."

"Do you think Regan killed this woman?" Lyman asked hesitantly.

"I think I need to have a serious conversation with her, and that will be one of my first questions."

She got back in the elevator and pushed the button for the lobby. She'd been diplomatic with the doctor, but the truth was that she didn't need to ask any questions to know what happened. Regan had killed Trish Whitmore. And she might not be done.

CHAPTER TWENTY FOUR

Susannah Valentine was exhausted.

She'd spent the night at the station pursuing leads, ultimately getting about three hours of fitful sleep on a lumpy couch in the break room. Jim Nettles pulled out a cot from the closet and snored nearby. Karen Bray skipped sleep entirely, instead going home for an hour to check on her young son, who was fast asleep, and make him Mickey Mouse-shaped pancakes that her husband could heat up in the morning.

But despite working as the early morning darkness gave way to sunrise, she, Bray, and Nettles had mostly been running in circles. Of the other nine victims of the attack besides Holly Valdez who were currently in the hospital, only two had regained consciousness so far, and neither could offer a description of the person who poisoned them. In fact, neither even knew that they *had* been poisoned in the moment.

So the three detectives were reduced to poring over recent criminal and university academic files, looking for any charges or dismissals related to the intentional, improper use of volatile chemicals. There were over two dozen such instances in the last year alone, but almost all of them related to fires or explosions. Nothing even close to the more sophisticated attack from yesterday cropped up.

They finally caught a break around 7:15. The crime lab had identified the poison used on the victims: a massively amplified version of Intocostrin, a synthetic form of the neurotoxin, curare.

"The strange thing is that curare typically works by entering the bloodstream," explained the lab tech they spoke to. "But it looks like your killer found a way to combine two other chemicals into a liquid so concentrated that it could do the same damage via the skin. Intocostrin also might explain the broken ribs we found in most of the victims."

"How so?" Susannah asked.

"The toxin works by causing asphyxiation, due to muscle paralysis, including of the diaphragm," he said. "It's possible that in the early stages, before they lost all muscle control, their bodies would seize up violently as they desperately fought for air they couldn't get. The contractions could be powerful enough to break bones."

They were all quiet for several seconds after hearing that. Bray snapped out of it first.

"Let's find Jamil," she said.

They grabbed the researcher, who had apparently been helping Ryan Hernandez and Jessie Hunt gather a list of nannies who might have killed some woman in El Segundo, and put him to work. It didn't take him long to get some hits.

"We're in luck," he said, as Susannah, Bray, and Nettles stood over the monitor he was sitting at. "Because these chemicals are so volatile, all facilities with access to them are tracked in a database run by the CDC's Agency for Toxic Substances and Disease Registry. According to the records, there are lots of labs that have one or the other of these two chemicals. But there are only fourteen within a hundred miles of Los Angeles that have both."

"What about outside that range or via mail?" Susannah asked.

"No on the latter," Jamil said definitively. "Shipping those kinds of materials though the mail together is not only illegal, it would raise red flags. The company who got the request would have to report it to the ATSDR—no way that your perp would risk that. As to labs outside a hundred miles, it's certainly possible. Heck, your killer could have come from Florida with the materials three years ago. But we have to start somewhere, right?"

"He's right," Bray said, "If this attack was planned that far in advance, then we're probably screwed regardless. We have to hope our attacker is local. Let's split these facilities up and check them out in person."

"You don't want to call first?" Nettles asked.

"We could," she replied. "And under normal circumstances, I'd say that's a good first step. But I worry that we'll get caught up in bureaucratic mazes that way. The labs need to understand the magnitude of the situation and that can be better conveyed through in-person visits from people with badges and guns."

"I agree," Susannah said. "Besides, it sounds like stealing these kinds of materials from a lab isn't like shoplifting from a convenience store. My guess is that our killer needed help from someone on the inside. And to determine who offered that help, we need to interview people, look in their eyes, see who seems shifty."

"Good points," Bray said. "So let's split these places up. Each of us will go with two officers in a squad car. That's all we can spare until someone gets a quality hit. Sound good to everyone?"

Nettles nodded. Susannah did the same. After endless hours of thumb-twiddling, she was just happy to have a mission.

*

The mission had turned into drudgery.

It was approaching lunchtime and Susannah was on her fifth and final lab of the day. The previous four had been comprised of soul-deadening conversations with operations managers and heads of security about detailed, redundant procedures that had been put in place to ensure that the exact kinds of chemicals she was looking for never left without duplicate, verifiable approvals.

As she and the two officers accompanying her sat in the visitor waiting room at B.U. Labs in Norwalk, she texted with Bray and Nettles, who were having no more success than her. Nettles, who had been assigned four facilities, had just left his final lab and was headed back to the station. Bray was en route to her last one. Neither seemed optimistic.

The door to the waiting room opened and a middle-aged guy with thinning black hair, wearing a white dress shirt that fought his considerable paunch, stepped out. He wore a tie with multiple images of Beaker, the character from *The Muppet Show*.

"Detective Valentine," he said, extending his hand to shake hers and doing an admirable job of trying to keep his eyes above her neck. "I'm Mark Weir, the operations manager here at Bounty Unlimited Labs. I was told you have an urgent issue to discuss."

"That's right, Mr. Weir," Susannah said. After muddling through with the other labs, she knew much better now how to get straight to what she needed. "Have you discovered any discrepancies in the listed and actual supplies of these chemicals in recent weeks?"

She handed over a piece of paper with the chemicals, whose names she still couldn't properly pronounce. Weir looked at the paper, and then back up at her. His stunned expression told her this visit would be different.

"How did you know?" he asked, dumbfounded.

"Are you saying that there's a discrepancy?"

"Yes," he said, ushering her out of the waiting room.

"You guys stay here," she said to the uniformed officers. "But keep your radio channel open. I'll let you know if there's anything going on."

She joined Weir in a small vestibule off the waiting room that split out into four narrow hallways. He looked around to make sure there was no one in earshot before speaking. Susannah tried to hide the growing anticipation she felt. She didn't want to tip anything off, but she was sure: something big was coming.

"We do a complete inventory review every Friday after lunch," he said in a hushed voice. "Our last one showed a small variance in the catalogued and actual supply of both those chemicals. We did a second review yesterday and came up with the same issue so we initiated a formal inquiry this morning."

"What did you find?" Susannah asked.

"Nothing definitive," he said. "The best explanation we have so far is that some portion of the materials were used but not properly logged. A lab tech in our biochem unit said that his terminal went down briefly last Tuesday when he was cataloguing pending and used vials. He thinks the data may have been lost at that time."

"Has that been confirmed?" Susannah asked.

"Our IT folks are working on that now actually," Weir said. "They verified that his system had an unexpected shutdown but are trying to determine if any data was lost, and if so, whether it can be salvaged."

"What's the tech's name?" she pressed.

"Phil Russell."

"Is he here now?"

"Yes," Weird answered. "He's been moved off biochem into our agriculture unit until this is resolved."

"Can you take me to him?" Susannah asked.

"Of course, follow me."

"Valentine here," she said into her radio to the cops in the waiting room. "We may have a decent lead here. Officer Braden, meet me in the agriculture warehouse. Medavoy, return to your vehicle and keep the car running."

Mark Weir led her down one of the claustrophobic halls, which eventually opened up into a large warehouse with open workspaces and a rows of tables with computer monitors and equipment that Susannah couldn't begin to identify.

"What can you tell me about Phil Russell?" she asked as they cut quickly through the warehouse.

"Until about two hours ago, not much at all," Weir admitted. "But a lot more now since I've been reviewing his file. Phillip Russell is twenty-five, got his degree in Bioengineering from Cal Tech. He was working on his master's when he got a DUI two years ago. If not for that, I assure you he wouldn't be working as a lab technician at a company that specializes in animal feed."

"Why does an animal feed company have a biochem unit at all?" Susannah asked.

He smiled condescendingly.

"Manufacturing the perfect balance of nutritional elements in feed is a more complicated process than it sounds. Plus, we need to ensure that the feed isn't susceptible to absorbing pesticides, which means having pesticide components in-house to test. That was what Russell was working on."

"Any disciplinary problems with him?" Susannah asked, refusing to let Weir's patronizing tone send her off course, "Disagreements with co-workers, disputes with managers, requests for paycheck advances?"

"There's nothing like that in the file," he said. "For the first year he was here, he had to submit to weekly drug tests because of the DUI. But that ended last April and there haven't been any red flags since."

He stopped walking abruptly. So did Susannah.

"That's him in the lab coat with his back to us," Weir said, pointing at a tall, skinny blond guy at the back corner of the warehouse. He was holding a glass slide up to the warehouse skylight.

"Care to make the introductions?" Susannah asked.

Weir, who suddenly looked nervous, nodded and started toward Russell.

"In the warehouse now, Detective," Officer Braden said over the radio.

Susannah looked back over her shoulder and saw the broad-shouldered cop near the entry door, about seventy yards away.

"Come on over, Braden," she said waving to identify herself. "I'm about to chat with our first interesting prospect of the day. Can you hear me, Medavoy?"

"Loud and clear," he confirmed. "I'm in the car now."

"Excellent," she replied. "Can you run this guy through the system and see if anything pops? Name is Phillip Russell—twenty-five, Cal Tech grad, DUI about two years ago."

"Will do," Medavoy said.

Weir led her over to Russell, who was hunched over a microscope, oblivious to their presence. Weir coughed dramatically to get his attention.

"Excuse me, Phil," he said.

The young man stood up and turned around to face them. He was pale-skinned with glasses and bad acne. His blond hair was unkempt and his brown eyes were beady.

"Phil," Weir said uncomfortably. "I'd like to introduce you to Detective Susannah Valentine. She has some questions for you."

The guy's little eyes got surprisingly wide as he took in Susannah, along with Weir's description of her job.

"Okay," he said meekly.

"Mr. Russell," she said, getting straight to the point, "I want to talk to you about the missing chemicals from last week."

He shook his head in agitation.

"I already told Mr. Weir and the security folks that it was a computer hiccup. I don't actually think there will turn out to be any discrepancy in on-site stock."

"Nonetheless," Susannah said, "you'd acknowledge that if those two chemicals were missing and in the same place, it could pose problems, right?"

"Um...," he began, before suddenly breaking into a sneezing jag. "Can we talk about this in a few minutes? I just realized that I really have to go to the bathroom. I have a nervous bladder."

"Maybe after we're done," Susannah said, disinclined to let up on the pressure. Perhaps his physical discomfort would lead to a greater willingness to be forthcoming.

"I really have to go to the bathroom," he insisted. "I feel like I'm going to throw up."

"There's a trash can right there, Mr. Russell," Susannah said, pointing at the plastic bin by his table.

"I can't do that here," he said, turning and shuffling quickly toward the restroom about twenty feet away.

Susannah was just about to order him to come back when he suddenly veered left and began running toward the exit at the corner of the warehouse. Susannah, who was already on the balls of her feet in anticipation, took off after him.

CHAPTER TWENTY FIVE

Jessie arrived back at the Crane house just a few minutes before Ryan did.

She saw him coming and got out of her car to wave him down.

"Just park here," she told him. "I'm not sure if Regan's come back from the doctor yet and I don't want to get too close to the house in case she's on the lookout."

Ryan parked and joined her in the street.

"I have Beth getting access to her phone GPS data right now," he said. "She thinks she'll have it within the hour. But I'm worried that might take too long. By then Regan could be on a flight or almost to the border. She's a Mexican national. What do you think the chances are that their government would extradite a rape victim for killing her attacker's wife? I'm guessing not great."

"I'm worried it might be worse than that," Jessie countered.

"What do you mean?"

"What if Trish wasn't the intended target?" Jessie theorized. "What if she came over to the Whitmore house early yesterday morning hoping to find Roger, but he wasn't there because he spent the night at the office? What if she took her anger out on the person who just happened to be there, who didn't try to stop what happened?"

"You're thinking she might still be going after her original target?" Ryan wondered.

"It makes sense," Jessie replied. "She just learned that the doctor who saw her wanted to report the rape. She might be worried that it's still a possibility. And she might figure that once the police get that report, it won't take long for them to question her and potentially connect her back to the Whitmores. She knows she'd be the prime suspect in Trish's death. She might be thinking that if she's going to get arrested for that anyway, she may as well finish the job and go after the person who hurt her in the first place."

"So would she go to their house and wait for him there?" Ryan surmised, "Maybe his office?"

"I doubt she'd try the office," Jessie said. "She'd know she'd never get past security. I could see her hanging out on his street, but after a while she'd realize he wasn't going there, that he wouldn't just go back right away to the home where his wife was murdered yesterday."

"So she'd try to find out where he was staying now," Ryan surmised. "Maybe use the au pair community to get an address. It wouldn't be hard. A few calls and texts would do it."

"Probably," Jessie agreed.

"So I guess we're going back to Aunt Nancy's."

"I think so," Jessie agreed, "but let me make a call first."

She dialed Dorian Crane's number and put the call on speaker. The woman picked up on the first ring.

"Hi, Mrs. Crane," Jessie said, trying not to sound too frazzled, "its Jessie Hunt."

"Hello, Ms. Hunt," she replied, clearly concerned about something. "Did you find Regan at Dr. Lyman's?"

"I'm afraid not," Jessie told her. "I thought she might have come back to the house."

"No, she hasn't," Dorian said anxiously. "And I'm starting to get worried. She isn't answering my calls. I'm concerned that whatever this au pair issue is that you can't tell me about might be serious. Is she in danger?"

"I hope not," Jessie said as she and Ryan got into his car. "But if she comes home, would you please give me a call? I'd really like to chat with her."

"Of course, right away," Dorian promised.

By the time Jessie hung up, Ryan had pulled out and was on his way to Aunt Nancy's. On the drive over, Jessie called Roger Whitmore. Even though he was a rapist, he needed to be warned that his life might be in danger. It went straight to voicemail. So she tried Beth. She answered right away.

"Is Whitmore still at the station?" Jessie asked.

"No, he left soon after Detective Hernandez did."

"Any luck on locating Regan's phone yet?"

"It's still in process," Beth answered. "Jamil is crazed with the Plaza killings stuff so he can't help and I'm new to this. But I should have something for you in the next fifteen minutes."

Jessie didn't want to tell her that might be way too late.

"Okay, thanks Beth. Keep us posted."

She hung up just as Ryan arrived on Aunt Nancy's street and parked a few houses down from her house. They dashed over as they inserted their ear buds. They were so in sync with each other that they didn't even have to discuss the plan they intended to put in place. Ryan called Jessie so they could hear each other. Once the call connected, Jessie went to the front door while Ryan hopped the fence leading to the back. She knocked on the door, trying not to sound too desperate. Aunt Nancy answered within seconds.

"Hello, Ms. Hunt," she said without any of the warmth from earlier. "I didn't expect to see you again, after what you did."

"What do you mean?" Jessie asked, perplexed.

"Roger told me that you arrested Shannon for Trish's murder," she said sharply. "I don't know how you think that sweet girl could have done anything so horrid."

In the background, Jessie could hear cartoons coming from a different room and assumed the kids were home, so she kept her voice down.

"Is Roger here now?" she asked. "I'd like to talk to him to clear all that up."

"No, he's come and gone."

"Do you know where he went?"

"He grabbed a bag; said he wanted to get a few pictures of Trish back at the house so the kids would have them," she said. "They miss her terribly."

"I'm sure they do," Jessie replied, trying to keep her voice level. "Thank you."

"You should be saying 'I'm sorry,'" Aunt Nancy retorted.

Jessie couldn't dispute the point. She might owe Shannon Stanfield a major apology when this was all done, but that wasn't her priority now.

"One more thing, do you recognize this woman?" she asked, holding up her phone with the picture of Regan on it.

"I do. She stopped by just a little while ago. She wanted to offer her condolences on behalf of the other au pairs in the neighborhood," Nancy said, pointing at a bouquet of flowers in a vase on the foyer table. "She had these, wanted to give them to Roger. But since he wasn't here, I promised to pass along the kind wishes."

"Did you mention that he was going to be stopping back at his house?" Jessie asked.

"I did actually," Aunt Nancy said. "He called on his way back from seeing Shannon at the police station, asking if I had a bag he could borrow to collect the pictures. I told him I did. Then that girl arrived. She offered to take the flowers over to the other house but I suggested she leave them here. It seemed inappropriate for her to stop by there while he was in that state of mind, don't you agree?"

"I do," Jessie said, trying to rein in the adrenaline coursing through her. "So let me make sure I have this right—Roger called to say he was coming by to pick up a bag for the pictures, then this au pair stopped by with the flowers, at which time you mentioned that he'd be going to the house on Hillcrest. After that, Roger arrived, picked up the bag and left for the house. Do I have all that correct?"

"You do," Aunt Nancy said.

"How long ago did he leave?"

"Not more than five minutes ago," Aunt Nancy answered.

"Thanks so much," Jessie said, already turning to head back down the path as she called out, "I promise to make things right with Shannon as soon as I can."

She was waiting in the car when Ryan returned. He started it up and pulled out without needing to be told where to go. Jessie tried to call Whitmore again, but it continued to go to voicemail.

"We'll never make it in time," Ryan said as he accelerated well past the speed limit for residential streets. "If she's been lying in wait for him, he might already be dead."

"Maybe she's waiting for him to come into the room where she's hiding," Jessie suggested. "There might still be time."

But she feared he was right. Five minutes was a long time. By now, Regan might have killed him and left the house. They just had to hope Whitmore was taking his time going from room to room.

Or I could warn him.

"I'm going to call Regan," she said suddenly, as Ryan pulled onto Hillcrest.

"You didn't already try that?" he asked.

"I didn't want to give her a heads up that we were looking for her," she explained as she dialed the number. "But if Whitmore hears her phone ring, he might realize he's not alone in the house and bail. Maybe I could even talk her down before she does anything."

Ryan drove all the up to the end of the cul-de-sac and parked next to Whitmore's car in the driveway. As they hopped out, the call connected. Jessie heard Regan's recorded voice.

"It went straight to voicemail," she told him, hanging up.

"She probably turned it off for that very reason, so it didn't give her away," he said as they stood in the driveway. "How do we want to do this?"

"Let me try the front door in case he went in that way," Jessie said, heading over and delicately turning the handle. It gave way.

"Okay, you go in here," Ryan said quietly. "I'll use the side entrance like last time when we found Shannon. Let's open a phone line and stay in contact. Sound good?"

"Yes," she whispered back, "But hurry—we're out of time here."

He nodded and hurried off to the side gate. Jessie put in her ear buds again and called him. He answered right away.

"Approaching the kitchen door," he said in a hushed voice. "It's slightly open. And one pane of the glass window has been smashed out."

"If Whitmore came in through the front, then that must have been Regan," she replied. "Be careful, Ryan."

"Will do," he pledged. "You do the same. Going in now."

Jessie waited one more beat, then unholstered her gun, took a deep breath, and stepped inside.

CHAPTER TWENTY SIX

Susannah watched Phil Russell disappear through the warehouse door but she was moving fast, and got through it before it even closed.

The door led outside, to a large courtyard with stone benches mixed in among topiary bushes cut into the shapes of farm animals. He was just dashing past what looked like a large pig. She broke into a sprint, taking an angle around a goat to make up the distance between them.

Russell wasn't in great shape and he seemed to be petering out even before she got to him. She hurdled over a bench just past what looked like a flock of chickens and leapt at the guy, tackling him from behind. She rolled over him and popped up, ready for whatever he might do. But he wasn't doing anything.

Instead, the gangly guy lay on his stomach, groaning in between fits of wheezing. Officer Braden arrived moments later to cuff him and pull him to his feet. That's when Russell followed through on his threat from before and threw up.

"Have him sit on the bench," Susannah instructed when he was done, wincing at the sight of the pathetic creature in front of her. She waited until he was breathing close to normally again before asking, "What the hell was that all about?"

"I'm sorry," he huffed. "I just kind of panicked."

"Why?" she asked, hoping he might reveal something without having to be led.

"I don't know," he muttered, his head downcast. "It's been a rough few days. I didn't get much sleep last night."

"Why not?" she pressed.

He looked up and she knew without a doubt that Phil Russell was involved in what happened yesterday.

"Because of the attack," he answered. "That's why you're here, isn't it?"

"Yes, Phil," she told him. "That's why I'm here."

She thought he might spill everything right then and there but he didn't.

"Do I need a lawyer?"

"I don't know," she said as Mark Weir finally caught up to them. Behind him were two security guards. "Do you need a lawyer? Did you commit a crime?"

"Not that one," he said emphatically.

Susannah sighed, debating how best to proceed. Russell wasn't the person in the footage from California Plaza. That was a small female. He was about as different as one could get from that. Maybe he was an accomplice but he wasn't the person behind all this. Still, she needed information from the guy and couldn't risk him shutting down.

"Here's what going to happen, Phil," she said. "Officer Braden here is going to read you your rights. After he does, you can remain silent or request a lawyer. But I'm going to be straight with you. It's clear that you are caught up in this somehow. You're on the hook. But if you didn't kill those people in the Plaza yesterday, your best bet is to answer my questions. The person responsible for this is still out there. If she—and we know it was a she—does this again and you had information that could have stopped her, you won't just be charged with something like improper handling of dangerous materials. You'll be charged as an accessory to multiple murders. You'll be convicted and you'll spend your life in prison. I'm not sure how'd you'd fare in a place like that, Phil. So once you've been read your rights, you let me know how you want to handle this."

As Braden Mirandized Russell, Susannah stepped away to check in with Officer Medavoy.

"Anything worthwhile I can use on the guy?" she asked.

"Afraid not, Detective," he told her. "Other than the DUI, he's clean. No violence, no threats against the government. The file's pretty boring, actually."

"Okay, thanks," she said, turning back to Russell as Braden finished up.

"With those rights in mind," the officer concluded, "are you willing to talk with us without an attorney present?"

Russell looked over at Susannah.

"Moment of truth," she said.

"Yes," he said resignedly, "I'm willing."

"What happened to the chemicals?" she asked without hesitation.

He wiped some drool from the corner of his mouth before speaking.

"Let me explain," he pleaded. "I connected with this girl on a dating app last week and we met up at a bar."

"What was the app?"

"NerdLove," he said sheepishly. "It's for fans of science and tech. She pinged me. We talked through the app. She sounded fun and smart so we agreed to meet up last Thursday night."

"Can you show me her profile?" Susannah asked.

"Not anymore," he said. "After the attack yesterday, I got nervous and looked her up. She'd deleted her profile. I'm sure it's still archived with the company but accessing it might take a while. I don't think anything in it was true anyway."

"Why not?"

"When I met her, I could tell a lot of stuff was made up. It wasn't as clear in her profile photo, but in person, her long, blonde hair was clearly a wig and it looked like she had colored contacts in. Her eyes were this super-intense, bright blue. When I called her by her name, she didn't respond right away, which made me think it might be fake."

"What name did she use?"

"Cher Horowitz," he said.

"It's fake," Susannah said definitively.

"How do you know?" he asked.

"That's the name of a character from a film called *Clueless*," she explained. "How was she dressed?"

"It was some kind of yellow, plaid outfit, with a miniskirt and a sport jacket."

"Okay," Susannah said, realizing that the woman had used everything about the movie character to mask her own identity. "What did she want?"

"At first we just talked, had a few drinks—maybe more than a few," he admitted. "Then out of nowhere, she blasted me with a threat. She said that she knew all about my DUI and that she had laced my drink with THC when I was in the bathroom. She told me that unless I did what she wanted, she would make an anonymous call to B.U. Labs, telling them that they should do an impromptu drug test on me. I'm sure you already know this, but THC can be detected in the body for months after use."

"What did you do?" Susannah asked.

"I begged her not to. I said that if I failed even a single test, that I would never get another job in the industry."

"But she knew that already, which was the whole point," Susannah surmised. "What did she want you to do?"

"She told me she was working on an experimental therapy to help victims of environmental exposure to lethal chemicals, but that she couldn't get funding because it outside of normal protocols. She said that she grew up in a small town that had been destroyed by exposure to cancer-causing agents. She told me that she just needed two chemicals in small quantities to conduct her study. All I had to do was get them from work the next day and give them to her in the amounts she needed. If I did, she promised not to make the anonymous call."

"So you did it?" Mark Weir asked, seething. "There was no computer glitch."

"No sir," Russell admitted.

"Where did you meet to give her the chemicals?" Susannah asked.

"We didn't," he said. "She instructed me to take the Angels Flight railway up to the tiny park right there, Angels Knoll, and drop them off in a specific recycling bin, and then take the next railway trip back down. There was big tourist group in the area at the time and it was really crowded. I never actually saw her."

"And you didn't hear from her again?"

"No," he said. "I wanted to believe her story about the environmental exposure therapy but deep down, I suspected it was crap. And when I heard the story about the deaths at California Plaza yesterday, I felt ill. I knew it had to be connected. I did a little research on what might happen if those chemicals could be somehow combined and realized that they…well, you already know. And with the Plaza being so close to Angels Flight, it felt like she was sending me a message: *you helped make this happen so you better keep your mouth shut.* And I did, until now."

Susannah tried to organize the thoughts in her head. The one that emerged, louder and clearer than the others was the most disheartening: as much information as Phil Russell had given her, she still didn't have a lot to go on. The app profile for "Cher Horowitz" might offer some clues once they reached out to the company, but not in time to stop an imminent attack. And because of "Cher's" disguise, his description of her was borderline useless.

"What was the name of the bar where you met?" she asked him.

"She picked it," Russell said, trying to remember. "It was named for some playing card—something like the Three of Clubs."

"Was it the Deuce of Spades?" Susannah asked, her heart sinking.

"Yeah, that was it," he confirmed. "How did you know?"

"Because that bar is over a hundred years old and hasn't been updated since Prohibition. Everything there is old school. They only take cash. They have old-timey registers. And they don't have any security cameras inside or out, which makes it a perfect choice for someone who doesn't want to be recorded. She knew exactly what she was doing."

Phil Russell's whole body slumped as he recognized that he'd been left holding the bag for a ghost. Susannah felt much like he looked and was having trouble hiding it. They had hit another dead end. Just then her phone rang with a number she didn't recognize.

"Take him to the car," she told Braden. "I'll be there in a minute."

She stepped away from the group to an isolated corner of the topiary courtyard and despite her misgivings, answered the call.

"This is Valentine," she said.

An automated voice spoke, making an unexpected request.

"Yes," Susannah answered reluctantly.

Then she listened as the person on the other end of the line began to speak. After a few seconds, her mouth dropped open in shock. But Susannah was so riveted that she didn't even notice.

CHAPTER TWENTY SEVEN

It was deathly quiet inside the Whitmore house.

As Jessie made her way past the foyer into the living room, her gun held firmly in her hands, she strained to hear any sound, without success. She moved on to the family room. After several seconds, Ryan spoke softly in her ear.

"Kitchen and dining room are clear," he said.

"Same for the living room and family room," Jessie told him. "I'm thinking that if Whitmore is gathering family photos small enough to put in a bag, he's probably in a bedroom. I think we should try upstairs."

"Agreed," Ryan said. "Why don't you take the main staircase and I'll take the hidden one leading up from the kitchen?"

"Meet you there," she said just as she arrived at the bottom of the stairs.

She tried to stay quiet as she moved up the steps but urgency was starting to take priority over stealth. Considering Regan's athletic background and her rage, all it would likely take was one powerful swing from a baseball bat or a fireplace poker to end things for Roger Whitmore.

She had just reached the second floor landing when she heard it: the sound of grunting and gasping one floor up, as if there was some kind of struggle going on. She raced up to the third floor as quickly as she could while still trying to avoid loudly announcing her presence.

"There's something going on in one of the bedrooms," she muttered once she reached the third floor landing. "I hear groaning and heavy breathing."

"I can't hear anything in this stairwell," Ryan replied. "It's like it's soundproof. But I'm almost to the third floor."

"I think it's coming from the main bedroom," she said as she scurried down the hallway, moving past Shannon's room and the mirror across from it that had helped exonerate her. "Be careful when you go in."

She arrived at the bedroom door. The grunting and gasping was unmistakable now. The door had been pulled closed but still had the cracks from where Ryan had kicked it open that morning. The handle hung limp and useless. It looked like a soft push would open it, hopefully silently. She didn't want to make any noise that would give Regan time to react. Jessie took a deep breath, shoved the door open, and peered inside.

For a second, she thought they were having sex. Regan was lying with her back on the bed and Roger Whitmore was on top of her, bouncing up and down forcefully. But then she realized she was seeing something very different.

As she moved into the bedroom, she saw that Whitmore was choking Regan and that the bouncing was caused by her kicking her legs wildly as she struggled to get free. Jessie was just starting to move toward them when the hidden door shot open and Ryan burst through it, stumbling slightly as he came in.

Whitmore looked to his right and grabbed something on the bed beside him. It was a gun. He pointed it at Ryan with his right hand while his left stayed on Regan's neck. Ryan regained his footing, took in the situation—including Jessie, unnoticed in the doorway behind Whitmore—and immediately spoke.

"Stay cool, Roger," he said calmly. "I'm going to put my weapon down on the ground, okay?"

"It won't do you any good," Whitmore hissed. "You know I can't let you live."

"You shoot me and your kids lose two parents," Ryan reminded him.

"I don't think so," Whitmore said with manic relish. "That's not how it will look to the cops that show up to the scene. They'll find you dead, shot with this gun by the psycho who killed Trish and tried to kill me too. You walked in on her attacking me; she shot you. I wrestled the gun away from her and managed to kill her before calling 911, in the futile hope that they could save you. It's a real tragedy."

Jessie knew that in Whitmore's mind, he had the perfect plan and nothing Ryan could say would stop him from putting it into action. He might shoot at any second. That meant she had to act now. She started toward him. As she did, Ryan screamed out.

"Please don't kill me," he begged. "I'm getting married soon!"

His booming voice drowned out the sound of her footsteps as she came up fast behind Whitmore and slammed him in the back of the skull with the butt of her gun. He toppled forward toward Regan and hadn't even landed on her before Jessie had torn the gun from his wobbly fingers and tossed it on the floor.

"Ohhh," he moaned as she rolled him off the au pair onto his back. His eyes were cloudy and dazed.

Ryan was beside her in a second, pulling the man off the bed, rolling him onto his stomach and cuffing him. On the bed, Regan tried to breathe but kept coughing. Jessie helped her to a seated position.

"Just take small breaths at first," she advised the girl. "When you can do that, take deeper ones."

Regan nodded and did as instructed. After about a minute, she seemed strong enough to speak.

"Who are you?' she croaked.

"My name is Jessie Hunt," she told her. "This is Detective Ryan Hernandez. We work with the Los Angeles Police Department."

Regan smiled weakly.

"Thank God you showed up when you did," she said, her Mexican accent now more clearly pronounced. "He was going to kill me."

"I guess that's what happens when you murder someone's wife with a meat tenderizer, Regan," Jessie said matter-of-factly as she snapped handcuffs on the girl's wrists.

"What?"

"Detective Hernandez, do you want to do the honors?"

"Sure," he said once he was sure that Whitmore wasn't going anywhere.

He read Regan Navarro her rights, noting that she was under arrest for murder and concluding by asking if she was willing to talk. She didn't need time to think about it.

"Yes, but only after you arrest him," she answered emphatically, nodding over at Whitmore. "He was waiting for me when I showed up here. You saw—he was choking me to death."

In a flash, Jessie realized what must have happened.

"Don't worry, we'll be charging him too," she said slowly as she put the pieces together in her head.

"What for?" Whitmore growled, coming to his senses now. "I was only defending myself."

"I don't think so, Roger," Jessie said. "Even if you hadn't told Detective Hernandez how you planned to stage the scene, you'd be in bad legal shape."

"What do you mean?" he demanded.

"Well, let's think about it," she said, smiling down at him as he lay on the floor. "You called Aunt Nancy on the way back from visiting Shannon at the police station, asking for a bag to collect family photos for the kids. But you're no dummy. Once you knew we were investigating au pairs that you'd slept with as potential suspects in Trish's murder, you must have figured out which one was most likely to have killed her."

Jessie paused briefly, letting the moment linger. Normally, she would have followed up by saying that Regan was the most likely to come after them because she was the one he raped while his wife looked on. But that would have broken her promise to Dr. Lyman. So she carefully danced around the truth.

"You realized it was the girl who was so unhappy with her experience that she gave the money to a women's shelter. I wonder why she did that," she said, before pressing on quickly. "Whatever the reason, you had to know that it was only a matter of time before we found Regan and learned about that night. Worse, you had to suspect that she'd be coming after you next."

"I don't know what you're talking about," Whitmore insisted.

"But you lucked out," Jessie continued, ignoring him. "Regan showed up at Aunt Nancy's house offering her condolences, although let's be real—she probably had other, more nefarious plans in mind if you'd been there. She left disappointed, but you were ecstatic. You likely pulled up just as Regan was leaving the house. You waited until she left and asked Aunt Nancy about her. She told you that Regan had mentioned going by your house to express her sympathy and suddenly you knew exactly where to find her. Even better, if she was lying in wait to take you out, you could catch her by surprise and do the same thing to her. The best part is that you could claim self-defense. After all, she was in your house and, as the authorities would eventually learn, she'd killed your wife. Now she'd be out of the picture, unable to cast any aspersions on you or your wife's character. You'd be free to lead something resembling a normal life. Have I got it about right, Roger?"

He didn't respond.

"It's really kind of amazing," she added. "You both came here to kill each other and now you'll both be spending the rest of your lives in prison."

"His death would be justice," Regan shouted. "He deserves to be with his bitch wife. I only regret that I didn't get to turn his face into pudding too."

"Is that what happened?" Jessie asked her, noticing that at some point Ryan had started recording everything on his phone. "Roger wasn't your intended victim? Did you mean to kill Trish all along?"

The question seemed to hit Regan like a punch and she slumped down on the bed.

"No," she said softly, "when I came by yesterday morning, I don't know what I wanted to do. I thought of secretly recording them confessing on my phone. I knocked on the door and was shocked when she let me in. She said he was at work but asked if I wanted coffee."

"What did you do?" Jessie asked.

"I said 'yes' and came in. But once we got in the kitchen, she turned nasty. She was so arrogant." Regan stopped for a second, as if unsure if she could get the next words out. But then a flash of fury passed over her face and she went on. "I told her that they raped me. She said that I had wanted it. I reminded her that I was crying the whole time. But she didn't care. She was so smug and said that the money they'd put in my account would tell a different story, that I had consented."

"You did, you little whore!" Whitmore snarled.

"You shut up," Ryan said with a tone that made the man close his mouth tight.

"You raped me!" Regan shouted at him, before turning to Jessie. "He's a monster, but you know what? His wife was worse. She's the one who selected me. She told me that she liked my "exotic" look. She said they just wanted to get to know me better. I was flattered. But when I got to the house and they told me what they really wanted, that they'd pay me to be with him, I said no."

"You were just playing hard to get," Whitmore snapped before Ryan's steely gaze shut him down again. Regan went on as if he hadn't spoken.

"That night we were in the kitchen. I asked to go to the restroom," she continued. "They said it was upstairs. When I was alone, I planned to call a friend to pick me up. I went up but the stairs didn't lead to a restroom. They led in here. Next thing I knew, he had snuck up behind me. He covered my mouth and threw me on this bed. He shoved a scarf in my mouth and pinned me down. The whole time, his wife was talking. She said no one had ever backed out on them and I wouldn't be the first. She said that once he 'broke' me, I'd come back for more. She egged him on, told him what to do to me, exactly how she wanted him to violate me. She watched like it was a Broadway show. She cheered him on."

The room was quiet. Jessie felt sick to her stomach. Regan went on.

"Then they made me give them my Venmo account and they sent me the money. They said that would prove I agreed to everything. They said they'd had a good time and looked forward to our next 'visit.' He even drove me home like it was date or something."

"What did you do next?" Jessie asked, hating herself a little bit for pushing for a more complete confession from someone who'd already been pushed so far.

"After he left, I felt like a piece of trash," she muttered. "I went to my room at the Cranes and fell asleep. When I woke up the next morning, I remembered the money. I felt dirty having it in my account so I gave it to a women's shelter that day. I sleepwalked through the whole weekend until Monday morning, when, well, you know what happened then. I punished her. She had to be punished. And so does he."

Jessie shook her head sadly at the girl and told her the truth.

"You're all going to be punished in the end."

CHAPTER TWENTY EIGHT

Jessie felt empty inside.

When she watched Regan walk into the women's holding cell at Central Station, there was none of the thrill that normally came from solving a case. Regan Navarro was a murderer but she'd been bullied into it by the very person she'd killed. Until the Whitmores selected her, she was just a normal girl trying to get by.

But the combustible combination of violence and cruelty visited upon her by the couple had sent her over the edge and made her snap. It didn't justify what she'd done but it did help explain it. Now her life was ruined. Jessie hoped she got a good lawyer.

The only solace she took was in being able to keep her promise to Dr. Lyman. Because Ryan had recorded Regan making the rape charge, there would be a new exam that would confirm everything Lyman said, without having to involve her at all. She was off the hook.

Whitmore was across the building in the men's holding area. She had no residual concern for him, although she did for his au pair, Shannon, who had just been released.

"Where will you go?" Jessie had asked her.

The young woman still seemed shell-shocked by what she'd learned about her employers but her answer was clear and unequivocal.

"I'm going to Aunt Nancy's," she said. "She's going to need all the help she can get. And like I said, I really love those kids."

Once she was gone, Jessie and Ryan ambled to the central outdoor courtyard in the middle of the station for a much needed break. They sat on the bench under the one tree that offered protection from the midday sun. Jessie exhaled deeply, allowing some of the stress of the day to disappear into the air with her breath.

"Please don't kill me. I'm getting married soon?" she said to Ryan teasingly, repeating the words he had shouted to distract Roger Whitmore so she could sneak up on him. "I didn't know you felt so passionately."

"Don't make fun of me," he cautioned, pretending to be hurt. "I needed to direct his attention away from you and I figured going with some heartfelt emotion might do the trick."

"Well, you touched my heart," she told him, touching her chest dramatically. "I guess this means we should make those nuptials a priority."

"Do you seriously want to do wedding planning right now," he asked, "or are you just trying to take your mind off the ugliness we witnessed in that bedroom earlier?"

"Can't it be a little bit of both?" she wondered.

"Sure," he replied. "Let's get into it. Are we still maxing out our guest list at twenty?"

"Yeah," she said. "If we invite that many people on short notice, I'm hoping that maybe we'll end up with just a dozen or so, the true believers."

"The true believers?" he repeated, trying not to laugh.

"You know what I mean," she told him. "I only want people there who care enough to adjust their schedules on a dime. I want to see some real commitment."

"You know that as long as you and I show up, everyone else is gravy," he reminded her playfully.

"That's one way to look at it," she countered. "Another is that making our guests sacrifice a little to be there will purify the occasion."

"You are messed up," he said, smiling. "Should we move onto venue? You still want something by the beach?"

"I do," she said. "I made a list of possible places."

"Jessie Hunt, as I live and breathe," he said dramatically. "Am I to understand that you are actually embracing this endeavor?"

"Don't push it, mister," she warned, fighting off a giggle.

"Next thing you'll tell me you've chosen a maid of honor," he continued, undeterred. "I know you were debating between Hannah and Kat."

"That debate is over," she assured him. "In the end it was an easy choice. Kat will understand if it's Hannah. The same couldn't be said if it was the other way around. I want my sister in a good place for this thing. Speaking of, I didn't tell you this but she called me last night."

"Really—what about?"

"She was very cryptic, wouldn't get into specifics," Jessie said. "But she wanted help knowing how I handle it when I have an instinct about a case but no facts to back it up."

"Why would she be interested in something like that?" Ryan asked.

"Like I said, she wasn't explicit, but I'm pretty sure she's trying to reconcile the suicide of the girl at Seasons with her inability to see it coming. Or maybe she did see signs but didn't act on them. She might be working through some guilt, wondering if there was more she could have done. To be honest, I find the fact that she's even grappling with those issues oddly…healthy."

"That's great, I guess," Ryan agreed.

"Yeah, now that I think about it, I actually want to check in with her to see how everything is going. Do you mind?"

"Go for it," Ryan replied.

She was just pulling out her phone when his rang. He held it up to show that the call was from Decker.

"Maybe you should hold off a minute," he said as he pushed the speaker button. "Yes, Captain?"

"You've officially wrapped up the Whitmore case, correct?" Decker asked without any preliminary greeting.

"Not quite," Ryan said. "There's still some paperwork to process. But everyone who needs to be locked up is, if that's what you mean?"

"That what I mean," Decker told him. "The paperwork can wait. This Plaza case is still active and we need all the help we can get. I want you and Hunt in my office right now."

*

When they walked into Decker's office, the captain wasn't alone. Sitting on the ratted-out couch against the far wall were Detectives Karen Bray and Jim Nettles. Jamil Winslow was standing in a corner, reviewing a document.

Jessie noted that none of them seemed to have slept much lately. Jamil, who was used to it, didn't look much different than usual, other than a layer of stubble on his normally clean-shaven face. Both Bray and Nettles had bags under their red, bleary eyes.

Captain Roy Decker always looked like death warmed over, and today was no different. His catcher's mitt of a face was weathered and worn out, so that the sixty-one year old looked more than a decade older than that. His hunched shoulder made his already concave chest even slouchier, so that he projected the vibe of a really tall hunchback. His gray hair, or what was left of it, splayed out in every direction. The one difference from every other day, which raised alarm bells for Jessie, was his eyes. Normally hawk-like and piercing, today they were dull and heavy. For them not to be fully alert, the exhaustion and stress of this case must really be taking a toll.

"What's going on?" Ryan asked in a concerned voice, obviously picking up on the same bone-tired desperation that she had.

"Shut the door," Decker instructed. "There's a lot to tell you and not much time to do it."

CHAPTER TWENTY NINE

Hannah tried to hide her irritation.

After her "moment" with Dr. Tam yesterday in his office, when she'd faked a meltdown and pretended that his presence was a source of security and comfort to her, she thought the dynamic in their therapy sessions might change. But it hadn't.

He still spoke to her condescendingly, as if she was a child.

"I just want her to respect my decisions," she told him in reference to Jessie. She had figured that discussing standard sisterly conflict was a safer topic than broaching her still-lurking desire to recreate the thrill she got from watching the life leak out of a man she'd shot.

"But how can you expect her to respect your choices when you make such poor ones, Hannah?" he wanted to know. "Your file shows that you repeatedly court trouble rather than seeking to de-escalate situations."

"As I mentioned earlier in the session, I've been working hard on that," she told him, trying not to come across as defensive. "But whatever happened to positive reinforcement?"

"Maybe you don't deserve that," he said, taking her by surprise. "Does a parent need to compliment a child every time they don't run out into the street? Or is it more appropriate to discipline them when they do? Some behaviors aren't praiseworthy; they're expected."

"But I'm not a toddler, Dr. Tam," she reminded him. "I don't need my hand swatted when I fall short of expectations."

"Don't you?" he wondered. "In many ways you are a child, Hannah. Your behavior reflects your emotionally stunted state. And until you prove that maturity isn't just a passing fancy, you're going to be treated as you deserve."

Hannah sensed something midway between frustration and anger rising in her chest and quickly forced it down before it was reflected in her body language. She let out a long, silent sigh. Dr. Tam glanced at his watch and she knew the session was nearing its end.

For her, it had been a failure so far. Not because she hadn't made any huge emotional breakthrough—she hadn't expected anything like that with this amateur. Rather, it was because she'd been hoping to discern where Dr. Tam kept the key for the desk drawer she'd found locked yesterday. She needed to know if anything in there was relevant to Merry Bartlett's death.

"Listen, Hannah, I'm worried about how combative you are today," Dr. Tam said, his tone as patronizing as his words. "I know I mentioned this before, but I'm seriously considering increasing the dose of your anti-anxiety medication. I think it may offer you the clarity you need to see things as they really are."

If she wasn't so appalled, Hannah would have been amused. She knew how those anti-anxiety drugs worked and it wasn't by providing clarity, it was by dulling her feelings to the point of numbness, something she was already intimately familiar with.

Jessie had told her that Dr. Lemmon would likely be back by the end of the week. But it was only Tuesday now. She couldn't risk being forced to take those pills and ending up near-catatonic. She needed to stay alert to pursue the truth about Merry. A few days from now, any relevant details might be lost to time or malfeasance. So she'd suck it up and smooth things over with this dumbass.

And then she had another thought—Dr. Tam was technically right. She was a minor, at least for a few more weeks until she turned eighteen. But the way he insisted on interacting with her, as if she was a little child instead of a near adult, seemed ill-advised and borderline creepy.

She couldn't help but wonder if that was his modus operandi, even when his patient was an adult. Merry wasn't the most emotionally mature person that she'd ever met, but she was twenty-three when she died. Had Dr. Tam treated her the same way, as if she was a youngster who required discipline and obedience? If so, how would he react if she didn't respond like he though she should? The thought sent a shiver through her.

"I take your point on the revised prescription, Dr. Tam," she said, standing up to indicate she knew the session was over, "but I'd like to try to work these things out on my own a little longer before we discuss upping my meds. After all, when I re-enter the real world, I'll be on my own. I won't be able to count on a pill to help me navigate challenging situations. Only changing behavior patterns will truly do that, don't you agree?"

He seemed to genuinely ponder the question. As he did, Hannah glanced over at his desk, again wondering how she might access that locked drawer. She noted his suit jacket draped over the desk chair and wondered if he might keep a key in one of its pockets, where it was easily accessible to him but not visible to others.

"We'll try a little longer," he conceded, pulling her attention away from the desk. "But if things don't improve, we'll have to revisit our approach."

"Fair enough," Hannah said, heading reluctantly for the door. She wanted to somehow stay in the room but there was no way to do that without drawing suspicion, so she gave up. "See you next time, Doctor."

She stepped out into the therapy wing waiting area. What she found there gave her renewed hope. Silvio was sitting in a chair, waiting to be called in for a session. She sat down next to him.

"Who is your appointment with?" she asked quietly.

"Dr. Perry," he told her, agitated. "But Elaine said she's running a little late. I hate that. I'm on time. She should be too."

"Why the delay?"

"I don't know," he muttered. "But it probably has something to do with the crying I could hear coming from her office. I'll bet the girl in there is having some annoying breakthrough that will make her session run way over."

Hannah smiled to herself. She had an idea.

"I'm really sorry about this girl's potential breakthrough making you wait," she replied tartly, "but I think I have a way to help you pass the time and get me closer to finding out what really happened with Merry. Are you up for it?"

"What would I have to do?" he asked cautiously.

"Nothing much," she told him. "Are you open to faking a seizure?"

His apprehensive expression turned into a half-smile.

"I *am* diabetic," he said.

She thought of all the sweet pastries he consumed at every meal and wondered how he wasn't in a coma. But that was a discussion for another time.

"All the better," she whispered enthusiastically. "No one will question it. Here's what I need you to do."

She explained her plan, expecting him to balk. But when she was done, his half-smile had morphed into a full one.

"Okay," she said, standing up, "Remember, wait for my sign to start."

He nodded, his feet bouncing up and down in excited anticipation. She walked over to Elaine, who was busily typing away.

"May I have the key to the restroom?" Hannah asked.

Elaine smiled absently and pointed at the spot where the key hung on a hook at the front of her desk. Hannah was just reaching for it when Silvio keeled over out of his chair and began to shake violently.

"Oh my God," she said urgently, "I think he's having a seizure."

Elaine looked over, horrified. Hannah could tell that the woman had no idea what to do.

"Go make sure he doesn't hurt himself," she ordered. "I'll get Dr. Tam."

Elaine nodded and rushed over to Silvio, kneeling beside him and trying to offer words of support. Hannah rapped on Dr. Tam's door and opened it without waiting for a response.

"Silvio's having some kind of seizure," she said, making sure to sound panicked. "He needs help."

Dr. Tam shot up out of his chair without a word, and dashed past her to join Elaine on the floor. Hannah didn't hesitate. She hurried over to his desk chair and started feeling around in the pockets of his suit jacket. She felt something in his inside breast pocket and pulled it out. It was a key. Gleefully, she tried it on the locked drawer. It worked. She yanked it open.

There was only one item inside, a leather-bound notebook. She opened and quickly discerned that it was a collection of notes on some of his patients. She flipped through it and found that the notes were in dated order.

There wasn't time to read anything in detail but scanning through the pages, it seemed that he had honed in on the more interesting patients, with especially complicated diagnoses. She even saw herself mentioned, and as much as she would have found reading his "analysis" of her entertaining, that wasn't why she was here.

Merry's name was in the book but there was one obvious difference between her entries and all the others. There was nothing written about her. Other than her name and the time and dates of her sessions, there was nothing—no review of their conversations or conclusions drawn from them. It was almost as if he didn't want any record of what happened in their sessions together.

Were they even therapy sessions? Or did something else transpire in their fifty-five minutes alone together, something he wouldn't dare write about and felt so protective of that he locked any reference to it away in a drawer, the key to which he apparently took home with him each night.

"Call for an ambulance," she heard Dr. Tam say from the waiting area. She knew that meant her time was up. She couldn't ask Silvio to keep up this charade any longer, especially if it might mean an unwanted trip to the hospital.

She put the notebook back in the drawer, locked it, and replaced the key in Dr. Tam's jacket. She was just about to run back out of the office when she noticed a small mini-fridge in the corner. On a hunch, she opened it and found several Gatorades inside. She grabbed one and ran out of the office, yelling, "Will this help?"

Dr. Tam looked up and nodded, waving her over.

"I knew you had a fridge and thought there might be something sugary in there," she said, hoping she sound appropriately alarmed.

"Good idea," Dr. Tam said, opening it and pouring some in the kid's mouth.

"He swallowed it," Hannah said excitedly, and then, using the words that were Silvio's cue that he could stop, added. "I think he's going to be okay."

Hearing them, Silvio's shaking began to slow and then subside altogether. He opened his eyes, making sure to appear bewildered.

"What happened?" he asked vaguely.

"You had a seizure," Dr. Tam said. "But you're going to be all right. Just keep drinking."

"I'm on hold for 911," Elaine said. "Should I keep trying?"

"He's seems to be improving," Dr. Tam said, turning to her. "You can hang up. We'll take him to the infirmary to monitor him and call back if needed."

With the doctor facing the other way, Silvio looked up at Hannah hopefully. She winked at him to let him know it had worked.

Of course, she didn't know that it had. She still had no idea what happened to Meredith Bartlett. But she was certain of two things, whether she had proof or not. First, Merry hadn't killed herself. And second, Dr. Tam was hiding something.

She was going to find out if the two were connected, no matter what it took.

CHAPTER THIRTY

"What makes you sure she's going to attack again?" Ryan asked.

Jessie had the same question. They'd spent the last ten minutes in Captain Decker's office, learning everything the others knew about the California Plaza killings. Unfortunately, it seemed that despite all the information they'd collected, they weren't much closer to catching this woman than they had been at this time yesterday.

"We're not sure," Karen Bray admitted. "But we have to operate as if this isn't an isolated incident. There's been no claim of responsibility, no explanation for the attack, which makes us worry that it might be random and the start of a pattern."

"One thing we know for sure," Nettles added, "is that based on what Susannah learned at B.U. Labs, Phillip Russell provided this woman with a sufficient quantity of those chemicals for at least one more similar incident, maybe two."

"Where is Valentine?" Jessie asked, finally getting a natural opening to broach the question that had been in the back of her head this whole time.

"She's following up on a lead," Decker said. "She said it's a long shot but that she'd update us if it turned into anything worthwhile."

"So what do we know for sure?" Ryan pressed.

"We know that this small, pale woman is smart enough to turn volatile chemical compounds into a liquid that kills people within seconds of touching their skin," Karen said.

"We also know she's a big fan of the movie, *Clueless*," Nettles added. "It seems to be extremely important to her for some reason."

"And," Jamil added from the corner, "we know that she planned this out far enough in advance to avoid cameras when she met with Phil Russell at the bar and nearly avoid any identification during the Plaza attack itself."

"That's not quite true," Jessie said more to herself than the others.

"What do you mean," asked Decker, who had stayed mostly quiet up until now.

"Well, she could have completely covered her face at the Plaza," Jessie replied, "but she didn't. Based on all her preparation, that doesn't seem like an oversight so much as an intentional choice."

"She was wearing a scarf," Nettles countered. "It could have just slipped off her face in all the commotion."

"Yeah, but the commotion didn't start until later," Jessie reminded him. "Portions of her face were already visible prior to that. Also, she spoke to that couple, what were there names again?"

"Holly Valdez and Alonzo Huertas," Jamil said.

"Right," she continued, a picture forming in her mind. "She could have avoided them entirely but she had an exchange with them. And Holly said that this woman spoke to both of them briefly, but only touched Alonzo. She could have touched Holly too when she pretended to stumble but didn't. Why not? By leaving Holly alone, she was leaving a witness alive who could describe her face and voice."

"That's right," Ryan added. "She had no way of knowing that Holly would get sick when she came across Alonzo lying in the street later. She let her live, even though she knew the woman might be able to partially identify her later."

"Almost as if she *wanted* a witness," Jessie muttered, "almost as if she wanted us to have some clues, just ones that would take a while to bear fruit."

"Same thing with the NerdLove dating app," Jamil said excitedly.

"What do you mean?" Captain Decker asked.

Jamil moved out of the corner.

"Just that if she was smart enough to know which chemicals she needed to get to make this poison, she had to know that them going missing from B.U. Labs would raise red flags and eventually be traced back to Russell. She knew that when we found him, the dating app would come up and that we'd look at it."

"But she deleted it," Nettles reminded him.

"Of course she did," Jamil said. "If she left her profile up, that would seem suspicious, considering how clever she'd been about everything else. So she removed it, knowing that we'd eventually be able to get an archived version of it from the company anyway, which we will. I got a text from someone there a few minutes ago saying they'd have it for us by the top of the hour. When we get that, even with her wig and colored lenses, we'll be able to use facial recognition to get a match. Based on the limited information we got from the plaza cameras about her bone structure and height, I've already narrowed down the potential attacker to just over 21,000 women."

"Is that all?" Nettles asked sarcastically.

"Considering how many women there are in this city," said Beth Ryerson forcefully, who had just joined them, "that's pretty amazing. We should know her real name within minutes of getting that profile photo."

"I stand corrected," Nettles said, holding up his hands in surrender.

"What have you got?" Jamil asked Beth, trying not smile at how she'd come to his defense.

"Like Detective Valentine suggested," she answered, trying not to smile back, "we did a search for any Cher Horowitzes in the greater L.A. area. There were seventeen. Three matched the estimated height and age range of our suspect but none fit with facial recognition. However, there's an anomaly."

"Go on," Decker ordered.

"I found an apartment rental under the name Cher Horowitz. There is no physically identifying information for the renter. The social security number is for a woman who died in 1982. And according to the building manager, she always paid her rent in cash in his mailbox. But he said she moved out yesterday, left him a polite note. The place is ten minutes north of here. Officers are en route now just in case she's still there."

"Did he give a description?" Nettles wanted to know.

"Not really," Beth answered. "He only met her once when she first got the place eight months ago and he doesn't remember anything other than that she was young and short."

"Dear God!" Karen said, "She's been planning this for that long?"

The others in the room mumbled similarly stunned words but Jessie didn't really hear them. Something Beth had said sparked a memory so deep that she wasn't sure she could retrieve it. "Cher Horowitz" rented an apartment eight months ago. That timing felt familiar and it wasn't the only thing that did.

When Karen had first described the nature of the California Plaza attack, a dim bulb of recognition had lit up in her head, only to fade as other facts were piled over it. She tried to remember what had piqued her interest in the first place.

The attacker had wandered into a public space and casually wiped poison on unsuspecting victims. Someone else had done something like that. She was sure of it.

She looked up, ready to ask Jamil to search the database for similar cases, but he was on the phone. From what he said, it sounded like he was talking to someone from the NerdLove dating app. Unwilling to wait for him to finish, she grabbed her own phone to see if a Google search might pull something up. When she turned it on, the first thing she noticed was the missed call from Andy Robinson. And in a rush of exhilaration, it all clicked into place.

"I think I've got it," she said loudly, cutting off all the cross-conversation.

"What?" Ryan asked. She could tell from his expression that he knew that she'd hit on something huge.

"I'm still working it out," she warned, "but I know who did this, or at least how to find her. The description of her attack sounded really familiar to me but I couldn't place why. When Andy Robinson helped out on the Livia Bucco case—the woman who macheted that girl to death in a YWCA shower a few weeks ago—we made a deal. She'd help out on any future cases involving women who served time at the Twin Towers Psych Unit. In exchange, I'd support a move to a different facility and related perks."

"This Andy Robinson is the woman who tried to kill you?" Beth confirmed. "You helped get her a cushier facility to live at?"

"I wasn't happy about it," Jessie admitted. "But if it saved lives, it was a small price to pay. But after that incident, I went back and reviewed the files of every woman who served time at Twin Towers with Andy, looking for possible future threats. I remember one patient who was inside for cutting the palms of her hands and then going into public places, hugging strangers and wiping them with her blood."

"I feel sick," Beth muttered.

"It's obviously disturbing," Jessie continued, "but I dismissed her as a major threat because she wasn't violent and because she'd been released for a long time without any further incidents. She was considered a success story."

"How long had she been out?" Ryan asked, though it was clear that he knew the answer.

"Eight months," Jessie said. "I would never have thought of it if I didn't just remember that I got a call this morning from the

Western Regional Women's Psychiatric Detention Center. That's where Andy was moved to. I didn't answer it because we were in the middle of our case. A suspect had just tried to run away. But she left a message. Listen."

Hi Jessie. Sorry to bother you but I was watching the news yesterday and something jumped out at me. I think I might have some useful information regarding the case you're currently working. Please reach out when you get a chance.

"I don't get it," Nettles said. "If this was about the woman you're thinking of who cut her hands, why wasn't she more specific?"

"I've wondered that too," Jessie admitted, "and I think there are a couple of reasons. First, she probably assumed I was assigned to the Plaza case, so she didn't need to get into details. It's in our jurisdiction and right in my wheelhouse. She couldn't have known that Ryan and I had been assigned to another case earlier that morning. That's why I didn't feel the need to call her back. I thought we had just caught the killer in the Whitmore case so there was no need."

"Okay," Karen said, "but you mentioned that there were two reasons she didn't get specific in her voicemail."

"Right," Jessie replied. "The other is that Andy Robinson never gives anything up for free," she replied. "She's always looking to get something in return. And if she has info on a case that left five people dead, she's holding on tight to that. It's precious. She knows she could ask for the moon and get it."

"But she called you hours ago," Ryan reminded her. "And she hasn't tried again since. What if we were to find this woman without her help? She has to know she'd lose all her leverage."

"That's a good question," Jessie said, "one that has me really worried."

No one had a quick response to that. Jamil finally interrupted the silence.

"The NerdLove people just sent me Cher's profile picture," he announced. "I'm inputting it into the facial recognition database now. It should only take a few minutes to get a hit."

"Whoever you find," Jessie told him, "she's going to be a former Twin Towers inmate, there for wiping blood on people in crowds, and who was released eight months ago. I'm sure of it."

"Captain," Nettles said, looking at a text he'd just received, "those officers that Beth mentioned are outside Cher Horowitz's apartment right now. Do you want them to breach?"

"No," Decker said. "Have them wait for Hazmat. We have no idea what this woman did to the place. We don't need our people walking into a trap."

"We've got a match," Jamil shouted, holding up his phone. "The real name of the girl from the dating app is Eden Roth. And like Ms. Hunt said, she was released from Twin Towers eight months ago after being placed there for…the blood thing. Her place is at the corner of Seventh and Main."

"That's literally a five minute walk from here," Ryan said.

Jessie had already started for the door when she replied.

"Two if we run."

CHAPTER THIRTY ONE

Jessie was less than a block from the address when she got an alert on her phone. She looked at it as she ran. It read: *Be advised. Officers on the scene—currently securing the perimeter.*

"Who the hell could have gotten there before us?" Ryan huffed from several yards behind her.

Jessie didn't reply but she was pretty sure she knew. There was only one person working this case who hadn't been with all of them in Decker's office: Susannah Valentine.

Sure enough, when they rounded the corner, there she was, standing at the entrance to the dilapidated apartment building, along with two uniformed officers. She looked as put-together as always, seeming more like a Victoria's Secret model slumming it than a police detective.

"How did you find this place?" she demanded after taking a few seconds to catch her breath.

"I'll explain later," Susannah said as Karen and Nettles arrived, along with four more uniformed officers, all panting. "Right now we've got to get up there."

"Fine," Jessie agreed. "Jamil says Eden Roth's apartment is 608."

"That's not where she is," Susannah said. "We need to go to 708."

"Jamil definitely said 608, Susannah," Ryan confirmed.

"Yes, that's Eden Roth's apartment. But it's going to be clean. I checked the tenant directory and the person listed directly above Roth's unit is Dionne Davenport."

Jessie felt her stomach drop slightly as she realized Susannah was almost certainly correct.

"Who the hell is that?" Nettles asked.

"That's the name of Cher Horowitz's best friend in *Clueless*," she explained. "Susannah's right. It makes a lot more sense for her to hole up there. That's the top floor, making for an easier escape if need be. How did you know to check the tenant directory?"

"I just followed up on a tip," Valentine answered. "We can get into all that later. Right now we need to get up there."

"Decker wants us to wait," Karen said. "Hazmat is on the way from the Horowitz apartment building. They should be here in less than ten minutes. Multiple ambulances are en route too. No sirens. They're two minutes out."

"Screw that," Susannah said. "We already have a dozen cops on the street. If she's home right now and looks down here, she's going to know something's up. And if she's already moved on to her next target, we need to get into her place to figure out what it is. The manager already gave me the key. Let's go!"

She entered the building without waiting for permission. Everyone else looked at Ryan, who was the senior detective on the scene. He could shut her down if he really wanted to but he seemed reluctant. Jessie understood why. Waiting was the smart, cautious move. But if they could keep Eden Roth contained in her apartment, she was less of a threat than if she got out in the open among civilians. It was still a risk to them, but much safer for the residents of the building and the public at large.

"Let's get up there," he finally said. "I'll take the hit if it goes bad."

He led the way and everyone followed. Once inside, he gave his instructions and the eleven of them split up, some taking different elevators to different floors. Jessie and Susannah took the stairs. On the way up, she wanted to ask the detective what lead had brought her here, but decided to hold off.

Catch a killer now, ask questions later.

When they arrived at the seventh floor, Ryan and Karen Bray were waiting.

"Are the others in place?" Jessie asked.

"Nettles is one floor down outside apartment 608 with two officers," Ryan told her. "Two more officers are on the roof. We left one more in the lobby and another by the first floor's back exit. One of the ambulances has arrived and the EMTs are coming up here now. But for the time being, it's just the four of us up here. Nettles is only going to breach if I give the word that we didn't find her up here. You all ready?"

Everyone nodded that they were. As they approached the apartment, Jessie tried to convince herself that Eden Roth wouldn't have booby-trapped it. The woman seemed to want big, public displays. Taking out a bunch of cops in a run-down apartment building didn't have the same panache. She wasn't sure that she entirely bought that. None of her profiler training and experience suggested that conclusion was a sure thing. But they were in it now.

Ryan silently indicated that he was going to kick in the door and that the others should move in afterward. Everyone understood, pulled out their weapons, and got into position. Ryan backed up to the wall opposite the entrance, then stepped forward and forcefully kicked the door next to the handle. It cracked but didn't give way. He reared back and kicked it again. This time, it flew open.

Susannah stepped in first, followed closely by Karen. Ryan was next. Jessie brought up the rear. By the time she was inside, she already heard Susannah yell "clear" from what looked to be a bedroom. Bray did the same from the second bedroom. Ryan was moving through the living room, his head spinning back and forth as he passed by the kitchen.

"Jessie, check behind the kitchen counter," he instructed.

She did. There was no one there.

Kitchen is clear," she announced.

"Living room is clea—," Ryan started to say before stopping mid-word.

She looked up to see him staring into an open doorway, his gun pointed at something she couldn't see. She quickly joined him. The open door was to the bathroom. At first she didn't get why he'd stopped talking. But then she saw it. In the reflection of the bathroom mirror, it was clear that someone was standing in the shower, though the curtain blocked a clear view.

"Come on out, Eden," he said firmly. "This is over. No one else has to get hurt."

A second later, Susannah and Karen were by their sides, their weapons also pointed at the bathroom doorway.

"Okay," Eden said in a docile but oddly happy voice. "Here I come."

She stepped out of the shower and into the doorway with her hands up, smiling broadly. It took Jessie a second to grasp what she was seeing. Eden Roth was a tiny thing—pale and skeletal, with thin brown hair and gray eyes. She was unarmed. She was also completely naked. But none of that was what grabbed Jessie's attention. Eden was also wearing plastic gloves.

"Be careful," she said urgently. "She's got gloves on. She could have already rubbed the Intocostrin on them."

"Maybe we should have waited for Hazmat to show up," Karen muttered under her breath.

"Hazmat won't get here in time," Eden said with a confidence that frightened Jessie. "It's too late."

"What do you mean, Eden?" she asked, trying to get the girl to engage.

"I have followed the Principles and protected the Principal," she said simply. "My work here is done."

Then without warning, she lowered her hands and hugged herself, rubbing the gloves down along the outsides of her arms.

"Dammit," Ryan said, pulling out his radio. "We need EMTs in unit 708, stat! Suspect may have wiped herself with a poisonous chemical agent."

As if to confirm his suspicion, Eden's whole body began to shiver. White, frothy spittle snuck out from between her lips. She stumbled backward, slamming her back into the sink behind her.

"What the hell can we do?" Karen shouted. "We can't get close to her to help when she's got those gloves on."

Eden looked at her, hearing the words but not seeming to totally comprehend them. Then, with great effort, she took a step toward them. Almost involuntarily, the whole group stepped back at once. Despite their training, it was hard not to let fear take over. Eden had the look of a zombie—mindless and relentless. Jessie inhaled sharply, trying to clear her mind and calm her nerves. Next to her, Susannah dropped to one knee and took aim.

"I'm going to take her out," she said flatly.

Jessie's mind raced. The detective sounded under control, but firing on this girl seemed like a last resort, not the first. It felt like a panicky move. There had to be another way. Eden took another wobbly step toward them. In that moment, Jessie had an idea.

"Wait," she shouted, holstering her gun and pulling out her taser. She pointed it at the girl and pulled the trigger. Eden shook briefly and violently before careening backward, slamming into the wall behind her and slumping to the floor. She was still.

Seconds later, two EMTs burst into the room with a stretcher and knelt down next to her.

"Be careful," Ryan ordered. "Whatever is on those gloves she's wearing did this. She could still twitch and get the stuff on you."

"Understood," one of the EMTs said. "We were warned in advance. Please clear the area."

They all moved to the corner of the living room, where they could keep their eyes on Eden without disrupting the EMTs' efforts to save her. Ryan and Karen watched the proceedings intently.

Jessie however, studied Susannah Valentine, wondering when the detective would come clean about just how she knew so much and got here so fast. Susannah clearly sensed Jessie staring at her but refused to make eye contact or even look up from the spot on the floor that suddenly seemed to have captured her attention.

If Jessie didn't know better, she'd think that the woman, in her moment of glory, was ashamed.

CHAPTER THIRTY TWO

It was just the three of them in Decker's office.
Jessie was in one of the uncomfortable, hard-backed chairs. Susannah Valentine was on the ratty couch, as far away from Jessie as she could get, and the Captain was seated behind his desk.
He'd called the two of them into his office for this private meeting, away from the others, who were out in the bullpen, completing the piles of case paperwork needed to officially close the case. He opened his mouth to speak when his phone rang. He put the call on speaker.
"Decker here," he said.
"Hi Captain, this is Murray," a clearly nervous officer said. "I'm at the hospital. I was ordered to call you directly with updates on Eden Roth whenever they were available."
"Yes, go ahead, Murray."
"One of the doctors just came out," he said. "She told me that Roth is unconscious and in critical condition. She said the EMTs did amazing work to keep her alive until they got here but that it may not be enough. I asked how long it would be before they know if she'll survive. She said she doubted she'd live through the night but that she was surprised she'd made it this long, so you never know. That's all I have for now."
"Okay, Murray," Decker said with a kindly tone he rarely used with detectives and profilers, "good work. Keep me posted on any changes."
He hung up and turned to Jessie and Susannah.
"We've got a bit of a situation here," he said.
"You don't say," Jessie replied, unable to keep the growing bitterness out of her voice.
"That's right, Hunt," he told her. "We're in a time crunch and I've got some important news for you."
From Susannah's downturned head, Jessie suspected the detective already knew what Decker was going to say. Then again, so did she.

"Let me save you some time, Captain," she said. "When I didn't call Andrea Robinson back this morning, she reached out to Detective Valentine here. Am I close?"

Decker looked at the detective, indicating that she should answer.

"That's right," Susannah said with a mix of guilt and defiance. "When you didn't respond, she called and asked me to come visit her at PDC, said she might have information crucial to the case."

"But there was a catch," Jessie deduced.

"Correct," Susannah acknowledged. "She told me that considering the magnitude of the case, she'd be foolish not to work something out that would benefit her. She said that she could only help if she had assurances that she'd be taken care of."

"And you agreed," Jessie guessed.

"I told her that if she gave me useful information, then I would take the request to Captain Decker. But she insisted that I go directly to Chief Laird and that I do it immediately, before she shared anything."

"Which you did," Jessie concluded.

"I didn't see that I had much choice, Jessie," Susannah said defensively. "Five people were dead. Ten more were in the hospital. Another attack seemed imminent. And after twenty-fours of investigation, we still had almost nothing to go on. So yes, I called Laird and told him her terms."

"Which were?"

Susannah seemed reluctant to continue, but knew she had to. When she spoke, she looked at her shoes.

"She wanted Laird to talk to the governor and get a promise to 'assist' her."

"How?" Jessie asked, feeling her chest tighten. "A pardon? Commute her sentence? She killed a man and tried to do the same thing to me."

"I know that," Susannah said, still looking down. "I was just the messenger. Anyway, her request wasn't that specific. She asked for 'consideration in light of her crucial assistance in saving lives and her ongoing efforts at rehabilitation.' She said to check with her doctors to get their opinions. I got the sense that she didn't want to be so transparent as to directly ask to be set free. She wanted to let the governor feel that he came to that decision on his own. But what was he going to do if she came through and helped us catch someone who'd done something this awful?"

"So he said yes?"

Susannah shrugged.

"He promised that any assistance she offered which led to the attacker's capture would be properly recognized," she said. "It wasn't hard to read between the lines."

"And then she told you?" Jessie pressed.

"Yes. She gave me Roth's name, told me that the attacks reminded her of the bloody hands routine she used to pull. She also said that the girl was brilliant and would never mix dangerous chemicals where she lived, both as a safety precaution and in case a social worker showed up at her place to check on how she was doing. She told me that Roth was obsessed with *Clueless*, which I'd already learned from talking to Phillip Russell, and that if she was doing the lab stuff somewhere else, that she might use the names of characters from the movie as pseudonyms instead of her own. That's how I knew to check the tenant list and found Dionne Davenport."

Jessie didn't respond. The detective kept going.

"I wanted to tell you all of it but we were pressed for time and—."

"And what?" Jessie asked.

"Laird insisted that I keep everyone out of the loop, especially you, until after we knew we had Roth. He didn't want you 'mucking it all up.'"

Jessie didn't know who to be more pissed at: Susannah Valentine or Chief Laird. Valentine was placing the blame on everyone else—Andy Robinson, Chief Laird, the Governor. But she had gone to see Andy knowing full well about the history she shared with Jessie.

Then again, at least she thought she was doing what she needed to in order to catch a killer. Laird's motives were muddier, as were his tactics, including manipulating Susannah into his political machinations, regardless of the consequences to Jessie or public safety.

But she saved most of her anger for the person who truly deserved it: Andrea Robinson. In that moment, a realization crystallized in her mind. Somehow, Andy had planned all of this. She suddenly recalled what Eden said back in that apartment: that she had protected the Principal.

Jessie couldn't prove that Andy was the Principal but she was certain of it. Andy was behind all of this and she'd done it from the confines of a lockdown mental facility. The magnitude of what this woman was capable of took her breath away—but only briefly.

"You know she's playing everyone," she said, addressing both Susannah and Captain Decker. "She had me going for a while too, thinking she was helping out just to make up for past sins and to maybe get a private room along the way. But it seems awfully convenient that both of these killers were women she interacted with while they were at Twin Towers together."

"What are you getting at?" Decker asked.

"Come on, Captain. Which is more likely—that she's helping out because of a sense of duty? Or that she brainwashed two vulnerable, unstable women into doing her bidding for her own personal gain?"

"I have to say, that sounds a little paranoid, Jessie," Susannah said.

"Really?" Jessie shot back. "You met her. Don't you think she's smart enough to do something like that? She almost got away with one murder and when I figured it out, she tried to kill me—and we were friends! There's nothing she's not willing to do to achieve her ends. And if she comes out of this mess looking like some kind of hero who helped save the city and salvaged her soul in the process, it's going to be hard to stop her when she decides to use that notoriety for whatever her real purpose is."

"What do you think that purpose is, Hunt?" Decker pressed.

"I don't know, Captain," she answered. "That's what's so scary. Especially when you think about how many other acolytes she might have groomed while she was in that hellhole. Remember what Eden said: 'I have followed the Principles and protected the Principal.' Who do you think the Principal is? What principles has she been teaching? For all we know, Andy Robinson has a whole sleeper cell of recently released mental patients just waiting to be activated, ready to do her bidding."

There was a loud knock on the door. Decker looked like he wasn't done with this conversation but he responded anyway.

"Come in!"

An officer poked his head in, looking apprehensive.

"Sorry Captain," he said, "but Chief Laird just called. He said he wants the folks that caught Eden Roth at headquarters in the next fifteen minutes. He's scheduled a press conference for 3:30."

"He wants to make sure it makes the evening news," Jessie muttered.

"All right, officer," Decker said, standing up. "Let him know that we'll gather the team and be right there."

The officer coughed nervously.

"What is it?" Decker asked, annoyed.

"I'm sorry again, sir, but he was very clear. The chief specifically said that he only wanted you and Detective Valentine to attend."

Decker opened his mouth and for a second Jessie though he might yell at the kid. But then he stopped himself.

"Thank you," he said, waving the officer away, before turning to Jessie. He seemed temporarily at a loss for words.

"It's okay, Captain," she whispered.

"I'm sorry, Hunt," he finally told her and without another word, walked out of the office.

Susannah Valentine stood up too.

"This isn't how I thought this would go," she insisted, before adding. "It's not what I wanted."

Jessie stayed in her chair.

"Are you sure about that?" she asked.

The detective didn't answer. Instead she walked out silently, leaving Jessie alone in the office. She sat there for several minutes, half-numb, unsure what to do next. She wasn't sure there *was* anything she could do.

But there was one thing she was sure of: a storm was coming and no one was prepared.

EPILOGUE

Zoe Bradway watched the evening news and felt giddy, almost light-headed.

The chief of police only made a cryptic reference to Andy Robinson during his press conference but Zoe noted it. And she knew what it meant. The Principal was closer than ever to freedom. And when she got it, the next stage would begin.

Zoe was ready. She'd been waiting five months since her release from Twin Towers, staying off the radar, patiently biding her time for when she would be called upon. She knew the code phrase that would activate her. And when she heard it, she would put her plan into place.

If the people of this city shook in terror at what Eden did yesterday, they were in for a nasty surprise. What was coming their way was much worse. She could hardly wait.

THE PERFECT MURDER
(A Jessie Hunt Psychological Suspense Thriller—Book Twenty One)

When a celebrity professor at an elite college in Los Angeles is found strangled, Jessie is called in to wade through his hidden life and abundance of secrets. Many people, it seemed, had reason to want him dead. But the true killer may be the most unlikely of all.

"A masterpiece of thriller and mystery. Blake Pierce did a magnificent job developing characters with a psychological side so well described that we feel inside their minds, follow their fears and cheer for their success. Full of twists, this book will keep you awake until the turn of the last page."
--Books and Movie Reviews, Roberto Mattos (re *Once Gone*)

THE PERFECT MURDER is book #21 in a new psychological suspense series by bestselling author Blake Pierce, which begins with *The Perfect Wife*, **a #1 bestseller (and free download) with over 5,000 five-star ratings and 1,000 five-star reviews.**

The college community is shocked when the unthinkable happens: a famous, untouchable professor has been found murdered on campus. From harassed students to aggrieved colleagues, his list of secret enemies is long. Too long.

The deeper Jessie digs, the more she realizes that nothing is as it seems.

And that this killer may just strike again.

A fast-paced psychological suspense thriller with unforgettable characters and heart-pounding suspense, THE JESSIE HUNT series is a riveting new series that will leave you turning pages late into the night.

Books 22-24 are also available!

Blake Pierce

Blake Pierce is the USA Today bestselling author of the RILEY PAGE mystery series, which includes seventeen books. Blake Pierce is also the author of the MACKENZIE WHITE mystery series, comprising fourteen books; of the AVERY BLACK mystery series, comprising six books; of the KERI LOCKE mystery series, comprising five books; of the MAKING OF RILEY PAIGE mystery series, comprising six books; of the KATE WISE mystery series, comprising seven books; of the CHLOE FINE psychological suspense mystery, comprising six books; of the JESSE HUNT psychological suspense thriller series, comprising twenty four books; of the AU PAIR psychological suspense thriller series, comprising three books; of the ZOE PRIME mystery series, comprising six books; of the ADELE SHARP mystery series, comprising fifteen books, of the EUROPEAN VOYAGE cozy mystery series, comprising four books; of the new LAURA FROST FBI suspense thriller, comprising nine books (and counting); of the new ELLA DARK FBI suspense thriller, comprising eleven books (and counting); of the A YEAR IN EUROPE cozy mystery series, comprising nine books, of the AVA GOLD mystery series, comprising six books (and counting); of the RACHEL GIFT mystery series, comprising six books (and counting); of the VALERIE LAW mystery series, comprising three books (and counting); and of the PAIGE KING mystery series, comprising three books (and counting).

An avid reader and lifelong fan of the mystery and thriller genres, Blake loves to hear from you, so please feel free to visit www.blakepierceauthor.com to learn more and stay in touch.

BOOKS BY BLAKE PIERCE

PAIGE KING MYSTERY SERIES
THE GIRL HE PINED (Book #1)
THE GIRL HE CHOSE (Book #2)
THE GIRL HE TOOK (Book #3)

VALERIE LAW MYSTERY SERIES
NO MERCY (Book #1)
NO PITY (Book #2)
NO FEAR (Book #3

RACHEL GIFT MYSTERY SERIES
HER LAST WISH (Book #1)
HER LAST CHANCE (Book #2)
HER LAST HOPE (Book #3)
HER LAST FEAR (Book #4)
HER LAST CHOICE (Book #5)
HER LAST BREATH (Book #6)

AVA GOLD MYSTERY SERIES
CITY OF PREY (Book #1)
CITY OF FEAR (Book #2)
CITY OF BONES (Book #3)
CITY OF GHOSTS (Book #4)
CITY OF DEATH (Book #5)
CITY OF VICE (Book #6)

A YEAR IN EUROPE
A MURDER IN PARIS (Book #1)
DEATH IN FLORENCE (Book #2)
VENGEANCE IN VIENNA (Book #3)
A FATALITY IN SPAIN (Book #4)

ELLA DARK FBI SUSPENSE THRILLER
GIRL, ALONE (Book #1)
GIRL, TAKEN (Book #2)

GIRL, HUNTED (Book #3)
GIRL, SILENCED (Book #4)
GIRL, VANISHED (Book 5)
GIRL ERASED (Book #6)
GIRL, FORSAKEN (Book #7)
GIRL, TRAPPED (Book #8)
GIRL, EXPENDABLE (Book #9)
GIRL, ESCAPED (Book #10)
GIRL, HIS (Book #11)

LAURA FROST FBI SUSPENSE THRILLER
ALREADY GONE (Book #1)
ALREADY SEEN (Book #2)
ALREADY TRAPPED (Book #3)
ALREADY MISSING (Book #4)
ALREADY DEAD (Book #5)
ALREADY TAKEN (Book #6)
ALREADY CHOSEN (Book #7)
ALREADY LOST (Book #8)
ALREADY HIS (Book #9)

EUROPEAN VOYAGE COZY MYSTERY SERIES
MURDER (AND BAKLAVA) (Book #1)
DEATH (AND APPLE STRUDEL) (Book #2)
CRIME (AND LAGER) (Book #3)
MISFORTUNE (AND GOUDA) (Book #4)
CALAMITY (AND A DANISH) (Book #5)
MAYHEM (AND HERRING) (Book #6)

ADELE SHARP MYSTERY SERIES
LEFT TO DIE (Book #1)
LEFT TO RUN (Book #2)
LEFT TO HIDE (Book #3)
LEFT TO KILL (Book #4)
LEFT TO MURDER (Book #5)
LEFT TO ENVY (Book #6)
LEFT TO LAPSE (Book #7)
LEFT TO VANISH (Book #8)
LEFT TO HUNT (Book #9)
LEFT TO FEAR (Book #10)

LEFT TO PREY (Book #11)
LEFT TO LURE (Book #12)
LEFT TO CRAVE (Book #13)
LEFT TO LOATHE (Book #14)
LEFT TO HARM (Book #15)

THE AU PAIR SERIES
ALMOST GONE (Book#1)
ALMOST LOST (Book #2)
ALMOST DEAD (Book #3)

ZOE PRIME MYSTERY SERIES
FACE OF DEATH (Book#1)
FACE OF MURDER (Book #2)
FACE OF FEAR (Book #3)
FACE OF MADNESS (Book #4)
FACE OF FURY (Book #5)
FACE OF DARKNESS (Book #6)

A JESSIE HUNT PSYCHOLOGICAL SUSPENSE SERIES
THE PERFECT WIFE (Book #1)
THE PERFECT BLOCK (Book #2)
THE PERFECT HOUSE (Book #3)
THE PERFECT SMILE (Book #4)
THE PERFECT LIE (Book #5)
THE PERFECT LOOK (Book #6)
THE PERFECT AFFAIR (Book #7)
THE PERFECT ALIBI (Book #8)
THE PERFECT NEIGHBOR (Book #9)
THE PERFECT DISGUISE (Book #10)
THE PERFECT SECRET (Book #11)
THE PERFECT FAÇADE (Book #12)
THE PERFECT IMPRESSION (Book #13)
THE PERFECT DECEIT (Book #14)
THE PERFECT MISTRESS (Book #15)
THE PERFECT IMAGE (Book #16)
THE PERFECT VEIL (Book #17)
THE PERFECT INDISCRETION (Book #18)
THE PERFECT RUMOR (Book #19)
THE PERFECT COUPLE (Book #20)

THE PERFECT MURDER (Book #21)
THE PERFECT HUSBAND (Book #22)
THE PERFECT SCANDAL (Book #23)
THE PERFECT MASK (Book #24)

CHLOE FINE PSYCHOLOGICAL SUSPENSE SERIES
NEXT DOOR (Book #1)
A NEIGHBOR'S LIE (Book #2)
CUL DE SAC (Book #3)
SILENT NEIGHBOR (Book #4)
HOMECOMING (Book #5)
TINTED WINDOWS (Book #6)

KATE WISE MYSTERY SERIES
IF SHE KNEW (Book #1)
IF SHE SAW (Book #2)
IF SHE RAN (Book #3)
IF SHE HID (Book #4)
IF SHE FLED (Book #5)
IF SHE FEARED (Book #6)
IF SHE HEARD (Book #7)

THE MAKING OF RILEY PAIGE SERIES
WATCHING (Book #1)
WAITING (Book #2)
LURING (Book #3)
TAKING (Book #4)
STALKING (Book #5)
KILLING (Book #6)

RILEY PAIGE MYSTERY SERIES
ONCE GONE (Book #1)
ONCE TAKEN (Book #2)
ONCE CRAVED (Book #3)
ONCE LURED (Book #4)
ONCE HUNTED (Book #5)
ONCE PINED (Book #6)
ONCE FORSAKEN (Book #7)
ONCE COLD (Book #8)

ONCE STALKED (Book #9)
ONCE LOST (Book #10)
ONCE BURIED (Book #11)
ONCE BOUND (Book #12)
ONCE TRAPPED (Book #13)
ONCE DORMANT (Book #14)
ONCE SHUNNED (Book #15)
ONCE MISSED (Book #16)
ONCE CHOSEN (Book #17)

MACKENZIE WHITE MYSTERY SERIES
BEFORE HE KILLS (Book #1)
BEFORE HE SEES (Book #2)
BEFORE HE COVETS (Book #3)
BEFORE HE TAKES (Book #4)
BEFORE HE NEEDS (Book #5)
BEFORE HE FEELS (Book #6)
BEFORE HE SINS (Book #7)
BEFORE HE HUNTS (Book #8)
BEFORE HE PREYS (Book #9)
BEFORE HE LONGS (Book #10)
BEFORE HE LAPSES (Book #11)
BEFORE HE ENVIES (Book #12)
BEFORE HE STALKS (Book #13)
BEFORE HE HARMS (Book #14)

AVERY BLACK MYSTERY SERIES
CAUSE TO KILL (Book #1)
CAUSE TO RUN (Book #2)
CAUSE TO HIDE (Book #3)
CAUSE TO FEAR (Book #4)
CAUSE TO SAVE (Book #5)
CAUSE TO DREAD (Book #6)

KERI LOCKE MYSTERY SERIES
A TRACE OF DEATH (Book #1)
A TRACE OF MURDER (Book #2)
A TRACE OF VICE (Book #3)
A TRACE OF CRIME (Book #4)
A TRACE OF HOPE (Book #5)

Made in United States
Orlando, FL
10 February 2025